WAR A̶̶̶̶̶̶̶̶̶̶
KOREA 1950

MIKE WEEDALL

outskirts
press

For the nurses of our armed forces who gave so much,
and for those who continue that noble tradition.

Korean Peninsula

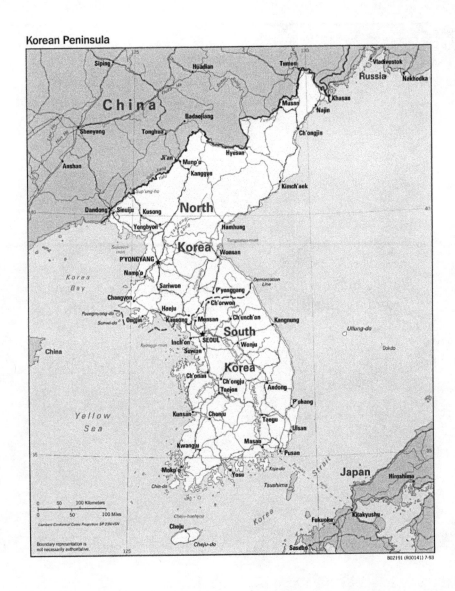

Siping • Huadian • Tumen • Vladivostok • Russia • Nakhodka

China • Musan • Khasan • Najin

Badaojiang

Shenyang • Tonghua • Ch'ongjin

Anshan • Ji'an • Manp'o • Hyesan
Kanggye

Sup'ung-ho • Kimch'aek

Dandong • Sinuiju • Kusong • North • Hamhung
Yongbyon

Korea • Wonsan

PYONGYANG

Namp'o

Sariwon • P'yonggang • Demarcation Line

Changyon • Ch'orwon
Haeju • Ch'unch'on • Kangnung

Paengnyong-do • Ongjin • Kaesong • Munsan • Ullung-do
Sunwi-do • Inch'on • SEOUL • South • Dokdo
Kyonggi-man • Suwon • Wonju

China • Korea

Ch'onan • Ch'ongju • Andong
Taejon

P'ohang

Yellow Sea • Kunsan • Chonju • Taegu • Ulsan

Kwangju • Masan
Pusan

Mokp'o • Yose • Koje-do • Strait • Japan • Hiroshima
Chin-do • Tsushima

Korea

0   50   100 Kilometers
0   50   100 Miles
Lambert Conformal Conic Projection SP 23N/45N

Cheju • Fukuoka • Kitakyushu

Boundary representation is not necessarily authoritative.

Cheju-haehyop

Cheju-do • Sasebo

802191 (R00141) 7-93

CHAPTER 1

"Are you alright, Lieutenant?" The young driver looked at her in the rearview mirror.

What could she say? All right? She hadn't been all right since the letter arrived seventy-two hours ago. Before that bombshell, the mess with Rob and his sister's baby was already overwhelming.

A wave of anxiety set off a round of nausea. But the green rolling hills of Central Massachusetts kept passing by. She fumbled for her rosary, fidgeting to find a comfortable position. Every mile in this old Army sedan with broken springs brought her closer to what she feared and didn't know how to manage. How could this be happening?

The driver spoke again. "How is your family handling your call-up?"

A wave of guilt hit Mary. This polite man was trying to start a conversation. She gave him a sympathetic look. "Not well, Private. I had to leave my two-month-old baby to be here."

"Wow! I'm sorry. Can the Army do this? I'm surprised that a mother with a baby would be called up, even with the Declaration of National Emergency."

Mary shifted in her seat again, still not finding a way to relax. The old car banged through another pothole, rattling her bones. *Not as simple as that, Private. I better figure out how to sweet-talk my way out during the medical exam. If that doesn't work, my problems will be bigger than anything at home.*

"Is it okay to call you Steve? Steve, you're a sweet guy, but I don't feel well. Maybe it's the early bus ride from Manchester, and now this . . . this drive. I'm going to nap since we've got a way to go."

"Yes, ma'am. Steve is fine. Get some rest. You have a full day ahead of you."

She leaned her head against the cool window. A tear slipped down her cheek that, hopefully, the driver didn't see. She fingered the rosary—a going-away present from her neighbor, Linda. *Just when I get used to being a mother, now this. Please, God, help me. I want to go home. Don't let this happen. Hail Mary, full of grace . . .*

MANCHESTER TIMES
NEWS BULLETIN
NORTH KOREAN INVASION CONTINUES

North Korean troops continue to advance and threaten to capture the entire Korean Peninsula following their June 25, 1950, surprise invasion. Elements of the US Eighth Army, currently occupying Japan, are being rushed to Korea. However, it is not clear that the US can put enough troops and equipment to prevent the North Koreans from overwhelming South Korean and American forces.

President Truman condemned the surprise attack and compared the invasion to Japan's sneak attack on Pearl Harbor in 1941. The President called upon the Soviet Union and China, North Korea's allies, to rein in the aggressor and have their forces return to the 38th parallel border established at the end of World War II. Truman also called for an emergency meeting of the United Nations Security Council to deal with this act of aggression.

CHAPTER 2

The private turned the car onto a narrow side road under a sky of puffy clouds. Mary could see Fort Devens in front of them. Ahead, traffic stopped at a glass booth with an unending row of military buildings behind. She didn't remember this entrance from years ago, but then she had been on a bus with other volunteers.

Steve flashed his badge at the checkpoint and handed the MP Mary's paperwork. The guard leaned into the car and saluted. "Welcome to Fort Devens, Lieutenant Belanger."

Mary saluted back, mouthing thank you.

Steve made two quick turns inside the base before parking in front of a long, tan building. "You'll get the exam here. I believe they're waiting for you."

They're waiting for me? Near the end of World War II, Mary spent hours sitting around with the other junior nurses before anyone even came to talk to them. No food. No rest. Then it took three days for complete processing before assignment to an Army rehabilitation hospital in New Jersey. *Maybe the Army had become more efficient.*

The private opened her door, then went to the trunk to retrieve her small bag. Mary leaned back, stretching stiff muscles, and followed Steve to the reception desk.

"Lieutenant," the attendant called. "They're waiting for you in Room GA-131 through that door. Private Brown will show you the way."

After a short walk, Steve pushed open the door to a medical exam room that reeked of antiseptic. When Mary entered, a nurse stood up.

"Welcome, Lieutenant Belanger. I'm Lieutenant Lucille King, Head of Nursing." The older, heavyset woman with a broad, friendly smile extended her hand, not bothering with a salute. "From now on, it's Lucy. We're informal here. I'll call the chief medical officer, who will work with us today. The base commander also wants to come by to greet you."

Lucy turned to face Steve. "Thank you, Private, for getting Lieutenant Belanger here today."

"Thank you, ma'am." He saluted the two women and turned to leave.

"Steve," Mary said. "I mean, Private Brown. Thank you for your help, and sorry I could not be better company. I hope we meet again."

"Oh, don't worry," Brown said, heading out the door. "I'll be seeing you soon."

Lucy hung up the phone. "The officers are on their way. We'll start the tests after that. In the meantime, might I get you some water? We'll be drawing blood, so I can only offer that."

Ready to start the tests? Things are happening faster than expected. I'd better figure out who can give me a deferral.

The door flew open. A tall officer stepped in. "I'm Captain Ben Heinz, Chief Medical Officer."

Mary jumped to salute.

"At ease, Lieutenant. Is it alright if I call you Mary?"

"Yes, sir. That's fine."

"Call me Ben. You've already met Lucy. As you know in the Army, we often just use last names, but for the exam we can relax a bit." The doctor extended his hand. Taking his fingers in hers, Mary felt warmth. He seemed pretty fit. The grey streaks in his dark black hair made him look mature and confident. *I wonder if this is the right guy to talk to. Those eyes are a gorgeous blue. He acts so sure of himself.*

Ben said, "When the base commander arrives, we should get formal."

Mary nodded.

"How was your trip? I know this must be a shock, getting called up on such short notice."

Before Mary could answer, the door opened, and an older officer sporting a uniform filled with ribbons entered. All three stood at attention and saluted.

"At ease," the man barked returning their salutes. "Lieutenant Belanger, I'm General Phillip Archer. Welcome to Fort Devens. Even though you're here for a short time, please let Captain Heinz or Lieutenant King know if there's anything we can do to make your stay more comfortable. I have the fullest confidence in their capabilities."

Mary immediately realized Archer would not be the right person to ask about a deferment. Generals never seemed to want to hear details. She'd have to raise her issue later with the doctor. *What does a brief stay mean? Maybe the Army thinks a few days is a brief time.*

Mary smiled. "Thank you, General. Your people have been most helpful already, and I appreciate you stopping by."

The commanding officer puffed up. "Lieutenant, it's my pleasure. I don't normally have the opportunity to greet call-ups, but since I already had a meeting here in the hospital, I couldn't pass up the opportunity. You have a challenging mission ahead of you. On behalf of our fighting men, we would be lost without nurses like you. One cannot overstate a nurse's ability to save lives. I must add a personal note. When I was wounded in France, seeing the caring face of a nurse was as much of a healing factor for me as the surgery."

Archer turned to Heinz. "My apologies, Captain. Your skills

are invaluable, but not delivered in nearly the same comforting a manner."

"No need to apologize, General. I completely agree." Heinz gave Mary a wink.

The base commander turned back to Mary. "Since I'll not see you again, all my best, Lieutenant. Thank you for your service in the last war and now this little spat in Korea. Oh, and Captain Heinz, the Lieutenant's hair is not too long. No need to squeeze a haircut into the schedule today." With that, he breezed out.

After the General left, the three grinned at each other.

All business, that man. He even dared to critique my hair. No haircut needed? What does that mean? And what was that about my challenging mission? I better find some time to talk to Captain Heinz alone.

Ben was now all business. "Let's get the medical exam started. We'll begin by taking your vitals and history. You know the drill. I'll be back for my part of the exam in a few minutes. There will also be technicians doing X-rays for TB and such. I apologize for all the blood we'll take today. Before that happens, I have one more task to complete."

The doctor walked to the door. "Lieutenant Crosley, please come in."

A tall, slender nurse entered the room. Heinz asked her to stand back-to-back with Mary. He placed a ruler across their heads to compare heights. The Chief Medical Officer handed Lucy a yellow tape. "Please measure their inseams, torso, waist, and arms."

Lucy took the measurements and gave the paper to Crosley, who turned and silently left.

Ben smiled. "That's for your uniform. Since we don't have time to prepare a new uniform, we'll be altering Lieutenant Crosley's wardrobe for you to be available this afternoon. Anything you need immediately?"

Mary's head spun. *A uniform by this afternoon?* "Um, yes.

There's something I need to discuss about my family. And will there be lunch? I left New Hampshire early this morning and had nothing to eat. Suddenly, I'm really hungry."

The captain looked at his clipboard. "Nice hosts, we are." He flashed the paperwork her way. "A full day without lunch or dinner. Great planning, or I should say, the same old Army you left several years ago. Lucy, please get an orderly to bring the Lieutenant something to eat."

He smiled. "I'm afraid we're on such a tight timeline that we can't send you to the mess hall. Please give the orderly a sandwich order and what you want to drink. I hope you don't mind eating while we work. Lucy, when you put in that order, make sure they bring cookies for our guest. She deserves a little something nice for all we're putting her through."

Mary nodded. "I appreciate that. When could we discuss the family issue I have?"

"What is it?"

"My situation back home may get in the way of my serving. It'll take some time to explain. Is this the right time to get into it?"

Ben paused for a moment and gave a small smile that emphasized the cleft between his eyes. "Could we hold that discussion until later? I promise to do my best to find a solution. This afternoon, the base psychiatrist will assess you. If I can't help with your problem, maybe he can. Will that work?"

Mary bit her tongue. "Sure." She liked this officer a lot. Best to get him on her side. Army doctors generally would have done anything to ensure nurses were well cared for during the last war. Of course, there had been the occasional creeps. Ben seemed like one of the good ones.

Heinz gave a quick wave and was gone.

Lucy turned to Mary. "What would you like to order? Unfortunately, I believe they're out of lobster. Maybe something simpler?"

"Any kind of sandwich will do. Turkey, ham, whatever."

"You remember Army food. Order lobster and take whatever they put on your plate. I'll get an orderly to head over. In the meantime, please strip down and put on that gown. I'll be back in a few minutes."

While she unbuttoned her blouse, Mary thought about Heinz. *He seems like he cares about others. Even ordered cookies for me. Only a few hours ago, it tore my heart out to hand Cindy to my mom. It's like she knew I was leaving. This guy has got to help me.*

By mid-afternoon, Mary knew Ben had not exaggerated the packed schedule. In a whirlwind, she went from one test to the next, rapidly getting worn out. A turkey sandwich appeared with potato salad and iced tea. But not until mid-afternoon did she find a moment to take a bite. The plate of cookies, which staff helped themselves to, now held only a few.

Ben sat down, reaching for one of them. "We saw you were alone for a moment and couldn't have that. Please keep eating, but you'd better grab that last snack."

Mary smiled, moving the cookie next to her sandwich.

"The good news is you're in excellent health. Although several of the tests will take a few days to process, I'd be surprised if any indicate an issue. If the results reveal concerns, we'll be in touch about how to proceed. Normally we do a physical fitness test, but that will not be necessary since your medical results are clean. Any questions you have for me?"

Mary put her sandwich down, gathering her courage to plead her case. "There's the personal issue I mentioned earlier that I need to talk about."

"Go ahead."

Without realizing it, Mary had twisted her napkin into shreds. Fighting a sudden attack of nerves, she took a deep, slow breath. "I need a deferment. Forgive me if this is disjointed. I'm really nervous."

"What's going on?"

Heart racing, she pursed her lips. "I've got a baby. Well, it's not really my baby. That is, my husband and I didn't conceive Cindy. She's Sharon's baby. That's Rob's sister. Rob is my husband. Oh God, I'm making a mess of this."

"I'm with you so far. It's Sharon's baby. How did you end up with Cindy? She's the baby, right?"

Mary took a deep breath. "Yes, Sharon is a party girl. She got into alcohol and drugs and took off right after high school. Out of the blue, she showed up back home late in her pregnancy, saying she didn't know who the father might be. Our family took care of her. The day after she delivered, she disappeared and hasn't been seen since."

"Care for the infant fell to you?"

"My husband and his father decided I needed to quit my job at the hospital to care for her. I didn't like that idea, but I agreed to go along. For the past few months, I've been a full-time mom. Actually, more than full-time. Cindy is a troubled baby. She hardly sleeps and cries endlessly. It's been tough."

"You mentioned the mother used alcohol and drugs during pregnancy. It doesn't surprise me that the baby struggles. After all, everything your sister-in-law put in her blood ran through the baby."

Mary's eyes lit up. "That makes sense, although our pediatrician in Manchester said that couldn't be the cause."

"The science is evolving, and not yet proven." He looked at her. "After you got your call-up notice, did you reach out to explain your situation?"

Mary nodded. "The sergeant said since it wasn't a child I gave birth to or adopted, they couldn't grant a deferment. My only hope is for you to give me that deferral."

Ben stayed quiet for a long moment, tapping his fingers. Finally, he said, "I'm sorry for your situation. Unfortunately, my authority ends with an evaluation of your physical condition. You're an operating room nurse, which puts you in demand, given what is developing in Korea. I hate to be the one to say this if you haven't figured it out, but you'll fly out of Boston tomorrow morning to the West Coast. From there, it's on to Japan and then Korea."

Mary's heart sank. *I knew it. What I feared—not getting home to Cindy. Worse, being shipped to a combat zone.*

Without any thought, Mary plunged ahead. "I'm only twenty-five and an operating room nurse that hasn't worked for months since the baby arrived. Even when I did work, it's only a small hospital in Manchester where I helped with tonsils and simple stuff. I did the day shift and didn't see the tough cases that typically comes at night. And it's only last year I started training for the OR. I'm not qualified to be a combat nurse. In the last war, I did rehab work. I'd probably hurt more soldiers than help." She was sure Ben could hear her heart pounding.

Ben said nothing. An awkward silence filled the room. Spent, Mary dropped her head into her hands, fighting back the tears.

Ben put a hand on her shoulder. "The Army sees operating room on your record, and there are no further questions. I can only evaluate your physical condition, and you're in good health. Your emotional stress is clear, but that's the province of the psychiatrist. You'll have to plead your case with him. I'm sorry."

Ben paused at the door. He looked back at the attractive dark-haired woman struggling with her emotions, "Mary, I wish I could do more. You must be strong to have taken on that responsibility at home. Hopefully, that strength will serve you with what's ahead. Good luck with the base psychologist."

One more chance is all I have. He thinks I'm strong, but I'm not. I didn't even mention Rob's affair and that he refuses to help with the baby. Damn Rob. If he wouldn't help me with the baby, he's not likely to work with my mother. Those two

hate each other. I must sound like a fool saying I'm unquali-
fied to a senior officer. It's true, but what must Heinz think?
But really, combat surgeries?

Following another round of injections, Mary continued to wrestle with her situation. After a knock on the door, a small dark-haired man entered. "I'm Captain Allison, the base psychiatrist." After a perfunctory handshake, he quickly spread out a pile of papers. "This should be quick."

Without any explanation, he started to grill Mary with basic questions about herself. When he got to her family situation, there were a few simple yes or no queries. Then questions concerning how she slept—did she have repeated dreams? Any negatives from her previous service? Mary wrung her perspiring hands under the table, wondering how to steer the interview to her marriage and the baby.

"That should wrap it up. You're fit for service." Captain Allison quickly gathered his papers and rose.

Her stomach in a knot, Mary snapped, "Wait, I'm not well mentally. You never gave me a chance to explain my situation at home and the responsibilities I have caring for a baby."

Allison looked at her in surprise and sat back down. "Your medical records don't indicate you were ever pregnant. Did you adopt a baby and fail to report it? I thought you had no children. That's what it states in your personnel file."

"I didn't legally adopt a child, but there's a development you need to understand. It won't allow me to serve."

Allison raised his dark eyebrows, his look skeptical. "Tell me what's special because it's hard for me to see there's any mental condition that would keep you from serving."

She gathered her breath, fighting to control a wave of panic and launched into the same story she'd given Ben. The psychiatrist kept looking at his watch. *All he wants is to get done with me.*

When Mary finished, this time including the problems with her deceiving spouse, Allison stood again. "I'm sorry for your issues, especially with your husband, but the regulations are clear. Like the sergeant explained on the phone, there's no exemption for an informal child situation like you describe. You taking your sister-in-law's baby is noble, but the needs of the US Army and our country must be a priority. I'm sure your husband and mother will get the right help to care for your niece. Unless you've anything further to add, I will report you're capable of returning to service."

Frustration washed through her. Once alone, Mary slammed her fist down on the table. *No mental issues. How about the desire to murder a psychiatrist? The Army's needs are priority? Why did I let Rob talk me into staying in the Reserves? Easy money, he said, and we want money to buy a house. Now look what's going to happen. That's it. I'm out of options.*

Lucy came back to find Mary in tears and rubbing a bruised hand. She stepped behind, massaging Mary's neck and shoulders. "Ben filled me in on your problems. I'm assuming Allison offered no help. You're getting it on all fronts. I wish I could do more."

Mary reached back, grasping Lucy's hand. "Thank you. That damn psychiatrist didn't want to hear about my situation. You've been terrific, but I don't seem to have enough justification to go home to my baby."

"You're a special, caring woman. Have you arranged care for the baby?"

"We cobbled coverage together between my mother and neighbor. I guess they'll have to figure it out."

Lucy gave a sad smile. "I hate to keep piling it on, but there's an attorney outside. He'll administer the oath, bringing you back to active duty and start the mounds of paperwork I'm sure you remember."

"Am I really scheduled on a flight to San Francisco tomorrow morning and then to Korea? Is it that fast a track?"

"That's what the paperwork says. You're in a priority one category given what's developing."

"What have you heard about conditions there? Is it as terrible as folks say?"

"From what I hear, things are dire. Word is the South Korean Army pretty much disintegrated, and the US had only a few hundred soldiers in country when the North Koreans invaded. Troops are being rushed from Japan to stem the tide, but no one is sure that will be enough."

"Why is there a North and South Korea? I seem to remember a newspaper article showing the North is a communist country, and we support the democratic government in the south. Do I have that right?"

"You do. The North Koreans are allies of the Russians. Some say this invasion is to test the resolve of the US to stand up to communism. Fortunately, the United Nations may get involved with Uncle Sam taking the lead. Hence, the rush to move troops, equipment, and medical personnel." She smiled. "Hey, the attorney is waiting. Are you up to dealing with him, or do you want me to stall him for another five minutes?"

Another five minutes! Another five minutes! What I want is a stiff drink and several days to process what's happening. What good are another few moments? Mary heaved a sigh. "Tell him to come in."

"Okay, hon. After the lawyer, there will be someone to bring your uniforms. They've made up a kit for you. Like Ben mentioned, you're getting Crosley's uniforms since there's no time for new ones. When the bureaucracy catches up, you'll receive a uniform allowance down the road. Then you can get replacements or pocket the check. Remember to laundry-ink-out Crosley from the uniforms or you may never get your stuff back."

She looked at Mary. "After these last meetings, you can get

dinner and find your quarters for the night. Unfortunately, you'll be up early for the flight west. Private Brown will drive you."

The next hour and a half flew by. The first order of business was repeating the oath of allegiance she had sworn to in 1944. "To defend and protect the Constitution . . . ." Then the forms started. List all next of kin. Who would get what in case of death? What insurance coverage did she want?

The most challenging issue turned out to be how much pay she wanted to receive versus allotments she might send to her husband. Given the things Rob had done over the past weeks, Mary chose to receive a small monthly allotment in the field, with the rest deposited in a personal savings account. If Rob needed money, she could deal with him then.

Next, who would be the beneficiary of her life insurance? She started to say her spouse, but then listed her mother. If anything happened to Susan, she could change the beneficiary.

What religion did she belong to? Catholic. Any special requests the Army chaplains should know about? Frustration growing, Mary wondered how much longer this would go on. She felt close to collapse. A massive headache now throbbed. "No special requests on the religion front," Mary managed to say.

The lawyer pulled out more forms.

Lucy walked in with a chain and dog tags. "These came for you. Just like the last war, it has your essential information, including blood type. Sometimes this Army moves quickly, but not when you want them to."

Mary tried to smile, slipping the metal tags over her head.

The attorney reached for the next piece of paper. "This got separated from the rest of the financial forms. It's a power of attorney in case you're disabled. I assume that would be your spouse, but given your other choices, perhaps you'll select someone else."

"Put my mother down."

An hour later, Mary stumbled into her temporary quarters in an unoccupied barrack, carrying her new uniforms and loaded duffel bag. A spare room with a single bed and small desk heightened her aloneness. She rubbed her temples and collapsed on the bed. Closed eyes brought the barest of relief. Although she knew tomorrow morning would come too soon, she put that out of her mind. *Lucy said the mess hall closes in thirty minutes. I'll rest my eyes for a few, then run over. Did I pack aspirin? I'll look for that before I head out.*

Half-awake. Was that a knock at the door? The rapping grew louder, followed by footsteps moving away. Mary jumped up and threw the door open. Down the hall stood Captain Ben Heinz.

"Hi there. I apologize if I woke you up."

"No, you didn't." Her hand ran through tangled hair. "Guess I'm not a good liar. I was taking a catnap. It's been a torturous day."

"You've had a bad one, so I brought you something to eat. When I asked about the rest of your schedule and what time you'd be leaving tomorrow, I figured there's no way you could squeeze in dinner. I have more mess hall sandwiches, a few apples, juice, and even scrounged up more cookies."

A warm glow eased her fatigue. "You didn't have to do that, but I'm glad you did. I missed getting to the mess hall. You're an angel sent to save me from me."

"Never been called that before, but I could get used to it." He held out two paper bags. "I wish I had more. Maybe even those lobsters we keep requesting."

"You could bring me cod liver oil, and I'd drink it. I'd invite you in, but there's no place to sit. Might you want to visit in the lounge for a few minutes, or do you have a family to get home to?" She saw he wasn't wearing a ring.

"No one is waiting for me. I'll stay if you agree to eat. Doctor's orders."

"I'm not that hungry. But if it's prescription, maybe I can get one of those cookies down. Let me do a few quick things and meet you in the lounge."

In her room, Mary reached into her overflowing bag to find a hairbrush. Several swipes later, she realized the uselessness. Maybe lipstick, but where might that be? She smiled, recalling Ben had seen her frizzy hair a moment ago. And earlier in the day, he'd examined her naked.

In the barracks lounge, Mary asked Ben how he decided to become a doctor.

"I grew up in a small California town where my dad was the local physician. When he grabbed the medical bag on a stormy night, I hungered to go with him. I knew medical school would be in my future. Didn't realize being in the Army meant I'd never be staying in one place long enough to find the right relationship."

After more talk about why he chose the military and the bases where he served, he glanced at his watch. "It's already past eight. I've kept you up too long and haven't learned more about you."

"I wonder if we'll see each other again," Mary said. "I'm on my way out of the country and don't know when I'll get back. Whatever the future holds, thank you from the bottom of my heart for all you did today. You saved me with food twice. Since there's enough left for me to eat in the morning, you're an angel three times over."

Ben grinned. "My pleasure."

Mary smiled back. "You were gentle during my exam. But, most importantly, you've been a good listener to my troubles and confusion. Even though you couldn't grant me that deferment, all I can say is thank you."

"Who knows? We might run across each other in Korea. I've got a feeling I may follow you to Asia. From what I hear, there's a need for additional medical units. My preference would be to get out in the field, but that's a decision for the higher-ups."

"I can't wish for anybody to go to a war zone. If that's where you end up, your patients will win. You're a terrific doctor. Thank you."

Ben extended his hand. Mary stepped forward to give him a peck on his cheek instead. She was pleased when he returned the hug.

"Keep yourself safe, Lieutenant. You're a special lady."

After Ben left the barracks, she headed to her room, feeling worried about how forward she'd been. *Heck, nothing but a platonic hug and kiss. Rob did more than that behind my back. Besides, I'll probably never see Ben again.*

Mary looked at everything that needed packing and suddenly remembered she had to call home. She'd have to call collect from a payphone in the lounge since she didn't have enough change. Rob would undoubtedly complain about the cost. Something else for her to deal with.

CHAPTER 3

Settled on the airplane following the mad dash to the airport, Mary felt excited. Today was her first plane ride. Flying was something she had wanted to try. Above the broken clouds with the air smooth, she appreciated having the window seat. Everything looked so small from up here. The drone of the propellers was loud, and she hoped the businessman next to her would leave her alone.

She pushed back her seat. Airplanes were so much nicer than buses. A moment of guilt hit her for enjoying this new experience. The thought of last night's call with Susan came to mind.

The minute she got on the phone, her mother criticized Rob for not being home. He'd gone to look for a job that morning and hadn't returned. Mary wondered if her husband might be spending time with his lover, feeling ill at the thought.

"Mom, let's forget Rob. I need to fill you in on what's happened." After describing her attempts to seek a deferment, she took a deep breath. "I'm on my way to Korea. I never thought this could happen."

Her mother broke down crying. Mary felt her own eyes fill. After a moment of silence, Linda, her neighbor, came on. "Maar, you there?"

"It's good to hear your voice, Linda. Given that it's getting late, thanks for helping my mom. How is she?"

"Not well. She went into the living room, crying. I take it you don't have good news."

Mary repeated the basics.

"That's terrible. How are you holding up?"

"I'm exhausted and need to get to sleep. I have to leave at a god-awful hour in the morning and cannot stay on the phone long. I'm calling collect."

"Don't you dare worry about costs when you have the chance to phone. If Rob complains, I'll pay the bill myself."

"You're a good friend. How's the baby? I can't stop thinking about her."

Linda described the day's routine of caring for little Cindy. The rosy picture of the baby eased a bit of Mary's guilt.

"Thanks for being there with my mom. When you see Rob, tell him my news. I'll try to call tomorrow. After I leave the States, I'm unsure how often I can be in touch."

"Do you want to talk to your mother again before hanging up?"

"That would be nice."

Mary could sense her mother fighting back the tears. "Darling, I knew this would happen. It's unfair. I'm going to write a letter to President Truman. Maybe that will help. In the meantime, promise to take care and be safe. Do you hear?"

"I'll be safe. Like I told Linda, I'll try calling you from California tomorrow. I love you."

Her mother sobbed. "I love you too, darling."

As Mary walked through the bustling Chicago airport, she noticed appreciative male glances at her second-hand uniform. *This uniform is a tight fit but works. It's these too-large shoes stuffed with toilet paper that are a problem. Glad I*

brought underwear. Lucy said Army issue is as uncomfortable as ever.

Unsure of where to go, she asked an airline employee for directions.

"Looking for a romantic flight to Korea?" a brash voice interrupted.

Out of the crowd, two friendly faces in uniform smiled. The short brunette said, "We're probably on the same plane." She spoke with a thick southern accent.

Her companion added, "Don't pay any attention to this one. Her sanity disappeared a long time ago. Hi, I'm Barbara Thompson, and this is Julie Fellows."

Mary extended her hand, looking up at the older blonde with a gap between her front teeth. "Nice to meet you. I'm Mary Belanger from New Hampshire. I assume you're nurses like me."

Julie stepped close, linking arms with Mary. "Good detective work, Mary from New Hampshire. Let's go to San Francisco to find the brain this dizzy blonde thinks I lost."

When they deplaned in San Francisco, Mary spotted a young man in uniform holding a sign: Army Nurses Here. "Guess that's us, soldier."

The private responded with a salute.

Julie laughed, returning his salute. "Promise me this is the last formality while we're together. Got it, Private?"

"Yes, Lieutenant. I mean, ma'am."

Julie seemed to be feeling the effects of cocktails on the flight. Once in the air, she informed the stewardess that three nurses were on the way to serve the USA and the airline should bring alcohol. They were quickly served. Mary sipped hers. Julie had several.

"Someone will grab your checked bags," the nervous

private explained.

Julie's voice rang out. "Are there more nurses you're gathering? It must be a wonderful duty to come and collect beautiful women."

Mary felt embarrassed for the guy.

"Yes, ma'am. I'm a lucky guy. Five nurses arrived earlier and are waiting at our bus."

"This guy has nurses stashed everywhere," Julie announced.

Barbara laughed and rolled her eyes as the group left the terminal. Next to cars loading and unloading to the left, several uniformed nurses lounged by an old bus. Their checked bags soon arrived, and the nurses climbed in.

After a round of introductions, Mary learned she was the only reservist. The others were full-time Army reassigned from medical facilities around the United States.

One nurse asked the driver, "Where are we headed?"

"Fairfield-Suisun Air Force Base, ma'am. It's an hour north of here."

"What happens from there, driver?"

"I don't know, ma'am. My orders were to pick you up and return to the base pronto."

Once underway and with Julie's head resting on her shoulder, Mary felt her nervousness building. Her fingers automatically reached for the rosary. The excitement of the trip and meeting new people faded and now replaced by worry. Even the curiously dressed pedestrians on the crowded streets of San Francisco couldn't interest her. She imagined herself dropping a scalpel while a wounded man bled to death.

The bus edged through city traffic, which the driver enthusiastically cursed. With light fading, more than one nurse badgered the driver about dinner. "Hopefully, the Army doesn't think airline meals are sufficient for the day," one grumbled.

"I drive this bus, ma'am. Beyond that, they don't tell me anything."

Julie surprised everyone by lifting her head from Mary's

shoulder where she had napped. "And you're doing a helluva good job. We haven't crashed yet." The drunk nurse glanced at Mary with a crooked smile, then dropped back into sleep.

Fairfield-Suisun Air Base could be heard well before the bus reached a squat building checkpoint. Jets roared, coming and going, interspersed with loud prop cargo planes. The roar woke Julie, who complained she needed a restroom.

"Me too," Mary said. "We'll ask first thing when we get there."

"Good plan. This southern girl will lead you to a potty."

In front of a large silver Quonset Hut, the driver pulled the bus to a stop. "All out."

Mary rushed off the bus with Julie in tow. The two sprinted toward the building while the driver called, "You forgot your bags."

Inside the bare lobby, a tall, grey-haired Air Force officer stepped forward. "May I help you?"

The two ladies snapped to attention. Mary stared at the emblems on his shoulders, attempting to recall the specific rank. Julie stamped forward. "Where's the goddamn restroom, sir? We need it now."

The stunned officer stepped back. "Down the corridor, on the right."

Julie pulled Mary along, hustling to the restroom. "Guess I told him."

While washing up, Mary looked over. "We just met, so don't take this the wrong way because I love it. But is there anything you won't say?"

Julie gave a big grin. "Can you imagine being married to me? One happy husband back home is celebrating the communists starting a war. At last, quiet."

Mary laughed, reaching over to hug Julie. "I'm glad we met. Neither of us wants this assignment, but finding you with that crazy attitude has made my day. I hope we get posted together. Maybe you can teach me how to keep a husband in line." Her eyes filled with tears.

Julie pursed her lips and pulled Mary close. "Looks like there's a story. I want to hear all about it. We'd better get back, grab our bags, and find some food. Let me get a tissue for you."

They joined the group in a large meeting room with a small podium. Box lunches had already been handed out with bags piled in one corner. The Air Force officer they'd met earlier stepped forward. "I assume you found the facilities. There are meals over on the table. Sorry, we don't have more for you. By the way, I'm Captain Weltzer, Chief Medical Officer here at Fairfield-Suisun. Welcome."

Mary saluted, but the officer waved it off. "No need, Lieutenant."

After introducing themselves, the nurses grabbed the two remaining boxes on the table. Julie turned up her nose. "I've got a feeling these sandwiches will look good down the road, but not now."

The door opened, and a female officer joined Captain Weltzer. The two Air Force officers moved to the front. "Please stay seated and continue eating, but if I may have your attention. I'm Lieutenant Warner, head of Nursing Services. Let me welcome you to Fairfield-Suisun on behalf of the Air Force, which will be transporting you. I don't believe anyone has briefed you yet, but you'll board a flight to Hawaii when the last two nurses arrive."

A collective groan filled the room.

"I know it's the shits. All I can do is offer my sympathy. But, ladies, you're much needed. The fighting gets more intense each day. We believe the tide will turn once we get enough troops and equipment in theater. For now, the combat is extreme, and that means casualties. Many casualties."

The room went silent.

She went on. "There are nurses in Japan serving with the occupation forces. Some are now on the Korean Peninsula, but not enough to meet the need. You ladies will be the second wave to get into theater. What you've experienced to date will not slow down. After you fly to Hawaii, it'll be on to Guam, Japan, and final deployment in Korea. Ladies, this is difficult, but I can say without exaggeration that no one is more needed than you right now. On behalf of the Air Force, I thank you for your service and wish you well."

The nurses nervously glanced silently at each other. Even Julie looked serious.

Captain Weltzer stepped forward. "All I can do is echo what Lieutenant Warner explained about the priority of your mission. Please let us know if there is anything either of us can do in the next few hours before you depart. Get as much sleep as you can on the flights. There are several payphones around the building. Use them in the next few hours. It will be your last time speaking with families and loved ones. I wish you nothing but the best. May God watch over you."

Each nurse jumped up to hunt for telephones. Mary followed the pack that beat her out the door. Soon, she stood second in line for a phone. Her stomach did flip-flops since the woman ahead of her was taking forever, crying with her family in Arizona. *Calm down. In a moment, someone might have to wait for me to finish. If we get called to the plane, what if I don't get a chance to phone?*

Since it was past 11:00 p.m. in New Hampshire, Mary worried about who might be awake at home. She desperately wanted to talk with her mother and Linda to see if they had information about Rob. *If Rob is there, what should I say to him?*

With a last "I love you," the nurse in front of Mary hung up. "I apologize for taking so long. Being ripped from my family could not come at a worst time. I'm recently engaged, and my fiancé is upset, wishing we could have married before this."

Mary hugged the woman. "This is tough for all of us. Congratulations on being engaged, even if the wedding has to wait."

"Thanks. You'd better get your call in. No telling when they will tell us to head to the plane."

Mary dialed the operator, requesting a collect call. After several minutes, her mother answered, accepting the charges.

"Honey, I'm happy you called. How are you? You must be exhausted. What time is it? Are you in California? Wait . . . Linda is coaching me to stop asking questions and let you talk."

Mary laughed. "Wonderful to hear your voice. Linda is there, good. I'm at an airbase in California. They said we'll be boarding a flight to Hawaii soon. If I get called, I may have to run."

"Hawaii, that will be nice. Does that mean you don't have to go to Korea?"

"Hawaii is the first stop. After that, we go to Guam, Japan, and then Korea. They have us on the run."

"What time is it there? Aren't they going to let you sleep before you fly? You must be exhausted."

"We'll have to sleep on the plane. The Army is in a rush to get us to Korea. Tonight may be the last time I can talk to you. Tell me about the baby, and is Rob pulling his weight there?"

There was a pause. "The baby is fine, dear. She's sleeping right now, but we know how she likes to make sure whoever takes care of her is also asleep before joining the night owls. I'll put Linda on in a minute, and yes, Rob is here."

Damn, Rob is there. There would be no easy way to get the exact picture of what her husband might be up to. Maybe she could get intelligence from Linda with the right questions.

"Put Linda on. Then I'll speak with you again before we hang up."

"Here's Linda, and stay on the phone as long as possible. I don't care what it costs."

"Sure, Mom."

Linda came on. "Maar, Maar, our traveling gal. Did the trip go okay?"

"Flying is different, although it loses its glamour quickly. I'll be back on a plane for the next couple of days and would trade this excitement to be back home."

"You're on your way to Korea tonight? Wow! I'll light a candle for your safety. How long might you be there?"

"I'm not sure. A regular Army nurse said a foreign tour is typically nine months before you get a break. Maybe it works differently for a reservist. I have a few questions about Rob, but know he's right there. Let me ask yes or no questions, and you can answer. Okay?"

"Got it. Go ahead."

"Is he being a good boy and helping with the baby?"

"No, but hopefully, things will change."

"He wasn't home last night when I called. Did he eventually come home drunk?"

"Yes."

"Do you know if he's still seeing Mona?"

"I believe that's correct."

Damn, damn, damn. "I don't want to ask any more questions about that bastard. How are you? Are you getting a break from the baby when you need it? You're such a hero for helping my mother. Is Stan okay with that?"

"Little Cindy is doing fine, and it's a pleasure to help Susan. My husband supports what I'm doing. He'd better, if he knows what's good for him."

Mary laughed. Linda's irreverence made their friendship fun. "Before I forget, thank you for the going-away rosary. That note you included was sweet. I'm lucky to have a friend like you."

"Do you have an address where we can write? I have a clip from the newspaper about your deployment. I'll send it. You're already a local hero."

"Letters will be the only way to be in touch. Get a piece of paper, and I'll give you the Army mailing address that gets stuff forwarded to me. Please write and send pictures. That way, I can watch Cindy grow."

"I'll get paper. Rob's right here, and he wants to talk. I'll be back."

Mary bit her lip hard, wishing she didn't have to talk to her husband.

"Hi, hon, how are you doing? You must be tired. Susan said you're flying to Hawaii and then on to Korea. That sounds awful."

Her stomach twisted. Mary stayed silent. A couple of nurses waved while walking by. Mary leaned her head against the wall.

"Mary, are you there?"

"Yes, I'm here." Mary drew the phone close, speaking in a quiet voice. "I'm in a barracks hallway. There are people all around. I don't want others to listen in. Can you hear me when I speak this softly?"

"I can hear you. Great connection for long distance."

"You've hurt me terribly, and it's not just me suffering. Your selfishness affects my mother and Linda, and all they must do to care for your niece. In the meantime, you continue to drink and fool around with Mona. Before I left, you promised me you would straighten out, but it doesn't appear you have. Maybe you never will."

She hurried on, not wanting to give Rob a chance to make excuses. "I don't want to talk with you now. What you're doing, shifting responsibility for our niece to my mother is selfish. You need to stop your drinking and fooling around."

"Hon, I had a bad first day with you gone. It's hard for me to be left behind when you're off on a new adventure. We discussed things here today, and I'll not make the same mistakes again. Please . . ."

Mary didn't hear the rest of what her husband said. A call for all nurses to prepare for immediate departure came from down the hall. *Damn. He's still talking.* "Rob, stop! They're calling us for our flight. I have to go. Get my mother on the phone."

"But, hon—"

"Put my mother on, now!"

After a brief silence, Susan took the phone. "Rob said you have to leave. Is that true?"

"Yes, I have to go. I want you to know I love you, and I'll stay safe. Thank you for taking care of the baby. That means the world to me. I've never said it before, but you're the best mother a daughter could have."

Mary fought tears, listening to her mother sob.

Linda was on the phone. "What's the mailing address before you go?"

Mary wiped her eyes and passed alongthe information. "I love you, Lin."

"Love you, Maar. We'll be in touch." The line went dead.

Mary turned to see the Air Force Senior Nurse, who patted her shoulder. "Goodbyes are the worst. Come on. It's time to get you going. Everyone else is ready. You'll have to finish your dinner in the air."

MANCHESTER TIMES
NEWS BULLETIN
MACARTHUR NAMED SUPREME
COMMANDER IN KOREA FIGHT

With the United Nations Security Council vote to declare an emergency and intervene in South Korea, General Douglas MacArthur was named to lead UN Forces in Korea. MacArthur kept his role as Commander of the Occupation of Japan.

The long-standing boycott of the Security Council by the Soviet Union avoided a possible veto to intervene in the Korean conflict. Numerous countries pledged equipment or troops to fight under the UN flag. The first military contingent from the Philippines is already on its way to join the US Eighth Army in Korea.

South Korean and American troops protect a fifty-mile perimeter on the Korean Peninsula's southern tip. However, it is unclear whether they can assemble sufficient forces in time to keep the North Korean Army from capturing the entire country.

CHAPTER 4

The pilot hadn't exaggerated when he announced it would be a rough ride to Korea from Japan. Unlike the passenger-friendly planes that carried the nurses across the Pacific, this cargo plane was not designed for traveler comfort. A bench ran along each side of the fuselage, with equipment strapped down in the middle. Mary couldn't take her eyes off the straining straps that held huge metal containers in place. With every bounce and bang, the straps snapped during the roller coaster ride. If any broke, the passengers would need more than a few nurses to treat the injuries.

Next to her, Julie bit her nails. Despite her own queasiness, Mary smiled and patted Julie's hand. Conversation was impossible, given the deafening noise from the two massive engines. Even with earplugs, her head buzzed with the vibrations reverberating throughout her body.

Today, July 24, was nine days since the postman brought his life-changing delivery. How many people had the Army uprooted so abruptly, she wondered. Scuttlebutt from the flight crew painted a picture of terrible combat casualties ahead. Anxiety and fear filled her when she thought of the medical emergencies coming closer. She worked her rosary hard, praying again for assistance to meet the challenge.

Julie continued going to town on her nails. Mary had discovered her new friend was not the brash and devil-may-care woman she first presented. Instead, she was a woman with the same doubts and worries Mary wrestled with. In several terrible moments flying into Guam, the pilot had announced they were lost and might have to ditch in the ocean. Julie lost it, clinging to Mary and crying, "Maybe this is what God planned. That way, I can't botch treatments."

While the passengers prepared for the worst, the pilot suddenly announced the landing strip was in sight, and they would be on the ground in a few minutes. Mary's hand still ached from her friend's clutching.

On the long flights, Julie shared some of her story. Raised in a rural Alabama town, Julie's parents were alcoholics. When her mother and father were in their cups, it was time for a little girl to hide. Although her older brother and sister secretly fled home, Julie didn't blame them. But it left her alone to face a worsening situation. Many nights she fled to a closet and cried herself to sleep.

The longing for affection may have contributed to Julie getting pregnant at seventeen, then sneaking off to get married. Her fiancé never showed up at the courthouse, leaving her to slink home and face more abuse. When she lost the baby, Julie punished herself daily for failing the unborn child. Several months later, Julie saw a poster advertising the Army Nurse Corps. With high school completed, she enlisted.

The discipline of the Army became something Julie relished. Never wanting to see her parents again, her heart ached to find her lost brother and sister. The husband she mentioned—there was no such person. Only a crazy statement from a lonely person trying to get a laugh. She told Mary, "I feel I'm a success on my own, having the freedom to do what I want. One day, I'll find a man who won't leave me at the altar. In the meantime, I'll take care of myself."

That made it easy for Mary to share the details of her relationship.

"Leave the bastard," her new friend concluded. "You're far too good for that kind of treatment. Maybe there's a way for you to get custody once you're back home. After all, a few adoption agencies are starting to allow single women to apply. Why not you?"

The bouncing cargo plane took a sudden dip, causing many to grab onto their bench. The air pressure grew and grew, hurting the ears. With no windows, it was a surprise when the aircraft banged and bumped onto the runway. The engine noise somehow grew more deafening during taxiing. Finally, the mammoth engines shut down, replaced by blessed quiet.

Over the PA system, the pilot apologized for the rough trip. "We stayed lower than usual because of reports that North Korean fighters might be in the area. A couple of our jet jockeys were above us to make sure we stayed safe. Let me welcome you to Pusan, the garden spot of Korea."

The stairway rolled against the plane, and the door swung open. Mary took her first breath at the top of the stairs, causing her to gag. The air temperature was stifling, and the putrid smell caused several nurses to cover their mouths with handkerchiefs. Immediately, flies swarmed. No matter how the nurses waved their arms, it proved useless.

Slightly dizzy from the travel, she stood on the dirt runway. Her eyes tried to blink away the dust while she panned the horizon. In every direction, countless personnel and equipment moved. An endless line of planes waited for unloading. The massive activity created a thick haze of dust that invaded her lungs. In the air, she could see planes lined up to land—the roar from cargo airplanes waiting for takeoff added to her growing headache. In the distance, through the haze, stark brown mountains stood void of any vegetation.

An officer approached, carrying a sign indicating the nurses were to follow him. Because of the noise level, the soldier had to yell. "Your bags are on their way. All newcomers have the same reaction when they first arrive. Most of the stench is because local farmers use human feces to fertilize their fields. That means the local population defecates in open trenches and fields. Since this facility is next to farms, the odor is powerful. It gets worse when you leave the base. I hate to say it, but you'll get used to the smell and the flies. Tonight, you meet the mosquitoes. Please follow me."

Sweat dripped off Mary. She flailed her arms, trying to keep the insects off. Dust and sweat mixed on her face. *I need cold water. How can anyone work in this noise and heat? New Hampshire gets humid, but not like this.*

Soaked through from the walk, the nurses reached a large tent where their guide held a door flap open. Even though stuffy inside, it was a relief to be out of the blistering sun with fewer flies. Clammy and ready to collapse, Mary headed for water jugs on a table. *Just a few minutes here and already worn out.*

Two officers strode in, one calling, "Ten hut!"

The nurses jumped to attention. The senior officer announced, "At ease, ladies. Find a seat. For those getting drinks, please continue." Short and in his early fifties, he commanded the room with the rigid bearing of a career military man. A small gut hung over his belt.

"My name is Major Phillips, head of the 100th Mobile Army Surgical Hospital. We're stationed north of here in Taegu." He looked tired, his voice gravelly. Deep furrows ran above his eyes, definitely a serious man. "Major Samuelson, head of Medical Services, couldn't make it today and asked me to greet you. Captain Brown, who leads the Medical Air Transport Service, is to my right. It's with pleasure that we welcome you."

Once the nurses settled, Philips continued. "I cannot tell you how you're needed. I'm aware of the quick reassignments and the brutal travel. Honestly, what you've experienced is nothing compared to what we'll be asking of you over the next months.

"The sum of it is, the North Koreans caught the South Korean Army with their pants down. It's been hell ever since. Once General MacArthur organized our defense, we started to slow the enemy's advance. There's a fifty-mile buffer between here and where combat takes place north of Taegu. We hope to stop the North Korean advance and eventually push them back. For now, that is uncertain."

He paused and scanned every nurse's eyes, all hanging on his words. "Let me be clear. You're in an active combat zone. Once you're with your unit, briefings on procedures to be aware of will be provided. You'll also receive appropriate equipment, including helmets and vests. Of course, we hope you'll never need all of that materiel, but the unexpected can quickly happen."

"Of the twelve of you, four will be assigned to Captain Brown to work on air transports. That means caring for wounded being shipped back to Japan. I know that flight can be rough, but I'm sure you four will do a bang-up job. If you're wondering why we're assigning Army personnel to an Air Force operation, the simple answer is we need trained people immediately. We'll decide down the road if you four will be permanent or just temporary. Captain, please call your people and take them for flight orientation."

"Thank you. I join Major Phillips in welcoming you to Korea. Lieutenants Wallace, Griffin, Henderson, and Truance, please follow me. For you others, I leave you in the Major's good care."

Those four rose, gathering their things. Hugs and quick goodbyes ensued.

Major Phillips addressed the remaining nurses. "The rest of you will be assigned to either of two MASH Units. Per your training, Mobile Army Surgical Hospital testing occurred at the end of the last war. That experience showed a thirty percent drop in combat fatalities. Getting our wounded quickly to first-rate professionals like yourselves gives each serviceman the best chance to survive. That means MASH units operate close behind the front."

"Four of you will join the 100th MASH with me, with the remaining nurses assigned to the Eighth MASH. I mentioned that the 100th is operating in Taegu. There's a train leaving in the morning to get us there. The following will become part of my unit: Lieutenants Jackson, Franks, Fellows, and Belanger. For those reporting to the Eighth, a jeep will take you to their staging area. For the nurses heading to the 100th, you won the lottery and will see action first. Before turning you over to my aide, I'm sure you have questions. What might I answer?"

The eight women glanced nervously at each other before Julie raised her hand. "Major, what advice do you have for us joining the MASH units? And is there a way for a girl to get a shower with all these men around?"

The others laughed at Julie's question, along with the Major. "Lieutenant, there are no showers due to a shortage of water. Because of the poor quality of local water, we are limited by what we can ship from Japan. We're still scaling up supply operations. The bulk of what we can bring we prioritize for the front. You'll find access to limited water you can put in your helmets for sponge baths. That's the best we can do for now."

"As for your first question, I don't have any words of wisdom. We'll ask a lot of you daily, usually more than you think you can give. I see in Taegu how our nurses do whatever is necessary. I'm sure all of you will rise to that level of performance. Anything else?"

He nodded at the silence. "Lieutenant Bowers will be here shortly to help draw your equipment and get you to your quarters. In the meantime, please remain seated and at ease. Good luck to each of you. For the four joining my unit, if I can get things wrapped up here, I might see you on the train tomorrow."

The nurses huddled after the officer left, asking about their experience serving in MASH units. None had worked in one during the last months of World War II, but each had taken part in training during field exercises. All knew the real thing would not resemble any exercise.

One nurse said, "The four heading to Air Transport duty will be better off. When they're not flying, they'll be based in Japan and have access to hot water and American-style food. Plus, they will be nowhere near the front lines."

Mary silently thought to herself, *I'm glad I didn't get that air assignment. Constantly back and forth to Japan on flights like that one that got me here sounds awful. Even if the flights aren't bumpy, I'd be on my feet no matter the conditions. With only one or two nurses on each plane to care for a load of wounded men and medical emergencies, no thanks. My unit may be close to the front, but at least my feet will be on the ground. Now that I know where I'm going, what did that major mean about them asking a lot of us?*

Fifteen minutes later, Lieutenant Bowers led the eight nurses to the supply tent. One-piece dark green fatigues for work in the field came first. Frustration rose among the nurses. "These fatigues are far too big. Could you please get us smaller sizes, Sergeant?"

Through the half-smoked cigarette hanging out of his mouth, he said, "Sorry, ma'am. We only have men's sizes. You'll have to make do and write your congressman."

Too big was an understatement, Mary thought. She asked to trade in her boots since they were also far too large. "No boots available, Lieutenant."

The equipment for each nurse slowly piled up. Helmets, again, too large. Gas masks, one size, no matter the differences in facial shape. A heavy flak vest. Bedroll. Canteen. Mess gear. Mosquito net.

"Will we be issued rifles, Sergeant?" Mary asked.

"No rifles or ammunition, ladies. That way, you can't shoot me when you try to carry all this gear out of here."

Nurses assigned to the Eighth loaded into jeeps amid another round of goodbyes. The remaining four labored to carry their equipment in the unrelenting heat and dust to their temporary quarters. Lieutenant Bowers didn't offer to help. When they thankfully reached a tent marked "For Women Only," they found several rows of cots with a musty odor, one blanket, and a bare pillow on each bunk.

"I don't think there's anyone else in here tonight. Take whichever cot you want," said Bowers. "The mess tent is back the way we came for dinner and breakfast. The train is at 0900. A truck will take you to the station departing at 0800. Good evening."

The women moved to claim cots. "Mary, over here," Julie called. "Let's grab these two."

Julie immediately headed out to search for the nearest bathroom. Mary dropped onto the cot, wiping her face with a handkerchief. *How will I get all this shit in my duffle? Thank goodness they didn't give us a gun.*

Sweat dripped down her face, adding to the feeling of total exhaustion. The stark conditions of the tent and the incessant din of the airbase heightened the pounding in her head. She felt awful. *I'm filthy. Have a sponge bath since there's no showers. Use your helmet? How much good is that going to do? I wish I had aspirin.* She stared at the tent roof, wishing she was anywhere else.

Julie came bouncing in. "You don't want to see the latrine setup for women, but I should show you where they are."

Mary somehow managed to sit up, running her hand through her damp hair. "Let's get back to the mess tent. I need to find water and aspirin." The two stepped toward the door.

Mary spied a long purple centipede crawling on the dirt floor. She suppressed a desire to scream, cautiously stepping over the creature.

Covered by a mosquito net, Mary wondered if sleep would ever come. The roar of planes coming and going never let up, and the temperature didn't seem to drop. Her light pajamas, damp with sweat, clung to her. Any relief from the sponge bath was long gone. In the dim light, the strange bugs and mosquitos outside the netting were too numerous to count. Once the sun had gone down, the insects seemed to coordinate their direct attack.

Mary hoped she wouldn't have to go to the bathroom during the night and expose herself to the bugs. Julie hadn't exaggerated about the terrible latrines. The rustling from nearby cots meant others were suffering the same difficulties.

With her eyes closed, Mary conjured the image of Cindy. The baby would be starting a new day on the other side of the world. When New Hampshire weather was hot and sticky, she and the baby had played in water under a big tree. Mary thought back to days growing up when her mother did the same. Her chest tightened with thoughts about what she might face tomorrow. *These are the last hours before being thrown into God knows what. Maybe there won't be fighting when I get to my new unit. I'll have to explain my lack of experience. I need to sleep, but can't stop thinking. Damn, my legs itch. Isn't this netting supposed to keep the bugs out? Are these fleas?*

CHAPTER 5

After breakfast, the nurses assembled next to a large canvas-covered truck. A soldier helped the four nurses load into the back. Mary settling near the tailgate. A guard jumped up and took the seat opposite her. His rifle rested on his lap, pointing out.

Still groggy after a fitful night, Mary took everything in around her like a terrible movie. Breakfast had been awful. The base's stench, the instant eggs, spam, soggy toast, and weak coffee, had done nothing to ease her despair. She'd forced herself to take small bites.

One soldier at the table remarked, "Better get used to that, ma'am. This crap is daily breakfast until we get out of this hellhole."

With a sudden jerk, the truck took off, causing Mary to grab the bench to avoid falling out. She watched a cloud of dust follow the vehicle which joined the larger plume enveloping the air base. The first drop of sweat rolled down her nose, mixing with the grime. At least the truck's motion created a slight breeze, keeping the flies temporarily at bay. But the terrible odor worsened as the truck drew close to the base gate.

Besides the aroma of human waste, the smell of burning charcoal now mixed in. Fumes from the grilling brought back memories of happier times cooking in the backyard. When she mentioned this to the guard, he explained that charcoal was the primary cooking fuel of most Koreans. Mary thanked him for the information, all the time scratching flea bites under the ill-fitting fatigues.

Past the guard house, the nurses got their first look at real Korea. A mass of people wearing loose-fitting pants and tops spilled into the road. They looked much smaller than most Americans, and their patchwork clothes showed extreme poverty. Many walked barefoot. A few wore cut-up truck tires as makeshift shoes. Almost all the older men had long grey beards. Several wore incredibly tall black hats. Women staggered under the weight of a child or two with a full sack on their backs or heads. Their pointed straw hats seemed practical, given the strength of the sun. Children ran everywhere, many crying—a few older ones cooked in tin cans over straw fires.

Further on, Mary spotted an enormous bull-like animal led by a man. "Water buffalo," the guard explained. It was mammoth but seemed docile at the same time. Another mile on, in a ditch, a human body lay with several rats at work. She gagged down her breakfast and turned away. The guard shook his head.

The truck picked up speed, crossing canals with floating human waste and dead animals. Mary wondered why only the nurses were reacting. Finally, she asked the soldier, "You don't seem bothered by this place. Is it a matter of getting used to things?"

Tiredly, the guard looked back. "A day doesn't pass where I don't struggle to adjust. One day easy occupation duty in Japan, and then this. Yeah, I got used to the smell. There's not much choice."

"What about the dust? Does that get better?"

"Ma'am, when it rains, all this will turn to mud. Then you'll wish for dust. Get used to the color we wear here—shit brown."

Mary smiled weakly and turned her attention to the town. The truck maneuvered carefully through busy, narrow streets teeming with people. She recalled movie nights in Manchester and the short travelogs shown before the main feature. In those films, nothing resembled what was before her. How could this be the same planet that held New Hampshire?

Most Koreans waved, many yelling when they spotted the American women. The nurses were an event. Suddenly, a sharp turn caused her to slide into the guard while the driver blasted the horn. With a lurch, they stopped. Several armed American guards appeared with weapons at the ready, checking the passengers in the vehicle. Waved on, the truck eased past the checkpoint into the rail yard.

A loud hiss from an old steam engine that looked like it belonged in a museum pierced the air. The guard jumped from the truck to help the nurses with their packs. "End of this part of the journey, ladies. This train isn't the Orient Express, but it's the easiest way to travel in Korea. I hope your trip goes safely."

The four nurses stepped into a sea of jostling bodies. Hundreds of American combat troops in full battledress moved toward the train. Several tanks rested on flatcars. On the roof of each railcar sat machine gunners surrounded by sandbags.

The women pushed their way through the crowd of military personnel. From the soldiers, catcalls started.

"They must be nurses."

"Nurse, nurse, I'm hurt. Help me."

"Forget him, ma'am, over here. I'm the one who needs help."

"Hey, beautiful, how did Hollywood let you get away?"

The women looked at each other, rolled their eyes, and continued to struggle forward.

An officer stepped over and ordered, "You men, quiet down and get to where you belong." He checked the list on his clipboard. "I assume they assigned you four to the 100th MASH, correct?"

"Yes, sir, " they responded in unison.

"You'll be in the second car, sitting toward the back. If there's any shooting at the train, it's typically at the engine. The first rail car has more chance of taking fire. Let me get a few men to help you with those duffels and equipment."

Volunteers surrounded the officer.

The four nurses climbed into their assigned coach and were getting settled when several officers entered. The women jumped up to salute. The senior officer said, "At ease, ladies— no need to stand on formality with us moving to the front. Although this train lacks amenities, let us know if we can get anything to make you more comfortable. By the way, if there's any shooting, hit the deck."

A sharp blast of the whistle, and the train lurched forward. The chaotic station passed out of sight within minutes, along with Pusan and its ramshackle huts. A more open countryside soon came into view. The rhythmic rocking of the train took the edge off Mary's nervousness.

She pressed against the window, surprised by how green the countryside farms looked. With hazy mountains in the distance, the train edged between flooded fields with rows of plants sticking out. Numerous men wearing those broad hats worked in knee-deep water. More water buffalos pulled carts along paths in the distance.

Mary looked at the officers huddled around maps and noted Major Phillips was not among them. Although her new commanding officer had spoken yesterday for only a few minutes, he'd impressed her with his confidence and manner. She closed her eyes to try and sleep, but the smell of burning coal, the lurching car, and the squealing wheels made that impossible. The nagging worries and fears returned. Her belly roiled and would not settle. The train rolled on.

In the early afternoon, they reached Taegu. One officer commented, "Half a day to go forty-five miles on this so-called railroad. When you see the condition of Korean roads, you'll understand why this is better."

The senior officer joined the nurses. "Welcome to Taegu, ladies. Let us help you with your bags."

Glad for the assistance, the small party pushed through the throng that filled Taegu Station. When they reached the main entrance, Julie called, "Over there. Someone has a sign for the 100th MASH. Tell the guys to bring our gear this way."

The officers said a last goodbye and wished them luck. Two guards from MASH checked each nurse's name, then picked up as much equipment as they could. Outside the station building, a Korean jumped out and knocked Ann Jackson down, attempting to rip her shoulder bag from her grasp. On one knee, Ann fought back, struggling with the man. The soldiers dropped what they were carrying, chasing the thief away. The would-be bandit disappeared into the crowd as the guards helped Ann up. "You all right, Lieutenant?"

Shaken, she responded, "I'm okay. Does that happen often?"

The GI picked up his packs and said, "People here have nothing and often have to steal to feed their families. What is in your bag might get that kid more than his family makes in a month. Some of it could also end up in the hands of North Korean partisans operating behind our lines. Good job hanging onto it, ma'am."

Mary and Julie grimaced at each other and rearranged their grip on their bags. Soon, another canvas-covered truck and more armed soldiers came into view. Two guards took up positions in the rear with the nurses and baggage.

The truck bounced along. Like in Pusan, crowded streets and poor peasants passed by. Here, more Koreans filled the road carrying children and loads of possessions. The teeming number of desperate people pushing and jostling overwhelmed Mary. A tired soldier explained that most were refugees fleeing the war. For the first time, she heard the low rumble of artillery in the distance. *How close might actual fighting be?*

After a series of turns, the truck entered a part of town filled with well-kept homes. Although smaller than typical houses back home, this part of the city was home to a wealthier class. Only a few minutes later, the vehicle stopped at a security checkpoint. Once cleared, the truck labored up a long hill, stopping in front of a two-story, white building with peeling, faded paint. It appeared to be an old school with playground equipment on the side.

The moment Mary jumped down from the truck, she felt paralyzed. Just ahead, orderlies unloaded stretchers of the wounded from a line of ambulances. Although still some distance away, Mary recognized heavily bandaged wounds soaked with blood. A stretcher trailed blood onto the leg of an orderly when he lowered the soldier onto the ground. She fought for breath, seeing too many who needed immediate attention.

To the left, a couple of orderlies strung up a tarp to provide shade for the line of helpless men lying under the relentless sun. Nearby, two nurses assisted a doctor conducting examinations. One of those women, covered in blood, spied the newly arrived nurses. She nodded a greeting. Mary wondered if she should drop her gear and go over to help. Another ambulance bringing more casualties crept past, honking its horn and forcing Mary to jump out of the way. *Damn, I almost became a casualty.*

An orderly emerged from the hospital and walked over to the new arrivals. "Welcome to the 100th. You can see we're hard at it. Your hands are needed immediately. First Lieutenant

Bates, our head of nursing, requests you report to her. Leave all your gear here. We'll get it to your quarters. The lieutenant is working in the OR on the second floor. Please come this way."

The new nurses followed the orderly into the building. Inside, the metallic smell of open wounds, mixed with antiseptic, swept over them. Mary felt dizzy and reached for the wall to steady herself. In a corridor leading to stairs, she saw patients fill every spot on the floor, each with a colored tag on his toe or stretcher. A nurse in blood-spattered fatigues carrying soaked dressings stepped out of a side room. She murmured, "Welcome to the circus."

Mary tried to steady her breathing following the group up the stairs. Ahead she could see the operating rooms. More men with seeping bandages or missing limbs lay on stretchers along the sidewalls, nurses cutting off their uniforms to prep for surgery. An exhausted nurse looked up at the new arrivals. "We're glad to see you—been at this for fourteen hours. Your arrival couldn't come at a better time."

The new nurses gave quick greetings, then caught up to the orderly.

Besides the stench of wounds and dirt, a realization struck Mary. Despite being surrounded by a multitude of seriously wounded, except for an occasional moan or stifled cry of pain, silence ruled. Their grimaces and facial contortions told how these men suffered. It stunned her to see these wounded bravely dealing with the worst moments of their lives.

At pre-op, where staff scrubbed up, the orderly pulled back a curtain and stepped into the first operating area. "The new nurses are here. What do you want them to do?"

David Walsh, head surgeon, and chief medical officer looked up from his patient. "Have them mask up and stand by the door—no need for them to scrub. Then you can go, Charlie. Thanks for your help."

The orderly turned. "You heard the captain. Masks are on

the shelf behind you."

Mary's hands shook, making it hard to cover her face properly. The four edged around the curtain into the OR. Before them stood an operating table. Off to the right stood a second where a bear of a man worked. One anesthesiologist moved between both tables, the floor slick with blood. Death's smell mixed in the stagnant air.

The head surgeon worked quietly for a moment. "That should do it, Sally. Would you mind closing him? Oh, these are your new people. I'll do the closing. First, you need to introduce yourself and give them assignments."

"I can do the closing, Doctor. You could use a break."

"I'm fine—talk to your people. I got this."

Covered with splattered blood, Lieutenant Sally Bates turned. "Welcome. We're glad you're here. But you've walked into a bit of a mess. No telling how long the casualties will keep arriving, meaning we have to put you to work."

The four murmured variations of "No problem, ma'am."

"We're informal here. I'm Sally, and that man sewing is Dave. He's our chief surgeon. You can meet the rest later. Two of you are experienced OR nurses. Please identify yourselves."

Mary's heart sank. She and Ann Jackson slowly raised their arms.

"You two scrub and gown up, then get back in here. There's no running water, but you'll find a jerry can and soap where you got the masks. You others report to triage outside to help there and learn the system. I'm sure you saw it when you entered the hospital. Please get to it."

Julie locked eyes with Mary. Anxiety washed over their faces. Standing outside the curtain, Mary touched her friend's arm. "You'll be fine."

Julie gave a quick hug. "You too," as she rushed out.

With a surgical gown on and washing up, Mary thought, *You'll do fine, but I'm not sure I will.* Weak in the knees and her stomach doing flips, Mary concentrated on thoroughly cleaning before donning surgical gloves.

Back in the OR, the surgeon called "Litter." That signaled orderlies to bring the next patient. An orderly quickly replaced the soiled linens with a fresh set. Within seconds, the next man, who had no legs, lay on the table. The operating team started unwrapping bandages from the bloody stumps. Eyes wide, Mary swallowed hard, choking down bile.

Without looking up, Dave sensed the new arrivals. "One of you get over there and work with that big galoot. We call him Bones because his are inordinately large. Ignore his size. He's a pussycat, although he doesn't like anyone to know that."

A loud "Meow" carried from the nearby operating table. Being closer, Ann glanced at Mary, then stepped over.

Mary stepped closer to the senior surgeon's table, slipping on the blood-drenched floor. She regained her balance, noticing that the operating table was nothing more than a board held up by two sawhorses. The surgeon caught her glance. "Careful there. The floor can get slick from all these operations. Like our fancy equipment? The portable operating tables haven't caught up with us. By the way, Sally, I need more bricks under the table legs. My back is aching from bending over."

Lieutenant Bates barked at an orderly. "You heard the doctor. Scout out something to raise the table and check with the other surgeons to see if they need the same."

The tall, hefty surgeon at the next table said, "I don't have a problem. I work on my knees."

A few chuckles came from around the room. At the same time, fresh, sterilized surgical tools and X-rays appeared.

From behind his mask, Dave looked directly into Mary's eyes. "What's your name?" The surgeon turned to the X-rays. Simultaneously, the anesthesiologist put the patient under.

"Lieutenant Mary Belanger, Captain."

"I like that, Sally. Finally, a bit of respect around here. This should be straightforward with the amputations, then ligating of the arteries. I don't see any other injuries. X-rays looked clean to me. What do you see?"

"It does look straightforward," Sally responded. "No other breaks or wounds. Poor bastard probably stepped on a land mine."

"Chet, tell me when you have him ready."

"All set."

The surgeon and senior nurse leaned down to work on the soldier. After a few minutes, Dave asked, "Where were you stationed, Mary? And by the way, it's Dave from here on. Until you get in trouble—then it's Captain David Walsh. Are you a troublemaker, Mary?"

"No, sir. I mean, no, Dave." Mary smelled burning flesh as the surgeon and nurse cauterized blood vessels. Head spinning, she fought dizziness and trembling legs.

"That's too bad, Mary. I had higher hopes for you."

A small laugh escaped her.

"Where were you stationed?"

"I'm in the Reserves, not regular Army."

Dave raised his head, eyes smiling above his mask. "Lucky lady. One day living a quiet life, then you get a terrible letter. Where did the Army pluck you from?"

"Manchester, New Hampshire."

"Beautiful country. The mosquitoes there are almost as bad as here. . . . I take that back. Korean mosquitoes have New Hampshire beaten by a mile. Work in the local hospital?"

"Yes, but not for the past two months. I left because I started caring for a baby."

Both Dave and Sally lifted their heads.

Mary said, "I'm not the mother. My sister-in-law gave birth and then disappeared, so we took the baby. When I got called up, there's no exemption for a surrogate parent." In a burst of nervousness, she went on. "I've not been in an OR for a couple of months. Even then, I worked the day shift and rarely saw extreme cases—mostly tonsils and simple procedures. None of the patients I worked with died or even came close."

Dave returned to stitching wounds. "Tonsils can get complicated. Although it's been a while, it's like riding a bicycle after a long spell. It'll come back quickly. You should feel nervous. We all did when we got here. Okay, Sally, I think we're done. If you and Mary could apply the dressings on what's left of this poor guy's legs, I'd appreciate that."

Heart racing, Mary stepped forward to stand next to the senior nurse. Sally pointed out the dressings and antiseptic. Mary's hands shook, taking the bandages as she started to wrap the stump. *I can't believe this is happening.* Biting down hard on her lip, she tried to copy how the senior nurse was doing the wrapping.

"Be sure to apply lots of pressure," Sally said. "We want to reduce the chance of excessive bleeding and don't want this guy to visit us a second time."

After she applied the dressings, Mary looked down, her hands visibly trembling. Sally and Dave watched.

"That's a good start, even for the most experienced," Dave said. "You'll be fine with a little time."

"Thank you, Doctor. I'm very nervous and don't want to hurt anybody."

"None of us do, Mary. As I said, we were all overwhelmed when we walked into this factory." After the surgeon called "Litter," orderlies carried the finished patient out. Then, another stretcher moved in while orderlies changed sheets, positioned clean surgical tools, and posted X-rays.

Dave faced Mary. "I believe in diving right in and getting you wet. I'd like you to assist me in the next surgery. Sally will stand by. At times she might help, if for no other reason than I'm a tough guy to work with. Don't take that intervention personally. We need to get you trained as fast as possible. Are you willing to give it a try?"

"Do you think this is a good idea?" Sally asked. "Maybe I should send her to clean-up duty since she's inexperienced, and there's no way to avoid death in this place. I can sort out her situation later."

Yes, yes, yes! Please. I can't do this. Please God, get me out of here.

With the patient already on the table, Mary stared at a gaping wound in his middle, exposing stomach and intestines. She heard herself somehow say, "I'll do my best, sir."

"That the spirit. I know you can do it. We'll be okay, Sally, Even with this nasty one to start. Make the rest look like a piece of cake. Okay, first look, perforated bowel and stomach. There's dirt and shredded clothing driven in that we need to clean. I'm going to sew up the lower part of the stomach after cleaning, then stitch up the bowel. It looks like I may have to remove part of the intestines. Chet, is the patient ready?"

"Patient is out. Vital signs stable."

"Let's go. Mary, please give me a medium clamp."

Mary reached for the surgical tray, feeling Sally's comforting hand on her back. The senior nurse's other hand snaked around, pointing to the right piece of equipment.

"There's no more after this one," the orderly reported.

"Thank goodness," Sally said from the other surgical table, where she was assisting Ann. It had been a few patients since Sally stood close to coach Mary. "This is as bad as we've seen it—about eighteen hours since the first wounded arrived. Things are under control here. I'm going to check on triage and post-op."

Relief flooded Mary with the finish line finally in view— one more operation to survive. With the senior nurse moving away, things must be acceptable. Soaked to the bone under her surgical gown from the heat and stress, she thought, *Please, don't let me screw up this last one.*

Dave shook his head, staring at the injured man on the

table. "Another abdominal, although the medics cleaned this guy's wounds well. Perforated spleen. It looks like a sniper hit him since the exit wound is clean. Chet, is he ready?"

"Our last victim is out."

Dave made the cuts and quickly had the damaged area of the spleen ready for stitching. Suddenly, the artery next to the spleen burst, sending a fountain of blood into the surgeon's eyes. Dave dropped his tools and staggered back, desperately trying to clear his vision. Mary panicked, realizing the patient would die if the artery continued to bleed. Without hesitation, she snatched a clamp from the surgical tray and sealed off the ruptured artery.

From the next table, Bones called, "Dave, you need me? Ann, take over here." The big surgeon rushed over while an orderly finished cleaning Dave's eyes. Both doctors looked at the open wound where Mary held the clamp.

With the emergency past, Bones headed back to his table, saying, "Bet that doesn't happen with tonsils."

Dave stood next to the patient. "Damn fine work, New Hampshire. You saved this man's life."

Sitting on a stair outside the makeshift hospital, waves of nausea washed over Mary. After the last operation, Sally had shown the new arrivals clean-up procedures and how to prepare equipment for the subsequent surgeries.

Now outside in the gathering dark and fighting back the tears, Mary welcomed a cooling breeze. Her mind replayed the many American boys' awful wounds and ruined bodies. Wrung out after four hours of surgery, she realized each operation had averaged fifteen minutes. *How had the other nurses worked fourteen hours before the new staff arrived? Will I have the strength to do that? At least no one died on our table today.*

Mary felt a hand on her back. Sally and Ann Jackson moved

close. "You look a little tuckered out," Sally said. "Get to the nurses' quarters down the hill for rest and something to eat."

"I'm not tired and can help you with the laundry," Ann offered.

"No, you two need a break after all your traveling. I hate to say it, but there'll probably be no let-up tomorrow. Charge up your batteries. I'm glad artillery isn't firing. Maybe we'll get lucky and have a lighter day."

"Laundry?" Mary gasped. "On top of everything, now you have to do laundry?"

"We have a couple of locals who help, but I want to ensure it gets done correctly and that we have enough. One thing we're consistently short of is clean linens. We need to tear up sheets if we don't have enough bandages. Plus, I have to get these floors hosed down. Enough for now. You two go get chow and sleep."

Ann asked, "If I might inquire, ma'am, when do you sleep?"

Sally gave a tired smile. "We have a saying around here. I'll sleep when I'm dead. In the meantime, you two get going."

Mary and Ann started down the hill. Their new boss called, "Both of you, great work, especially for your first day. Today was worse than usual. We typically have two docs at a table, but there were too many wounded. Thanks for stepping right in. And Mary, quick thinking to clamp off that artery. Well done."

"Thanks," Mary said. Seeing Sally without a face mask, she wondered if the senior nurse was the one who needed a break. She had short blond hair and an ultrathin build, but what stood out most were the deep worry lines and dark bags around her eyes. Sally seemed to be in a trance-like state.

Down the hill at their quarters, a nurse pointed Ann and Mary toward bunks where their gear lay. With no showers available, Mary stepped out of her soaked uniform to change into dry clothes. The other nurses invited her for dinner, but Mary only wanted to lie down. After encouraging her to reconsider, one older nurse said, "Get some sleep. We'll bring something back for when you're feeling better."

After putting up the mosquito netting, Mary collapsed on her cot. Although it was quiet in the tent, replays of the surgeries wouldn't stop. The moments when Sally had to intervene made Mary shudder. She could hear the senior nurse's instructions over and over again.

Julie burst into quarters, coming to kneel next to Mary. "When I didn't see you in the chow line, they said you were too tired to eat. I wanted to make sure you're okay. You look beat. How did it go today? I'll be honest: when our new boss assigned me to triage, I counted my blessings."

From under the mosquito netting, Mary took her friend's hand. "It's tougher than I even expected. I'm not used to such extreme wounds and the pace of everything. How can I keep up? All those damaged young men on the table depend on me. Dave and Sally are supportive, but I can't imagine being in surgery again tomorrow."

Her friend squeezed Mary's hand. "I heard you did fine and even saved your surgeon's bacon. Don't be hard on yourself. I learned in triage that life and death are what this place is about. Those tags on wounded guys—that's us deciding who gets what treatment and when. If a patient is not going to survive, we load them up with morphine and put a black tag on the stretcher. It's . . ." Julie broke into a full sob, grabbing Mary's hand.

Mary reached deep for the energy to stand up and push aside the netting. She took Julie in her arms. "We'll be okay," Mary heard herself say. "Some we're treating are only eighteen years old. We have to be there for them."

CHAPTER 6

A loud barrage of artillery fire pierced the nighttime silence. Once it started, there was no letup. Although a distance away, something was happening out there.

Mary scanned the room of sleeping nurses, although none seemed to notice the sound. Exhaustion eventually won out, allowing her to fall back to sleep. All too soon, she felt her foot shaken.

The senior nurse stood at the foot of her bunk. "Wounded on the way. Time to get ready for the onslaught." Sally moved on to wake the next nurse.

That's not enough sleep. The sun's already up. I can't move.

Mary rubbed her eyes. She now remembered last night that another nurse said the senior nurse would conduct a supply inventory after laundry. *Did that woman ever sleep?*

Sally came back. "Unless you object, Dave wants you to assist today. He likes how you work and that you're a quick learner."

Panic ran through Mary. Sally recognized the look. "Don't worry. I'll stay close. We're here to help each other, but you're the first nurse Dave requested. That says a lot coming from our head surgeon. His table is Surgery One, which will also be your title."

Mary tried to smile.

Sally continued. "Did you get enough rest? I see you skipped dinner. Better hustle to the mess hall and get something in your stomach. It looks like another long day."

"Ma'am, maybe I dreamed this, but I remember waking last night with the artillery heavier and closer. Did I imagine that?"

"The North Koreans attack at night, meaning that's when the bulk of the fighting happens. They do this to neutralize our Air Force, which controls the skies during daylight hours. That's why we're getting casualties now from the nighttime fighting. Unfortunately, our lines are not holding, and combat is closer. You'd better get a move on, or you'll miss chow."

Mary jumped up to put herself in high gear, then glanced down at her duffel. She had yet to unpack pictures of Cindy, her mom, of home. That would have to wait.

The loudspeaker system barked to life—five minutes to ambulances. Mary shoveled in the instant eggs and spam, chewing as fast as possible. With one more forkful stuffed into her mouth, she bolted from the table and sprinted to OR. In her pockets were two apples and several candy bars a nurse had left the previous evening.

In pre-op, Dave was scrubbing. "There you are. I wondered if you walked back to Manchester after the baptism by fire we gave you."

"No, sir, simply a tough time waking up. I admit this is all stressful. Hopefully, I can do better today."

"You did great yesterday and will be fine today. All this was new for all of us a few weeks ago. You picked it up fast. All right, I can hear the first ambulances pulling in. Someone will be on the table in a few minutes. Chet's already in there with the gas. Join us when you're ready."

A couple of minutes later, Mary stood at the operating table.

Bones came over and introduced himself as Jackson Wright. "I apologize for not coming over yesterday, but we were a bit occupied. That's Wally, heading this way, who also works anesthesia. You new ladies were popular, and we had to have you back. Let me know if there's anything I can do to help you get settled."

Dave interrupted, "Bones, stay over where you belong and leave this poor woman alone. It's bad enough that now Ann has to put up with you."

The hulking surgeon walked back to his table. "Only jealousy from the smaller males in our unit. Pure envy."

A grey-haired doctor replaced Bones. "Roger Anderson, Mary. Glad to meet you. You probably met my assistant, Judy, in your powder room. We often are part of Surgery One, but we were down the hall yesterday because of the load. Hopefully, we won't get that stretched today."

Mary gave a quizzical look to Judy, who gave a wry grin. "These docs think they're hilarious coming up with names like the powder room for the miserable places we sleep."

Everyone stopped speaking when orderlies placed the first patient on the table. The senior surgeon winced, looking down at the damaged body.

"Both legs gone, and a serious abdominal wound. Left arm may not be recoverable. Facial lacerations and scalp wounds. I'm surprised this guy didn't get a black tag. He's obviously a fighter to make it this far—time for us to fight for him. There are no X-rays, but there's not much left to take a picture of. Chet, let me know when you have him ready. Roger, I'll start work on his abdomen. You focus on his legs."

Chet said, "A few more seconds. With him having only a single arm, I had to swing the blood pressure cuff around. He's ready to go and as stable as anyone can be in that condition."

Mary realized she had yet to take a full breath. She fought

to clear her head when Dave asked for the first instrument. Her hand felt heavy, reaching for the surgical tray. Sally again stood behind her, giving her a friendly pat. Mary passed the first tool.

Seven and a half hours later, an orderly reported only a few remaining cases. With the casualty load more manageable than the day before, Mary welcomed the breaks to rest and have food brought in every few hours. At the first break, she felt too ill to eat anything, forcing herself to drink water to stay hydrated. Her appetite allowed an apple and a couple of candy bars by the next break. Then, time to scrub up again.

With only a few more surgeries, Dave told the orderly to funnel those to the other tables since he needed to process paperwork. Roger and Judy said they would see who needed a break or help. From the next table, Bones shook his head. "There goes typical management. I have office work. The rest of you clean up this mess."

With his gown and gloves off, Dave called back, "I have lots of paperwork. Most of it related to you, Bones, and all the complaints about you goofing off."

The big doctor loudly said, "The more who file about me, the better chance to be assigned to a nice stockade stateside. This place is the real punishment."

"I hope you don't mind the irreverence," Dave said to Mary. "It helps keep us sane. By the way, well done today. Tomorrow we'll switch roles since that might be the only way to rattle you."

Sally came up from behind. "I agree. You two make a great team. Should we make it a regular?"

"Done," Dave said, heading out the door.

"Are you ready for a tour of this place, Mary? We've had you tied up in OR."

"I'd like to see the rest of the unit. I'm glad we had a shorter day than yesterday. Is this typical, or is it more like yesterday?"

"No telling," Sally said, leading her down the hall, past more rooms with operating tables. "Presently, we have six tables. Keep in mind that we get cases at all hours. There's always a surgical team on standby."

The two entered a large room containing post-op. Sally paused and lowered her voice. "Let me tell you what your duties mean if you support Dave. Because he's the chief medical officer, he has other responsibilities like now and may not always take a table. That might happen when casualties are lighter, although we haven't seen many days like that. When the brass shows up, Dave must play host. Then I may assign you to another surgeon or to work in triage or post-op. You might stock supplies, sterilize equipment, or even be on the dreaded laundry patrol. I promise we won't let you get bored."

"With a baby at home, I know how to deal with dirty laundry."

"It must be miserable leaving a child where you're the acting mother. Who is taking care of the baby now? I assume your husband works. How is he managing?"

Mary shook her head. "It's a complicated situation. I'll tell you the whole story when you're ready to watch me cry."

With a sympathetic look, "I want to hear everything. I need to know what's going on with my people. Want to grab chow tonight? Maybe we can find a corner of the mess hall with some privacy." She grinned. "I follow suit whenever someone cries around me."

"Sure, let me know what time to meet."

"1800 work? Are you okay with food now? I saw you eating a couple of apples during the breaks."

"I'm okay."

"Then let's get acquainted with post-op." Through a curtain and in a large open area where the patients woke from surgery, stretchers were almost shoulder to shoulder, with narrow aisles for nurses to maneuver.

"Ginny, over here," called Sally. A short brunette with a broad smile and sparkling brown eyes walked over. "This is Mary, one of our new stars. Have you met?"

"I dropped by to introduce myself last night, but I should have left you alone since only one of your eyes opened."

Mary reached out to shake her hand. "I think I remember you. Many people were coming by."

"We're glad to have you. Are you turning her over to us, ma'am?"

"She's yours, but only to get an overview of how things work. Mary's been in surgery already. I want her here for no more than an hour. Then send her back to me, and I'll continue her orientation." Sally headed out the door.

"You've been tied up in surgery. That means you've worked a post-op routine before, correct?"

"Yes. But I haven't worked in a hospital for months. So, assume I'm new to everything. That way, I'll get up to speed faster."

"All right, let's start where a patient comes out of surgery and into our waiting arms." Ginny headed to a side door when Mary tapped her shoulder.

"Before we start, our first surgery was a badly wounded guy with no legs and one arm. How's he doing? Is he still here, and might I see him?"

Ginny turned, looking directly at Mary. "No legs and one arm—that describes too many of our customers. I remember your guy since he was one of the first brought to us. Unfortunately, he died of a heart attack shortly after surgery. His system couldn't take it. We tried like hell to revive him, but no luck."

Mary felt the air go out of her. Her legs shook, and wasn't sure they would support her. "Since I became a nurse, that's the first patient I've lost."

Ginny looked away to give Mary a chance to recover. After a minute, "Ready to see the place?"

Mary nodded.

In the nurses' quarters, Mary felt not quite as wrung out as she had the previous day. Thankful for a quiet moment, she unpacked two framed photographs, placing them next to the kerosene lamp on the wood box nightstand. In one picture, her mother held Cindy, and the other was of herself and the baby. Her heart ached. *What are they up to right now? I hope Cindy is sleeping better at night and giving Mom a break. They are there, and somehow this is my new home. For how long?*

The door flew open, and Julie came over to Mary's bunk. She plopped down to look at the pictures. "It must be tough to look at them when stuck here. How are you doing?"

"I miss them. How are you doing?"

"Everyone tells me I'm doing fine, but it's staggering. When you think the load is manageable, more ambulances arrive. Sometimes I feel like a one-armed paperhanger. I've given more morphine shots in the past two days than ever before. We mark 'M' on foreheads to know who has gotten shots. In one case, a dying guy begged me to hold his hand. He kept repeating, 'Mama, Mama, I love you.'" Her head dropped to Mary's shoulder.

A nurse from the other side of their quarters joined them. "Tough way to say welcome. When you first experience this place, it's devastating. After some time, you numb up. Then it's only an unrelenting horror show. By the way, I'm Ellen. What can I do to show you around or share survival secrets?"

"I'm sorry I cried like that," Julie said, wiping her tears.

"No apologies needed. Crying is a standard practice. It helps keep us sane."

Mary smiled. "This old school is a better setup than I expected. I envisioned we'd be in tents."

"This school looks good now, but these buildings were a real dump when the first staff got here. We scrubbed every inch of this place for almost twenty-four straight hours. Then the patients arrived. There were no breaks. Be glad you missed that."

Julie said, "The offer for the tips for survival seems too juicy to pass up."

Ellen sat on a bunk facing the two. "Here are my rules. First, we've never come under direct fire yet, so actual survival hasn't been an issue. None of us wear our helmets or flak jackets, even though we're supposed to. Sally isn't enforcing that requirement. One day we may need them, so know where they are."

"When treating the wounded, one of the under-appreciated stresses of this job is the constant bending. The cots are extremely low. Take care of your back since it suffers a lot of abuse. Oh, and get elastic bands for your pant legs and sleeves—cuts down on the bites from fleas and mites." Ellen grinned.

"For day-to-day survival, sleep whenever you can. You may not feel tired, but no one sleeps when the wounded flood in. Charge your batteries when you have the opportunity—the same thing with food. There's no telling when you may have to miss one or two meals and rely on a candy bar. I always carry a few. It's one of the few free things Uncle Sam gives us."

"Water, oh joyous water. If you want a supply for washing or brushing your teeth, find an extra jerry can to keep by your bed. Make sure you cover it to minimize dust getting in. We ladies have been getting showers twice a week. They post the schedule. The men have separate shower times, but some guys can't follow a chart. If you find yourself next to a naked man, shut your eyes and take care of your own business."

The two new nurses stared in surprise. Julie chuckled, "If the right guy walks in, it doesn't have to be a negative."

The three laughed.

Ellen went on. "Unfortunately, Rock Hudson is not assigned to this unit. The few men I've seen in the buff I'm trying to forget. Dysentery—congratulations, you'll get it. We all do. Keep yourself and your hands as clean as possible, and hope for a mild case. Those are the big issues I can think of."

"What are the head nurse and chief medical officer like?" Julie asked.

"Sally's a good egg, but all Army and committed to whatever the doctors want. Put the gods first, and you'll have no problem with her. She loves unannounced inspections of our quarters. Fortunately, she hasn't been strict with that since things have gotten worse. We also worry about her since she never takes enough of a break. That means we must do what we can to care for her."

Ellen shifted position. "Dave is a great person to work with. The number of docs we're supposed to have is short; a couple here lack full qualifications. We have two interns from stateside Army hospitals they rushed here. Dave and the other docs are training them on the fly. That means the experienced surgeons are overloaded. With you new arrivals, we're fully staffed at eighteen nurses. About ninety other personnel work to support us, including orderlies, guards, cooks, and ambulance drivers. What else can I tell you?"

"That's good stuff," Mary said. "Important to know about our boss. She's been more than helpful when I took over in OR, but I can see how she would get stretched."

"I see you're partnering with Dave," Ellen said. "You already see what a talented surgeon he is. He'll do anything for anyone if it's within his power, but he has no clout in some areas. I predict that you will soon have a crush on the guy since every other nurse does."

Ellen stood up. "Why don't we look for jerry cans and water for you two? Our next shower is not for another day. Then we can wash up and hit the best chow within ten miles—the only chow within ten miles."

"Deal," the two nurses chimed in. Even though it would not be an actual shower, getting the built-up sweat and dirt off with a sponge bath sounded heavenly.

Sally and Mary found a deserted corner of the mess hall at dinner. Once settled, the senior nurse said, "Tell me your story. I'm all ears."

Mary launched into the details, including her philandering husband. Before she knew it, her tablemate had finished eating. Mary's food was untouched.

Sally jumped in. "Time for me to give you a break from talking. That way, you can start on your food. Everything coming down on you is awful. I regret you couldn't get a waiver. The baby must miss you terribly. But selfishly, we're lucky you ended up here. It's only been two days since you joined us, but I can already tell you're a skilled nurse. With what's happening in this war, we need people like you."

"How can you tell my quality of work after such a short time?"

Her companion leaned forward. "I've got a sense for this. What I see is a woman who questions herself. But when events demand performance, you jump in, like clamping off that artery when Dave got blinded. Sure, you're rusty, and no one can ever be prepared for the terrible conditions here. How fast you've come up to speed is impressive. You need to cut yourself a break and recognize how good you are. Then there's no telling how far you could go."

"That's nice of you to say, but I worry if I'm up to the standards needed."

Sally smiled. "Let's talk again in about a month. I'm sure I know what we'll see then. By the way, have you met our Catholic chaplain, Father Phil? Given your issues back home, he might be worth talking to."

CHAPTER 7

Not one to sit on a suggestion, Mary's commanding officer must have quickly approached the chaplain. The next afternoon, Ann told her a priest was waiting at the door looking for the new surgical nurse. "I told him I'm not Catholic. That means he must be looking for you."

Mary grabbed her duckbill hat and went out. After introductions, the chaplain suggested a trip to the mess hall to chat over coffee. Once settled, Mary nervously twisted her hands, wondering how to explain her circumstances. Embarrassed to discuss with a priest how she married a man so self-centered and unfaithful, she didn't know where and how to start. Her experience at home with the local parish priest led her to expect this would be a standard lecture about remaining an obedient wife and that the man of the house deserved support no matter what.

When Father Phil didn't start interrogating her, and instead launched into how he became a chaplain, Mary realized this might be a different kind of priest. At an early age, Phil knew the priesthood would be his calling. Although he struggled with some of the religion's tenets, he said young priests like himself had to push the church to evolve. Especially in a war zone, the flexibility to bring faith to all, including non-Catholics, drove him.

Mary smiled. "Flexibility and compassion are not words I heard at my local parish."

"You're not alone in that experience." He smiled and shifted subjects. "Since it's only been a few days, the horror and stress must be shocking. You see the worst of the worst in surgery. How are you holding up?"

"Not well, Father."

"Call me Phil."

"That'll be a new way for me to address a priest. Forgive me if I slip." She smiled. "To tell you the truth, I'm struggling. I came from a small hospital where traumas rarely occurred. Being in the Reserves, I didn't expect a call-up. Everyone has been supportive, but Father, I mean Phil, last night when I crawled into my cot and pulled the blanket over me, I cried a lot. I kept seeing the first patient who died on me. This is not why I chose nursing."

"You're not alone with the sorrow and suffering. Most in this unit have a hard time dealing with our jobs. I certainly do. Through the grapevine, I hear you're performing well. Lieutenant Bates said you're a welcome addition."

Mary pursed her lips. "Phil, you seem open to hearing difficult things. Mind if I take a chance to say something I bet most priests never want to hear?"

"Go ahead. No judgments from me."

"I cannot believe the inhumanity I see here, and it's not only the combatants. The poverty and suffering among civilians are overwhelming. Innocent people are caught in the middle of fighting when they only want to raise their families in peace. The church taught me our God is kind and loving. Is he here in Korea, or did he stay behind in the States?"

Phil took a moment and spoke softly. "I believe our God is compassionate, and I know he's here. He'd better be because he's needed more than ever with everything going on around us. We're taught there's evil in the world, and this appears to be the center of that. I cannot explain why God lets this happen. It tests our faith."

Mary bit her lip. "My faith is being put through the wringer. Religion is important to me, but what's happening is nothing I thought God would allow. I worked with recovering men in the last war, but this carnage up close is more than I can bear. Phil, I may fail the faith test."

"I can understand that and hope you don't. It's overwhelming. I'll be here and open to discussing whatever troubles you. Since there are often conflicts with surgery, if you want to receive the sacrament outside of mass, give me a heads-up. Anything else you want to talk about now?"

"I expected you came to see me because Sally is worried about my home situation. But you never brought that up."

"She did mention you were dealing with terrible issues. I'm open to discussing them, but only if you feel comfortable."

"Phil, I'd like to discuss them. I'm unsure what you can do, but if you've got the time, let me get another cup of coffee."

Back in quarters, Mary saw several nurses sitting together, reading letters, and passing around treats.

One called out. "Belanger, you're in time before all the brownies disappear. Our boss got a big box and insists we eat them. By the way, there are a couple of letters for you on your bunk."

Although wanting to get right to those letters, Mary grabbed a treat and looked at shared photographs. After taking the last brownie, she headed to her cot. Two envelopes—one each from her mother and Linda. Nothing from her husband.

Mary tore open the letter from Susan.

Dear Mary,

I wrote this a few days after you left and may have to control myself from writing too many letters. We all miss you, especially the baby.

Things here are fine. Well, maybe not fine. Rob lost his job and is looking for new employment. He didn't share what happened, but Rob's father called and said his son should return to the family business. The two of them had a big fight, with Rob slamming down the phone, saying he'd never work with his father again. What a scene! In the meantime, Rob said he has savings to tide him over. Wasn't that money you two intended for a down payment on a house?

Cindy is doing well, although I struggle with not sleeping the night through. Thankfully, Linda is here every day to help. That means I get a good nap in. Our neighbor has been such a blessing since Rob is not around much.

I hear our little princess stirring. I'll wrap this up and write again soon. If you need anything, please tell me, and I will send it along. Forgive me for how much I cried on the phone. I'm scared something will happen to you over there. Be safe. I pray for you every night.

Love, Mom

That husband of mine lost his job again, and he's not helping care for his niece. All the work is falling to my mother and Linda. Now Rob will spend our savings because he cannot hold a job.

Mary tried to stop grinding her teeth, thinking about her irresponsible husband. She took several deep breaths, rubbed her jaw to relieve the cramping, and then opened Linda's letter.

Dear Maar,

Have you met any cute doctors yet? It's probably more awful than I can imagine, but I hope there are a few positives.

I pray you'll still like me after this letter because I'm about to unload on your husband. It turns out he got fired right after you left, although he tried to tell us he quit. He proved a lousy liar since his stories were conflicting. Eventually, he admitted being fired, saying a personality conflict with his boss made it necessary.

My Stan knows your hubby's ex-boss. Over beers, Stan learned Rob got fired because he was missing work. The Personnel Department Manager followed Rob on a supposed sales call, but he ended up at Mona's. When Rob tried to deny slipping off to see his mistress, they gave him the heave-ho.

It pains me to share this with you, but you need to know what is happening. Since being fired, Rob doesn't stick around the house to help with the baby. Most nights, he comes home sauced. Thank God your mother is there. I'm trying to help her during the daytime.

I want to be clear. How much time I spend with your mom is not a problem. You know how Stan and I want a baby, but cannot conceive. Helping with Cindy is something I enjoy. So I don't want to hear any objections since it's my labor of love.

Your mother is doing remarkably well. Even though it's been a short time, I swear the baby is raising Susan's energy level and improving her overall health. Stan and I will make sure she continues to do well.

I wish I didn't have to share news about Rob. Even though you cannot do much about it, you must understand the whole picture. Write when you get a chance.

If you find a cute doctor, kiss him and say I made you do it.

Love, Lin

Tears slipped down Mary's cheeks. When she glanced up, Ann was watching. Mary grabbed her blanket, pulled it over her head, and slid down onto her cot.

A while later, Mary felt better enough to sit up. When she did, she saw several nurses huddled, looking her way. When they made eye contact, the group moved toward her.

Ann sat on the cot and pulled Mary in her arms. "We don't know what's in those letters or why the chaplain sought you out, but there's some shit going on. Just know we're here for you."

By now, Ginny sat on the other side of Mary. Two others sat facing Mary. "If you don't want to talk, that's fine. But we're in this together and need each other to make it through. It can't hurt to have a bit of girl talk. We might even be able to help."

Mary broke into a sob, leaning on Ann. After a moment, she lifted her head and wiped her eyes. "I appreciate you coming over. The thought that I can share is already helping. Are you sure you want to hear my story? We all struggle with issues. I don't want to be a burden on the unit."

Ann reached over to wipe the last tear from Mary's face. "Too late to chase us away, Belanger. The 100th Ladies Support Group is in session. What in the hell was in those letters?"

CHAPTER 8

Over the next few days, Mary settled into a routine. First thing each day were rushes of the wounded, typically in the early morning hours after night-time fighting, followed by breaks when each side regrouped. Surprised at how she was adjusting to the extreme conditions and the unrelenting pace, Mary's confidence grew.

The emotional support from others in the unit also bolstered her. Consensus ruled Rob a lost cause. No one had an answer as to what to do with the baby long-term, but the care her mother and neighbor provided meant Mary had time to figure things out.

In the meantime, the fighting crept closer. Once distant, the artillery grew louder, and the ground shook occasionally. One corpsman explained, "When we hear the whine of incoming shells and see the flashes, it's time to get bug-out fever."

"What's that?" Mary asked.

"Bugging out is when we know it's time to pack our bags and save our asses. We had a lot of practice at quick withdrawals when the Pusan Perimeter shrank to fifty miles. Thank goodness the US Navy controls the seas and keeps us from being surrounded with nowhere to run."

Rumors flew that there might be a North Korean break-through. American hope for a turnaround came with the ar-rival of more troops from Allied countries under the aegis of the United Nations. These fighting units presented another challenge to the 100th MASH, who were now treating patients where language could be a barrier. A translator accompanied the wounded when possible, but sometimes wasn't available. Communications in triage and recovery became a game of pantomime.

Another positive development for medical care came with the first fully equipped hospital ship, the *Consolation*, now anchored in Pusan Harbor. The vessel brought much-need-ed state-of-the-art medical facilities closer to treating the wounded once MASH stabilized. As a result, instead of all the wounded being flown to Japan, the worst cases received care on the ship.

The grueling demands on the 100th did not let up, how-ever. When not facing a flood of wounded, the nurses wrestled with fatigue and life's inconveniences. One issue in particu-lar irritated Mary—how she had to labor to keep her fatigues somewhat clean. If she missed getting clothes into the regu-lar laundry schedule, washing uniforms in her helmet became another chore. With the still limited showers, her helmet too often remained her bath. Like other nurses, Mary started to douse herself with perfume. Ann observed to the group, "I may be rank, but at least I smell like a lady of the night."

Anxiety grew throughout the MASH unit with the fight-ing closer. In the middle of more surgeries, Mary asked Dave about a term she'd heard a few times—meatball surgery. Without batting an eye, the surgeon explained, "That's what we do. We must be quick, doing whatever is necessary to sta-bilize patients. Save lives and get the next patient on the ta-ble. For example, we'd like to take more time for operations that might save a GI's leg. Since time is of the essence, we take the leg off. Then we send the guys to follow-up care and comprehensive treatment. Our job is to preserve life, hence the meatball terminology."

"I understand the approach and see that it's necessary. I hope we don't ever have to employ it back home."

"Unless a form of a mass disaster occurred, it's unlikely. Hopefully, there would be enough resources to take time with each patient."

Mary passed a scalpel. "If you're not too distracted, I have another question."

"Go ahead. Clamp."

"You got to grill me about my background when I first got here. Mind sharing a bit of yours?"

"Fair enough. Born of poor but honest parents. Oh, never mind that part of the story."

From the next table, Bones called, "Yes, on behalf of the rest of us trapped with you, please don't tell the rose-up-from-nothing story again. And be sure to skip the part where you saved your high school baseball team by hitting over two-hundred home runs every week."

Dave glanced over toward Bones. "Do you hear anything, Mary? All I hear is the wind whistling."

"Doctor, I hear nothing of substance."

Bones shook his head. "I tried, people, but we have to hear it again."

"As I started to say, my parents came to America from Ireland. They moved to Philadelphia because other family members lived there. So I'm a first-generation-born American—one of three children. I'm the oldest, with a sister four years younger and a brother five years younger. My sister is married and about to give birth to her first. Guess I'll miss that event. My little brother recently graduated from college and is starting a job teaching high school. I'm praying they don't institute a draft for this war where he might get snagged. There are already rumors of having to draft doctors because of the low enlistment rate."

From the next table: "Yeah, why are younger doctors much smarter than we were to avoid this place? What does that say about us?"

Dave ignored the comment. "I'm not married, but a wonderful lady is waiting for me. Her name is Allison. We're unofficially engaged with the plan to formalize that when I get back."

"How did you two meet?"

"It happened during my residency—a civilian nurse caught my eye. I enlisted right after college. That way, the Army would pay for medical school and training. One day, I'm doing standard surgeries on a base down in Alabama, then the North Koreans issued an invitation I couldn't refuse."

"You must miss her a lot."

"My heart aches for her. What we're doing here is life and death for these poor guys, but all I want is to go home. Like you, we're here for a nine-month rotation—counting the days and never wanting to see this place again. Despite the enticements they'll offer, I sometimes imagine walking out on the mandatory meeting with the reenlistment officer near the end of my tour. Okay, all done here. Could you please apply the dressings? I need to slug down a couple of cups of coffee before our next victim."

"I got it. Could you please bring me back a cup?"

Mary watched Dave head off. She remembered Ellen's prediction that she would get a crush on Dave. She wondered if that might be happening.

Under overcast skies, the next day brought a rush of wounded civilians. A village north of Taegu got caught in the fighting, with women and children getting the worst. The North Koreans typically killed or took men for slave labor. Among these civilian cases, most were burn victims. From the nearby ward came a cacophony of crying children and pleading mothers. In the OR, the helpless cries of infants filled Mary's ears. More than once, Dave admonished his nurse. "Focus here. Others are taking care of those children."

After finishing their last surgery, Dave said, "Okay, we'd better get in there and see what we can do to help."

She discarded her scrubs and gloves, rushing into the ward where most villagers were. The sight took her breath away. Forty or more women and children were in distress, with nurses and doctors struggling to keep up. The din of children crying and mothers calling out made it hard to hear. Flies attacked the open wounds and burns.

Mary spied Ginny, who was trying to get a mother with a severely burned face to go for treatment. The distraught woman was refusing to leave her child. Despite a translator arguing with the mother, the wounded woman refused to release her child.

Moving to the pile of spare cots, Mary hurried one back to the distraught mother. "Let's push the other cots back and squeeze this one in. Then we can move the child out of the way. Get what she needs, and we'll treat this woman here. I'll stay with these two. That work?"

When the translator finished, the woman nodded and lay beside her son, still clutching the child's arm. With her other hand, she grabbed Mary and spoke to the translator.

He shared, "Blessings on you."

"I'm on the way," Ginny said. "It looks like this woman won't let you go anywhere."

Mary patted the hand of the mother, who gradually loosened her hold. The suffering of the innocents tore at her heart. *Now is not the time to cry. I've got to hold it together and help these people.*

Sally arrived. "I know you're doing good work here but we need you outside. They drafted several corpsmen to load ammunition needed for the front. We have to lug stretchers."

Mary pulled away and stood. The distraught mother made a last lunge to grab her again. The small Korean woman wailed when Sally and Mary started to move away. Mary asked her commanding officer, "May I have another moment with this patient, ma'am?"

"Negative, Belanger, let's go."

Sally was already halfway out the door. Mary gave one last look at the child and pleading mother. Finally, Ginny arrived with the needed supplies and said, "I got this."

Without another glance, Mary rushed to catch up with her boss. Outside, another scene of chaos with too many wounded to count arriving. Two triage nurses labored by with a stretcher. One warned, "Be careful of your back. Lifting these guys is heavy work."

"Belanger, grab that end, and let's get this guy into pre-op."

Mary bent and struggled to lift her end of the stretcher to knee level. Sally already had her side of the pallet up to her waist level. "What are you doing back there? Are you trying to dump this hero on the ground? He's had a bad enough day already. Get with it, Belanger."

A stream of warm blood from the stretcher flowed onto Mary's leg while she fought to level her end. Sally had already stepped forward, forcing Mary to shuffle her feet to keep up. With an immediate shoulder ache and burning in her hands, Mary gritted her teeth, praying for the strength not to drop anyone.

Back in surgery the next day, Mary worked carefully because of the blisters on her hands and soreness throughout her body. On a positive note, they had evacuated the injured villagers.

Dave laughed. "I thought that mother would never let you go, and you'd end up having to evacuate with them. But your boss wouldn't let that happen. By the way, how are your hands?"

Before Mary could answer, Major Phillips stuck his head into surgery. "Orders just arrived. Our lines are falling back. We move out in eight hours. Schedule the surgeries appropriately, Dave." The commander moved on.

Mary looked up. "I assume this isn't a surprise to you."

"I'm shocked we didn't bug out sooner. After this patient, we'll take a break. I'll assess triage and sort things there. You find Sally and make sure she gets the word. Then get back here to see how long we keep doing surgeries. Those hands of yours are going to take another beating today."

Mary forced herself to focus on the patient. The North Koreans might arrive in eight hours. The condition of her hands no longer a concern.

CHAPTER 9

Under the stink of coal dust, the train lurched to a stop, throwing the two nurses off balance. Ann caught the corner of a stretcher. Mary fell against a wounded patient, causing him to moan. She balanced herself, then leaned over to ensure his dressings were not affected, apologizing. Through gritted teeth, he said, "I knew you had your eye on me, ma'am. Just a matter of time until you made your move."

"You had me figured out from the start, soldier. Your bandages are okay. Anything I can get you?"

"No, ma'am. Thank you."

Ann came over and asked if the two of them needed a chaperone. The injured man looked up. "Wow, two nurses chasing me."

Ann patted the man on his good shoulder. From the other end of the carriage came another voice. "Nurse, the pain is getting worse. Is there anything you can give me?"

Ann said, "I got this one."

Right then, the train bucked, then just as suddenly stopped. Both nurses fought to stay on their feet. A chorus of groans filled the car. Mary prayed this start-and-stop train to Pusan would finally get going. In this heat, the trip was brutal for the injured.

Outside, cries from fleeing refugees grew louder. Koreans surrounded the train, trying to get on board. Guards positioned at the end of each car pushed to keep the fleeing civilians at bay. A sudden burst of fire over the heads of refugees from on top of the carriage drove the crowd back. Only a few moments later, the crowd of Koreans edged toward the train again. *If the crowd storms the train, how will we be able to care for the patients? People may die.*

Mary told herself to ignore the events outside and conduct another round of checks. With everyone stable, she took a standing position at the coach's door to get a bit of rest. After another series of lurches, the train finally moved forward, leaving the mob behind. *I'm worn out. It hurts to stand. This muggy air is draining me. If I could rest my eyes for a minute, that would help. Dear Jesus, when will this be over?*

Memories of escaping Taegu played in her head. She and Dave completed two more operations. Mary then moved into post-op to prepare patients for travel. They put the wounded in the best shape in ambulances and trucks to evacuate over the terrible roads. The worst cases moved to the train.

Chaos appeared to rule, with support personnel breaking down and packing equipment. The nurses prepared emergency packs and started moving patients. Mary realized this crazy ballet was well planned.

After the wounded were loaded to take to the train, a few moments remained for nurses to sprint to their quarters and grab their gear. Mary threw things into her bag, then took a moment to wrap her framed photographs. Hefting her duffel, she spied her flak jacket and gas mask on the ground. They would have to be left.

She rushed out of the tent to find the truck's engine running and staff jumping into the back. Hands vaulted her up.

The truck started in a rush, moving the last of the staff to the train station. No one in the back could relax with the driver speeding away and blasting the horn. They grabbed onto whatever they could find to avoid being thrown out. Refugees filled the roads, jumping out of the way of the speeding truck. Doctors and nurses exchanged worried looks. Nobody spoke.

With the news of the approaching enemy, countless Koreans around them fought to escape with a few possessions. Many held out hands toward the passing truck, begging for a ride. In the background, the impact of artillery and the sounds of combat had never been closer.

At the train station, Mary discovered most patients were still on the ground. Progress loading the wounded proceeded slowly and painfully since the stretchers had to be carefully maneuvered into railcars. Amid the commotion, Sally directed the orderlies. The arriving nurses grabbed their gear and rushed over to the head nurse.

"Pile your gear over there. Orderlies will load it. We're putting two of you in each car. Here's the list. Figure out where you're assigned, then go. Each coach already has emergency supplies. Doctors will move through the train helping where needed." With that, Sally moved on, yelling at an orderly to be more careful.

Each nurse hustled to their assigned coach. At her railcar, Mary assisted in moving the wounded on board. Patients suffered because of the tight turns. A clever orderly suddenly knocked an intact window out with the butt of a rifle. Quickly, others did the same, considerably speeding the loading process.

Dust and noise filled the station. Soldiers fought to keep desperate civilians from rushing the train. Gunfire erupted outside the station. When the stretchers were finally laid across the tops of the seats, a whistle blast sounded, and the train moved south.

Mary opened her eyes to see Father Phil moving through the crowded railcar, talking to patients. She watched one soldier whisper in the priest's ear, with Phil leaning over to give a blessing. She made a mental note to closely monitor that patient, hoping the chaplain wasn't performing last rites.

When Phil reached Mary, he said, "Are you doing okay? You look beat."

Mary smiled. "You do too. I'm dead on my feet. This heat isn't making things any easier. Hopefully, there aren't more delays."

Just then the train braked hard, throwing Mary against the priest. "Sorry, Phil. Guess I cursed us with my last wish. I'd better check on our passengers, starting with the guy you were blessing."

The hours dragged. The train stopped more than it moved, often shuttled to sidings to allow supplies and troops to be rushed to the front. Back standing at one end of the carriage, Mary fought sleep. *I wish I could take off these boots. My feet have never hurt so much. Please, God, get this train going.*

With a start, Mary woke to find Bones holding her up. "Hey there, Mary, catching a catnap?"

She gathered herself, pulling out of the doctor's grip. *Falling asleep while on duty is terrible. Having a doctor catch me is even worse.* "Guess I did nod off. Thanks for saving me."

Bones smiled. "My pleasure. We're all the same—beat to a pulp. The good news is the Eighth MASH is waiting in Pusan to take over. Their unit is now operational, meaning we may get a break."

"That's fabulous news," Ann said, approaching them. "Doctor, a patient is bleeding more than I'd like. Could you look and see if we need to do something?"

Stifling a yawn, Mary struggled to follow Ann and Bones to the wounded man.

"All right," the doctor said after examining the patient. "I want to rewrap this wound, but first, let's see if I can get another stitch in. In the meantime, let's start a transfusion. Mary, get some plasma. Ann, you get the sewing kit and fresh bandages."

Mary turned to get the plasma and was surprised to see one of the wounded leaning on his elbow, trying to get off his stretcher. "I want to help. What can I do?" The soldier had lost both legs and was not aware of his efforts.

"I've got to get this guy settled down," Mary called to Ann and Bones. "One of you needs to get the plasma."

Mary reached the struggling man, gently helping him back down. "We've got it covered, soldier. One of our best doctors is taking care of things. You need to rest."

The man weakly fought her. "No, I need to help. That's my buddy there. I'm not hurt that bad; he's worse. I've got to be with him."

"Your friend is in expert hands. Let the doctor do his job. Does that sound okay?"

The man's eyes grew dark from the stretcher, looking harshly at her. "He'd better be okay, or I'll come after you. You hear me?"

Bones called, "Need any help over there?"

"No, we're fine," Mary said, reaching into her pocket for a sedative syringe. She held down the struggling soldier and slipped the needle into his arm. Mary smiled. "I promise your buddy will be okay. Time for you to take a little nap."

At long last, the train pulled into Pusan Station. Mary gave a deep sigh of relief. This ordeal was finally over. Outside, medical personnel from the Eighth scrambled. Two nurses stepped into the car, approaching Ann and Mary. "We're here to take over. I'm Maggie, and this is Sylvia. Any special instructions for these patients?"

Mary pushed back her hair, struggling to process what they had said. Ann talked about the patient Bones had treated, then described the wounded man who'd received the additional sedative. Mary mentioned the soldier Phil had blessed.

The new nurses quickly checked those patients, completing the handoff.

Mary didn't want to but forced herself to ask, "What can we do to help unload?"

Maggie said, "We're under orders not to allow you to do anything more. You've been through hell, and we've got it from here. Your unit is mustering for transportation to the rear. Thanks for the offer, but get out of here."

Ann stretched. "I'll not argue with that. Come on, Mary. Let's go get a martini or at least a beer."

Before leaving, Mary walked back to the GI she had landed on earlier in the trip.

"I knew you couldn't stay away, ma'am. I'm too handsome."

The GI, who looked about eighteen, was missing an arm and had severe burns on his face. He had a hard road ahead. It tore at Mary's heart.

"You're much too good-looking for me, soldier. You need to go chase down Dorothy Lamour. She's more your speed."

"Dorothy Lamour. I like that."

Mary patted his remaining arm. "God bless you."

Off the train, her legs almost buckled. A cool breeze brought a bit of relief. Around her, many patients were already unloaded and moving to ambulances. The new medical personnel looked fresh and eager.

Arm in arm with Ann, Mary walked a short distance. To her surprise, there stood Ben Heinz from Fort Devens. He was talking animatedly with Major Phillips. The 100th commander turned and walked away. With a deep breath, she stepped over. "Captain Heinz, we meet again. Remember me? Mary Belanger, the reluctant nurse."

"Mary, yes. My stars, they shipped you right to the front lines with the 100th? It's good to see you, although I can't imagine what you've been through. Are you okay?"

She looked at his uniform, realizing he'd been promoted. "Excuse me. I didn't see you're now a major. Congratulations on your promotion. I'm hanging in there. Exhausted, but okay."

"I command the Eighth and had better start earning my pay. We have a lot to do following the amazing work of your unit. You've earned a well-deserved R&R. When things calm down, might I find you to catch up? I especially want to hear what is happening with your baby."

"That would be terrific. You said we might cross paths over here. I can't believe it's happened. Enough of my prattling. Get to work, Major." Mary saluted.

Ben smiled, extending his hand, then headed into the crowd.

Mary found a newfound spring in her step. *He remembered the baby.*

MANCHESTER TIMES
NEWS BULLETIN
NORTH KOREANS CONTINUE SLOW MARCH SOUTH

Despite announcements from General MacArthur that United Nations forces were slowing advances by the enemy, Allied troops recently fell back from Taegu, narrowing the protective perimeter around Pusan. Local commanders expressed concern that South Korea could be lost without additional forces and equipment.

An Army representative expressed optimism that each passing day strengthened UN capabilities. "North Korean supply lines suffer because the US Air Force controls the skies and relentlessly attacks during daylight hours. American airpower is forcing enemy supply caravans to only travel at night without lights."

MacArthur expressed optimism the enemy would soon be stopped.

CHAPTER 10

Mary resisted her impulse to wake up. In the distance, she could hear the muted roar of the airbase. It helped that the 100th was stationed on a far corner of the base with relative quiet. Within the tent, she heard muffled conversations. When Mary reluctantly pushed herself onto her elbows, Julie gave a perky smile from the next cot. "There's our sleeping beauty. Given how long you've been snoozing, aren't you getting bed sores?"

"What time is it?"

"Almost 1500 hours. You've been out for over eleven hours. Guess you needed the release. We all did."

A couple of nurses chatting across the aisle of cots waved at Mary. Slowly standing, Mary felt her exhaustion. She sat down and rolled back under her blanket, giving in to the fatigue. "When do we have to report for duty?"

"No schedule. We're on break since the Eighth took over. The rumor at lunch is we'll have at least a few days off unless the North Koreans breakthrough. If that happens, we'll evacuate to Japan or become prisoners of war."

Mary forced herself to stand and stretch, running her hand through her stringy, dirty hair.

Julie noticed her disgust. "I was going to wake you soon.

Here's the treat—showers for women in an hour. They finally have enough water. We can luxuriate and put on clean clothes. Laundry goes out tonight, meaning we can get out of the fatigues we've been living in."

With that welcome news, hunger rumbled. Since there wouldn't be time to find something more substantial, Mary reached into her bathrobe pocket for a Tootsie Roll. After the shower, she'd visit the mess hall and hopefully find different snacks. She was getting sick of this brand of candy.

While the other nurses trickled in to prepare for showers, Mary opened her duffel to look for clean clothes. She discovered that the pictures of Cindy and her mother had the glass shattered. *If that's the only damage from that awful evacuation, lucky me.*

Back in quarters after washing up, the nurses luxuriated in what warm water and soap could do for morale. No loudspeaker announcing the next round of wounded was a gift from heaven. Instead, animated conversations and good-natured teasing had Mary joining in. With electricity available, Armed Forces Radio played the latest music in the background.

Knowing how his MASH unit was bearing the brunt, Mary's thoughts wandered to Ben. She whispered a silent prayer for their well-being—then a bonus prayer Ben would get to visit.

While Mary toweled her hair, a nurse burst in. "Hey everyone, movie night. *The Philadelphia Story* is playing. First showers and then a movie. Is this the life, or what?"

Several cots over, a nurse pulled two whiskey bottles out of her bag. "Here's how to make a movie better."

Someone else chimed in, "I talked to a few docs, and they have a bigger stash than that. I think this might be the best movie we've ever watched."

Mary leaned back to take another sip from her tin cup. Whoever said this would make the movie better knew what they were talking about. Outdoors, tonight even the mosquitoes were cooperating. She heard another nurse giggle, "No matter how attractive Katharine Hepburn is, it would be unlikely two guys as good-looking as Cary Grant and Jimmy Stewart would fight over the same woman. I would love her problem."

The soundtrack occasionally cut out, allowing for irreverent comments. Overall, a welcome way to pass a few hours with people Mary had come to like and respect.

When the film ended, the distant rumble of the airbase came back into focus. Between the shower, movie, whiskey, and knowing that sleep would be uninterrupted, Mary felt more relaxed than at any point since receiving her recall letter.

Several nurses stood. Julie lost her balance, falling against Mary. "Hey there, Jules. You okay?"

The drunk nurse straightened and slurred, "I'm fine, Lieutenant—never been better. But, listen, I think we need to move to where the docs are. They have more booze. Let's go."

"This is enough for me. Tomorrow, I have to function. Someone snagged a volleyball set, and matches will be in the afternoon. I'd love to get some exercise. So, it's off to the sack for me."

"You spoilsport. Hey, Doctors, here comes a thirsty nurse."

Mary smiled, watching her friend head over. Barely able to keep her eyes open, she felt fatigue fill every bone. Walking with a couple of comrades back to quarters, Mary enjoyed the small talk and relished the anticipation of losing herself to sleep.

Volleyball the next afternoon started as fun, but from Mary's perspective, the fun matches quickly morphed from friendly to overly competitive. Something she had observed all her life—get a game going, then guys' juices pumped.

On the sandy field, three men and three nurses made up each team. Mary's group competed for the right to play in the finals against the team led by Bones. No surprise that hulk of a man captained one finalist team. For such a big guy, he moved gracefully.

Set for the next point, Mary felt growing tiredness in her muscles. Tomorrow she'd be stiff, but it felt terrific to be moving. While the match was competitive, the trash-talking proved more fun, making everyone laugh. With the next positional rotation, she moved close to the net. From the other team, Dave said, "Belanger's at the net. Get the ball to her, and the point is ours."

She crouched into position. "Maybe you'll be the one that gets surprised."

A long, competitive point got underway. Twice, the ball came Mary's way, and both times she blocked it back over the net—then a wide shot angled toward the sideline. Lunging, she got her fists under the ball. On the ground, face down in the sand she heard a cheer erupt while her teammates rushed to help her up.

"Terrific shot. The ball ticked the net for a winner. Shot of the day," Ellen proclaimed.

Feeling elated, Mary enjoyed the spectators razzing her surgical partner. "Get it to Mary, eh, Dave? Time for Plan B, Doctor. Maybe even C."

In the end, Dave's team came out on top, pushing Mary's crew to the sidelines. A nurse handed her a cold beer, which went down smoothly. Even though the temperature was not as hot as in the past few weeks, her soaked T-shirt clung to her. In the shade, she sat back with a second cold one, secretly glad her team had lost. For the first time in weeks, she felt satisfied.

In the final match, she focused her attention on Dave. Such an attractive man and nothing but kind and supportive—so different from her husband. And what about Ben? It had been a surprise to see him at the train station. *Maybe I have my version of Cary Grant and Jimmy Stewart.*

The last rays of sunlight faded as a crackling fire melted marshmallows cooked on sticks. With the sun setting, Mary waved away the offer of another beer. *Where had the time gone? Thank goodness that fried chicken and chips arrived a while ago from the mess hall. I haven't had this much to drink in a long time. Time for bed to sleep this off.*

When she tried to stand, Mary slipped. Bones reached out to steady her. In his arms, she looked up, feeling dizzy. "Where did you come from? I'm okay. You can let go of me." Then, giggling, "Boy, you smell ripe. I bet we all do."

Bones loosened his grip but didn't take his arm away. "Easy, Lieutenant. I got to catch you on the train and have done it again. You can start calling me your guardian angel. I think you've had enough and should get back to quarters."

She stared at Bones' arm. "That's what I'm thinking. Time for me to go beddy-bye. Good night, Doctor."

"I'm heading that way. Why don't I walk with you and make sure you're alright?"

She bristled and said a little too loudly, "I'm fine, but let's go if you want to come along."

Mary wrestled out of his grip when she noticed several nurses watching. Ginny stood. "Mary, let me go with you.

Then I can come back." Ginny glanced sideways at Bones, who returned a sharp look.

"I'm fine, Ginny. Besides, I have a bodyguard with this mountain of a man." Mary giggled at her own joke. "He's bigger than you. That way I'm safer with him in case of attack. You stay and have fun."

After a couple of steps, Mary stumbled. Bones reached out to support her. Ginny bit her lip as the pair stepped away from the group.

Bones called back over his shoulder, "We're fine, Ginny. I got this."

Away from the fire and moving into darkness along a path overgrown with bushes, Mary felt the big man's body pressing against her side. Then the doctor leaned close, speaking softly.

What is he saying? I can barely hear him.

"The minute you walked in that first day, I knew you were special. It disappointed me when you got to work with Dave. You and I would make a better team. You're capable when things are tough, yet you make time pass because you're such good company. I bet your husband doesn't appreciate what a special person he has. It gets lonely here, and we should be selfish and grab pleasure where we can."

Mary struggled to understand his words. *Is this guy coming on to me? Complimenting me as a nurse? What did he mean about being selfish?*

They stepped out of the darkness when they reached the doctors' tents. Bones said, "This is my place. Come in. There's something I'd like to show you. I even have a bottle if you'd like another snort."

Her body stiffened in alarm. Pulling her arm away, "No, thanks. I don't want a drink. I need to get back to my bunk. I don't feel well."

"Okay, no drink, and we'll only be a minute. Inside is a picture I want you to see."

Bones gripped her arm and steered her firmly toward the

tent entrance. The big man reached down, flipped around a small sign on the door handle, and then pushed her inside.

In the dimly lit tent, Mary saw three bunks and scattered clothing. Her head spun, confused about what to do. *This is not good. Inside the tent of a senior officer. I remember as a junior nurse when that doctor got me alone in the laundry room. That was close, but what now? Shit.*

Mary wrestled her arm from his grasp, his alcohol breath too close. "What is it you want me to see?"

"Sure you don't want another drink?"

"No. I need to go."

"Come over here. I want you to see a picture of my football team."

Bones slid his hand to the small of her back, pushing her to a makeshift table where several pictures stood. She saw one of his family and wife. "Not that picture, this one." He moved his left arm around her from behind, pointing as his right arm snaked around her middle.

Tears filled Mary's eyes. *Why did I drink so much and get in this situation? Ginny's look now makes sense. I bet I'm not the first he's brought here. Doctors are the most important people in this unit. I don't want to create a scene by screaming.*

Mary struggled to free herself, but Bones had both arms around her. He pressed his groin against her backside, whispering in her ear. "Mary, you're the best-looking nurse in this unit. Everyone knows your husband is cheating on you. It's time to take care of yourself and have fun. We make a good team."

One of his hands cupped her breast. His other moved up her thigh. "Stop it. I'm married."

Bones became more aggressive. One hand slipped inside her T-shirt, resting on her bra. With his other hand, he pressed against her pubic bone. "Come on, Mary, relax. It'll feel good. If you stick with me, I'll make sure you're well taken care of in this god-awful place."

Mary fought to push his hands away. All her struggling didn't make the slightest impact. She felt him kiss her neck as the top button of her pants popped open.

A voice near the tent door said, "Oops, looks like somebody needs privacy, Dave. The warning signal is flipped."

"Damn that guy. At it again. Let's head back to the party."

Bones' hand flew over Mary's mouth. She bit down as hard as she could. A muffled cry escaped the injured doctor as he jerked his hand away. Mary called, "Doctor Walsh, Dave, come in. Bones is showing me his pictures, but I need to get back to my quarters."

Dave and Chet entered the tent. She yanked herself free of Bones. The two doctors watched Mary step back, straightening her shirt and buttoning her pants. She glared at Bones, who cradled his hand.

Standing as straight as possible, Mary ran her hand through her hair, taking a deep breath. "Thank you, Doctor, for showing me the photos. I especially enjoyed the one of your wife and family." She strode past the doctors. Chet grinned. Dave looked upset. Mary slammed the door open and ran back to her quarters.

Away from the doctors' tent, she wept with relief, realizing how close she had been to not getting away. *What are the doctors going to think of me now? Dave especially. How am I going to face him? That bastard Bones. What's he going to say to others about this? Such a good day—now this.*

With head throbbing and her stomach aching, Mary's first waking thought went back to the night before. *I wonder who knows? Bet the gossip chain is working overtime. God, I feel sick.*

Swinging her legs off the cot, she realized her clothes were still on. As she fought the cobwebs, Ginny walked her way with a cup. "This isn't the hair of the dog, but cold water might taste good."

Mary gulped it down, giving a painful smile. "Thanks for not bringing me more alcohol. That's more drinking than I've done in a long time."

"Yeah, this place can do that. We each have to find ways to deal with this mayhem, and alcohol can become a crutch. Want more water?"

"I'll get some in a moment. What time is it? Where is everybody?"

"They're out and about. No one knows how long we'll be on break, meaning people want to get things done like mail and shopping at the PX. It's almost noon."

Mary stood, listing to the right and fighting nausea. Her head spun. "Guess I better get my butt in gear and put something in my stomach."

Ginny leaned close. "Tell me to mind my business, but how did it go with Doctor Hands? I felt relieved when I got back to see you in bed. I figure he either lost his nerve, or you taught him a lesson."

"Doctor Hands, eh?" Mary grimaced as she fought dizziness. "Is his reputation that well-known? I had no idea. I should have been more careful."

"Don't beat yourself up. You had no way of knowing. I blame myself for not being more forceful about walking back with you. We're all trained to bend to what the doctors want. They're the gods."

"Is he the only doctor like that, or are there others I must watch out for?"

"He's the worst, but it serves a gal well to keep her eyes open unless you're into that sort of thing. Like alcohol, certain people use sex to cope with this place. You strike me as old-fashioned, no matter what you're dealing with back home."

"If Dave and Chet hadn't shown up, I don't think I could

have stopped Bones. Is Sally aware of his behavior? I should file a complaint."

Ginny sat down, pulling Mary next to her. "You might want to think twice about that. Miss Army is all about the docs. It might not go well if you file paperwork."

Mary felt her temper rise as she processed Ginny's comment. "It's the senior nurse's job to protect us. If Bones' behavior is going to change, someone has to speak up."

Ginny stood up. "Don't say I didn't warn you if you decide to talk to her. Sally can be nice when she thinks you're a team player but watch out if she believes there's a threat to the docs. Promise me you'll think about it. Right now, I've got to go meet a friend."

"Ma'am, do you have a moment?"

Sally looked up from a pile of files. "Sure. Come in. This shuffling of paper is never ending."

As Mary took a seat, the senior nurse smiled. "I heard you were a terror on the volleyball court. Well done. Good to show the men that women won't be pushed around."

"It's timely that you mention us not being taken advantage of. That's why I'm here. A doctor sexually assaulted me last night. I want to file a complaint."

The warm smile on the senior nurse's face vanished. She then leaned back in her chair. "What happened? I heard you got pretty soused last night."

Mary caught her breath. Word travels fast, but then her boss specialized in being on top of the details.

"I probably drank a little too much, but I didn't pass out or lose my senses. All of us were drinking, which doesn't give anyone the right to take advantage of another person."

Sally twisted strands of her hair as her eyes narrowed. "Tell me what happened. I heard you left the party with Doctor

Wright. What went on with you two?"

What went on with us? Ginny's warning loomed. With a deep breath, "Ma'am, Doctor Wright dragged me into his tent and tried to rape me. If Dave and Chet hadn't come along, he would have succeeded. I made it clear to Bones that I'm a married woman and wanted nothing to do with him, but he wouldn't quit. I couldn't stop him."

Mary fought back the tears filling her eyes as she sat up ramrod. Across the table, the senior nurse stared back. After a long minute, "Did you scream?"

"No. I got confused, but I told him to stop. He's a senior officer. I didn't want to embarrass him. I bit his hand when he tried to keep me from calling the doctors who were outside. Go look at his hand."

"I don't need to examine his hand. Let me get this straight. You were drunk and ended up in a doctor's quarters. You started to fool around, then didn't like how things were going. A couple of docs showed up, so you got out of there without harm. All you experienced is a little boys will be boys stuff. Right?"

Mary felt her face flush. *Boys will be boys! What if he had raped me? Is that boys will be boys?*

"Well, Lieutenant Belanger, am I correct? Is that what happened?"

"Yes, I mean no." Mary's mind flew. "He attacked me. If not interrupted, I'm sure he would have raped me. I couldn't stop him."

Sally leaned forward, picked up a pen, and turned her attention to the work on her desk. "But you didn't scream, and he didn't rape you. Anything else you want to complain about, Lieutenant?"

Mary watched as the woman focused on her paperwork. Then standing at full attention, "No further complaints, ma'am."

When Mary turned to go, she heard, "One more thing, Belanger."

The senior nurse's eyes drilled into Mary. "Part of my job is to keep this unit running in the worst conditions. The success of our mission depends on the doctors. That doesn't mean they have the impunity to do whatever they want, but you weren't physically harmed. I suggest you stay away from Doctor Wright or any men late at night after you've been drinking. Maybe sometimes you nurses wear your clothes too tight. Do you have a problem working with our head surgeon, Lieutenant?"

"No, ma'am."

"I suggest you focus on your job and forget about what happened. You're dismissed."

Mary thought about saluting. Instead, she spun on her heels and headed out of the tent. Behind, she heard Sally mutter, "I don't need a damn reserve nurse screwing up my unit."

Stepping into the bright sunshine, Mary tried to focus. Across the way, Julie smiled and waved. Mary turned the other way and headed off at a half-run.

Still feeling the effects of her hangover, Mary pulled the blanket over her face. *Are others laughing at me for getting mixed up with that big asshole? Why didn't anyone warn me about him? Why did I allow myself to get trapped? I should know better. I've never been a big drinker. The relief once we were safe and with everyone relaxing swept me along. No more alcohol for me.*

The image of Sally popped into Mary's thoughts. *Well, I feel harmed. Since I got here, everyone has been supportive. Now this, from my boss of all people. What might this mean with Dave? Sally asked if working with him might be an issue. What if I get reassigned? I don't want that.*

She felt a tug on her blanket. Mary tried to ignore whoever might be there. The pulling persisted.

"It's me, Ginny. I can guess what you're feeling. I tried to warn you about Sally. Lots of us have had to put up with her attitude. We're all on your side. It's not right what Bones gets away with, but that's the Army. You're a good person."

The cot shook as Mary wept.

Ginny went on. "For what it's worth, I have one more bit of advice. If you're considering going to Major Phillips, you'll likely get the same message that Sally gave you. Concern for women is one thing that sucks about this Army." Ginny gently stroked Mary's head through the blanket and walked away.

Many of the nurses reached out the next day. More than a few told stories about their struggles with Bones. Mary appreciated the support but was worried about how Bones would react when they saw each other.

It didn't take long. When Mary and two nurses left the mess hall, they heard a man call out. "Lieutenant Belanger, I mean, Mary, wait a minute."

The three stopped when Bones bounded up. "Ladies, you all look well. Mary, I have a gift for you."

The doctor extended his hand. Mary's eyes went blank as she struggled for breath. Not wanting to make eye contact, she looked down and spied a small box wrapped in newspaper. She was unsure how to react. Across the walkway, she noticed Sally taking in the scene. *I just want out of here.*

"Mary, there seems to be a misunderstanding between us from the other night. I want to make it up to you. If I did anything to upset you, that wasn't my intent."

Held in his bandaged hand, the wrapped box hung before her. Silently, Mary took the gift. "I need to get back to quarters, Doctor."

The three nurses departed, leaving Bones standing alone. After a few steps, Mary turned. Sally and the doctor stood with their heads together. She flipped the wrapped box into a trash can. Her companions burst into laughter, linked arms with her, and started to discuss how they planned to tell this story back at quarters.

I'm glad these two are with me. My legs are shaking from seeing that man. Will I ever get over this reaction?

In the early evening, a knock came from the door of the nurses' tent. Mary overheard Julie say, "Let me get her for you, Dave."

Mary's stomach knotted up.

"Your surgical partner is here to see you."

Mary grabbed her hat, not wanting to have this conversation within hearing distance of the other nurses. She feared that Dave would think less of her now. Hurridly, she pushed open the door and rushed past the senior surgeon.

He scrambled to catch up. "Hey, slow down there. I want to make sure you're okay."

She kept walking and looked over. "Sally doesn't think I'm okay and blames me for getting in that situation and threatening the effectiveness of you doctors. Sure, I made a mistake drinking too much. But I don't care if Bones is more important than me. It's not right what he did. Whenever I think about him touching me, I feel sick. Thank goodness you came along, and I appreciate that. But I'm humiliated you caught me in that situation."

Dave reached for her arm to slow her. Forced to stop, she stared at the ground.

"You're right. What Bones did was unacceptable, and he and I had it out. From now on, his table won't be near ours. I want him as far away from you as possible. He's not happy about that. We'll hear grumbling. I don't care. That's the way it'll be."

Mary lifted her head. "Why did you do that?"

"Because it's the best I can do. It's a poor excuse, but we're in a war zone. A formal complaint and starting an investigation with the old school attitude of our COs would lead to he said, she said. And I hate to admit it, but surgeons in these conditions are a priority. I wish it wasn't that way."

"You don't think I'm a slut for getting into that tussle with Bones? What about the other doctors?"

"Slut? Hell no. All the docs' money is on you in a future rematch. We've seen the stitches Bones needed on his hand. That wasn't foreplay; it's moxie."

With a small smile, she said, "I saw the bandage and wish I had done more. It serves him right."

"Bones is lucky we're on R&R. Otherwise, he'd have to explain to more people besides me why he's limited in the OR until he heals."

Mary looked deep into Dave's eyes. "Thank you. The more I think about what happened and how my CO slapped me down, I get angry. Sally is a dedicated nurse, but she's off-base on this issue. If I ever get to a position of responsibility, I'd pursue discipline in such a case."

"This unit needs you, and I need you, no matter what Sally says."

The two were quiet for a moment. Finally, Dave said, "How about we get a beer and laugh a little?"

"How about a cup of coffee? I'm taking a break from alcohol."

"Coffee it is. I'll even throw in a Butterfinger. Scuttlebutt is a shipment of them arrived, meaning we get a break from Tootsie Rolls."

Mail call the following day meant packages were quickly torn open and goodies passed around. Mary had a handful of letters, including one from Rob. *Read his first to get that out of the way. Then find the ones from Mom and Linda with the most recent postmarks.*

Dear Mary,
    I'm sorry for not writing sooner, but it's been busy here. If Susan hasn't already shared the news, I quit my job. It didn't work out since my boss had it in for me from day one. You wouldn't want me in an unpleasant situation. I'm sure I'll find something and make you proud.
    Things at home are fine. I'm doing all I can with the baby, but your mother and Linda won't let me near her. If you didn't hear, Linda has been taking care of the baby during the days while your mom rests from nighttime duty. Cindy continues to have trouble sleeping at nights. Linda has been a godsend.
    I want to assure you I've stopped seeing Mona. It's unfortunate that you found out about us right before you left, but there is nothing to worry about anymore. When you get home, we can get back to normal.
    I hope you're not working too hard.
    Love, Rob

She crumpled the letter, blood boiling. Quit his job—Linda made it clear in her last letter they'd fired Rob. More deception. Why should I believe he ended his affair if he's lying about his job? Then he has the nerve to write things can go back to normal. Her jaw locked up from clenching her teeth. After massaging the cramp and taking a deep breath, she opened the most recent letter from her mother.

Dear Mary,
    I'm writing with awful news. Rob's sister died yesterday. We received a call late last night from the

Boston Police. They found Sharon dead in an aban-doned apartment. There is no news about the cause.

Rob and his father are in Boston today to bring her home. When arrangements are complete for the service, I will send them to you. Could you possibly get leave and be here for the funeral? Linda told me it wouldn't be possible, but I must ask. If the Army doesn't let you travel, I understand. Please don't feel guilty if you can't get here.

That's enough for now. The baby is fine. Linda is doing more each day, and Stan also spends lots of time helping. I'm lucky to have the two of them.

Stay safe, honey. I love you and miss you, Mom.

Sharon, dead? Mary grabbed the letter from Rob and com-pared the postmarks. Rob mailed his three days earlier. That's why he hadn't mentioned her passing. Poor Rob. For all his flaws, he and Sharon had been inseparable growing up. Maybe they needed each other because of living with an overbearing father once their mother died.

Mary turned to Linda's letter. There might be more infor-mation about what happened to Sharon.

Dear Maar,

Oh boy, are things messed up here. Rob's sister died in Boston. Since your mom said she would cover that news in her letter, I won't repeat the little we know.

I'd not met your father-in-law, Richard, until now. That guy is a piece of work. The call from the Boston police came in late last night to Richard. I slept on your couch in case your mom needed help since Cindy had a rough day. Richard showed up yelling at Rob about how he would have to adopt the baby now that Sharon had died. He said Rob needed to stop screwing around with that tramp. Apparently, Richard knew of Rob's affair. Anyway, the yelling woke up Susan and the baby. After settling the baby, your mom came downstairs crying about you serving in a war while Rob is still cheating.

I promised not to sugarcoat things. It's an absolute circus with Sharon's passing. Here is the thing you must know.

Before your father-in-law headed to Boston with Rob, Richard said I should assure you he will make his son end his affair. He added that Rob would return to work at the family company and told Rob to shut up when he objected. Richard said he wanted to make sure you and Rob stayed together to adopt the baby.

Your father-in-law is something. I can see why his daughter turned away from the family. That man might also have contributed to why Rob is so self-centered. Maar, maybe in some ways it's better you're not here, but then I wish you were to help sort this out.

I'll write when I have more details. In the meantime, Stan and I will do whatever is needed to care for your mother and the baby.

Love, Lin

Mary dropped the letter and held her head in her hands. Rob's still cheating. With Sharon gone, who else but Rob and she could adopt the baby? She pounded her pillow, regretting marriage with such a deceitful husband. But what would happen to Cindy if she left the marriage?

Mary slid down on her bunk and covered herself to block out the world.

Dave and Mary walked back together from the mess tent after dinner. "I'm sorry about your latest news from home. It's tough enough having to serve in the middle of this mess, but adding the stress from home where you can't do anything is not fair."

"Thanks for saying that. If there's a chance to get leave and fly home, I'll grab that. But, given how conditions are deteriorating here, I doubt that's in the cards. Maybe if we get overrun by the North Koreans, that would get me out of here."

"Let's hope that doesn't happen. But I agree there's little likelihood of any of us getting leave. If there's anything I can do to help, please ask. It hurts to see you suffer this much."

Mary's physical attraction watching Dave play volleyball was now matched by a growing emotional pull. She leaned over and hugged her surgical partner. "Thanks. That means a lot to me. Since I started working with you, I know I have a friend. I'm learning whom I can trust—people like you and Father Phil." *Bet this hug will get back to my boss?*

"Glad to hear our chaplain is helpful, but isn't that his job?"

"I suppose. Compared to my previous Catholic priest experience, he's different. Although today when I visited with Phil, he didn't say everything I wanted to hear. After all, it's church law, so he can't be supportive of divorce."

"Have you started thinking you want a split? Those last letters you received sound tough, but I didn't know you were that far along in your thinking."

"I'm not sure what I want. In frustration, I blurted out the word divorce to Phil. Our chaplain encouraged me to give things more time. Maybe I'd get the same message back home. Our chaplain does it more nicely."

"Whatever you decide, Phil will be there to support you. On a lighter note, I never told you what a star you were in that volleyball game. Despite my jawing, you hit the best shot of the day."

Mary grinned. "Better not fire up a reservist. We can perform when challenged."

"I've noticed that since day one. What did you think of

the movie we saw? Whenever I looked over, you nurses were chattering."

"I enjoyed it after the awful things we'd experienced. The movie made for a great day. It was the first I'd seen in a long time."

"Tell me. You a Stewart fan or a Grant fan? Got a favorite?"

"Stewart. He's the perfect all-American guy. Really down to earth. Cary Grant is too sophisticated, but I loved his quips. Every woman would die to have that choice." Images of Ben and Dave popped into her mind.

Back at quarters, two new nurses stood by the tent, one Caucasian and one Negro.

"Hello, ladies," Dave said. "Looking for someone?"

"I'm Lieutenant Mildred Scott, and this is Lieutenant Grace Thomas," the older nurse said. "We're newly assigned to the 100th MASH, reporting to First Lieutenant Bates. Do you know where we can find her?"

Terrific, Mary thought. Two more pairs of hands. Sally said the 100th was at full staffing earlier, but maybe that had changed. Mildred looked stocky, probably an Army lifer from her ramrod posture and demeanor. Grace was much shorter, with dark brown eyes and coffee-colored skin. With her high cheekbones and curly hair, Mary thought Grace looked stunning.

"Sally's away working on supply issues. I'm Captain Dave Walsh, Chief Medical Officer, and Mary is one of our nurses. Mary, could I ask you to get our two newest team members settled? The senior nurse will be back tomorrow." He turned to go. "By the way, do either of you play volleyball? If you do, watch out for this woman. She's an animal on the court." With that, he moved on.

The two nurses gave Mary a funny look. "It's a long story," she said. "We're on a break and got in a bit of R&R. Come on, let me help with your bags and find cots."

Mildred and Grace located bunks an aisle over from Mary. A few nurses wandered in, leading to more introductions. Mary said, "Let's take a quick walk around to show you where the mess tent and other key spots are located." Julie bumped into them at the door on their way out of the tent.

"Ah, perfect timing," said Mary. "I'd like to introduce our newest nurses, Mildred and Grace." Julie shook Mildred's hand, then moved past Grace without a word. Mary watched her friend go to another nurse, lean close, and whisper.

Uncertain of how to react, Mary let it go.

After a short tour, they returned to the nurses' quarters. Inside the tent, Mary saw Julie huddling with two other nurses. At her bunk, Grace said, "What happened to my stuff? It's gone."

"We moved it to that cot over there," Julie said. "It's much quieter. You'll be alone and more comfortable."

All the nurses watched as Grace dropped her head and moved to the far corner. Once there, she stood, not moving, with her back to the group.

CHAPTER 11

Mary slipped out of quarters early, double-timing to the mess tent. She spied Sally reading reports in the corner of the half-empty mess. This would be their first one-on-one interaction since her complaint. Fortunately, no one was sitting near her CO. Mary took a deep breath and stepped close.

Sally looked up from her reading. "Surprised to see you up and about this early. You must be feeling better, although everyone should be relishing this break. Is there something I can do for you?"

Her boss gave a hard look while Mary stood at attention. "I regret having to bother you, ma'am, but there's an important issue I need to discuss. Is the present acceptable?"

"At ease and sit down. Did something happen at home? Nothing bad with the baby, I hope."

"Not that, ma'am." Mary wet her lips, searching for the right thing to say. *Here I am complaining again, and this time about a friend. Will she bite my head off? I don't know her feelings about race.*

Sally sensed the nervousness. "Hey there, I see something's bothering you. Start at the beginning. I promise to keep it confidential."

"The problem is you can't keep this confidential. I think

you need to take action right away."

"Tell me."

"Two new nurses arrived last night that I don't think you've met, right?"

"Correct. I've been on the run. They're on my list for this morning."

With another deep breath, "One of them is a Negro, Grace Thomas. I met her and Mildred, who is Caucasian, last night. I gave them a quick tour after Captain Walsh asked me to help."

"Go on."

"At first, the new nurses put their gear on empty bunks close to me. After I showed them around, we discovered someone, and I think it was Julie, had moved Grace's stuff to a far bunk. Mildred's gear wasn't moved. Julie said Grace would be happier by herself, but I could tell it hurt Grace. Julie has complained to other nurses about having a Negro in our unit. She even refused to shake hands with Grace when I first introduced them. I feel awful for Grace."

The head nurse leaned back. "Shit." Finally, she said, "Thanks for bringing this to my attention. This situation must be difficult for you, given that you and Julie are close. Your sense about this is correct. And I'm going to need help from you and the other nurses."

"What can I do? You're the commanding officer."

"This world would be easier if all I had to do is issue the order that you shall not be prejudiced. President Roosevelt ordered military desegregation in the last war, but did you see much change? Although President Truman has been clear about achieving full integration, altering opinions takes time."

Sally took a sip of her coffee. "Julie's from Alabama, where race relations are strained. Ultimately, our unit will be stronger once everyone accepts Grace as a nurse doing her best, but we'll have to work to get to that point."

Thank goodness she said the right thing. I can breathe

again. I don't know what I would've done if she'd brushed me off. "I'll try to help. What do you have in mind?"

"You're one of the leaders among the nurses. People respect you because you work with the senior surgeon. I need you to monitor tent talk. Where possible, speak up so that we give Grace a chance. If things get out of hand, give me a head's up. I don't want to issue a lot of commands unless needed. If necessary, I'll knock heads together. I want to avoid that."

Mary nodded.

Sally went on. "It'll be necessary for me to talk one-on-one with Julie to feel her out and send the message we're on the same team. I'll also need to discuss this with Grace. That make sense?"

"If you say so. I feel awful for Grace. I could tell she felt all by herself last night."

"Would you be willing to spend time with her? Demonstrate that you accept her. If you ask a few other nurses to help, maybe we can nip this in the bud."

Mary smiled. "Okay, I can do that. Thanks for letting me bother you in the middle of your work."

"Before you go, do you have another moment?"

"Sure." Mary sat back down.

Now Sally took a deep breath. "I was rough on you when you came about the incident with Doctor Wright. We're here to support the surgeons who are the critical players in our mission. Bones shouldn't have acted that way, but we're at war. We must overlook certain things for the welfare of the men we're trying to save. Since you got here, you've become one of the best nurses in the unit. Coming here today with your concerns exemplifies being a natural leader. When we first met, I said you'd succeed. Today is an example of that. Keep up the good work, but stay away from getting into a compromising position with doctors. Any questions?"

Mary's heart sank. *So, I'm doing great but don't do that again? Play by my rules, and you'll be okay. And if you have a personal problem, keep it to yourself.*

After a moment, she nodded. "No questions, ma'am."

Despite her desire to reach out immediately to Grace, Mary knew she had to get letters off.

She first penned a short one to her mother.

Thanks for your latest letter. It's terrible to hear about Sharon's death, but leave is impossible. Please keep me posted, and thanks for all you're doing to take care of the baby.

She wrote to her husband, " *I'm sorry to hear about your sister's passing. Sharon was a wonderful person at heart and just attracted to the wrong people. Despite all her struggles, she left us the gift of Cindy. My mother promises to keep me posted on funeral information.*

Now may not be the best time, but I must share how angry and disappointed I am with your lies. In your last letter, you said you'd quit your job. But I know they fired you for taking time away from work and spending it with Mona. You also said that your relationship with her ended. Now, it appears you're still cheating on me.

You deceived me before my call-up, and nothing has changed since I left. Don't write to me anymore. Things are tough enough here without having to put up with your dishonesty. When I get home, we can figure out our relationship. Until then, I don't want to hear from you.

The longest letter was to her best friend.

> *Thanks for your letters and for filling me in on all the details, no matter how difficult. I wrote Rob, instructing him not to write me anymore. I don't need that aggravation as long as I'm stuck here. In the meantime, I hope he won't take out his anger on you or my mom.*
>
> *I regret you had to meet Richard. The apple never falls far from the tree. Small chance those two can ever work together. It will be interesting to see if Richard can get Rob to stop carrying on with Mona. I don't care whether he does the more I think about it. Something has broken inside me.*
>
> *I struggle when I read about Richard saying Rob and I need to adopt Cindy to keep her in the family. I love that little girl, but would that love be enough for me to put up with a man I no longer respect?*
>
> *We're on a brief break. Dearest friend, please keep me posted. You're the one I most trust to tell me the truth. My mother said she couldn't cope without Stan and you. Thanks for all you are doing.*

She leaned back on her cot and thought about taking a nap. A few minutes later, the tent door slammed back, causing everyone to look over. Julie stormed into the tent and right toward Mary. "I heard you met with our CO at breakfast. Might I ask what the two of you were talking about?"

Stunned at Julie's directness and her nasty tone, Mary sat up, unsure how to respond. *Should I be honest and share what we discussed? Lying doesn't feel right. Maybe Sally's approach of taking it slow won't work.*

All the nurses in the tent were watching. Mary saw that Grace wasn't there.

"Julie, maybe we should head outside where we can talk."

"I don't want to talk privately. Everyone here can see that my so-called friend went behind my back to our boss. If you have a problem, say it to my face."

"I didn't go behind your back, but I did need to share my concerns about Grace being accepted. A minority joining a team can be challenging, but we need as many good nurses as possible. We've got to give Grace a chance."

"You did talk about me."

"I'm concerned you didn't seem open to meeting Grace and then moved her gear away from our bunks."

"How many Negroes live in New Hampshire? Ever work with one?"

"There are some, and no, I never had the opportunity. But we're all human, no matter what skin color, or whether Korean or American."

"You don't have the experience I do. Down south, Negroes are all over the place, and they cannot do the work whites do."

"Is it they cannot do the work, or are they not allowed to do it?"

The other nurses crept closer until they were only a few feet from the argument. With so many nurses watching, Mary struggled with how to defuse the situation. This wasn't the quiet start Sally wanted. *What should I do or say? Julie's right in my face.*

"Like I said, Julie, let's give Grace a chance. She seems like a nice person and wouldn't be here if she wasn't qualified."

"From my experience, we don't need those kinds of hands. I thought you were my friend. You ratted me out to the CO. Thanks a lot."

"I didn't rat you out. I went to get suggestions about how we can work together."

From two bunks over, Ann spoke up. "Julie, we need to accept the new gals. Like Mary said, we can use more help. This affects us all, not just you two."

Julie glared at Ann. Then the tent door opened. Sally

walked in with Mildred and Grace.

"At ease, ladies," the senior nurse ordered. "Although you should be relaxing, it's a bit loud in here. So let's tone things down."

The room fell silent. Mary looked over at Grace, who had her head down.

Sally continued. "I've been meeting with our new arrivals and know they'll be terrific additions. Their records are superlative. Both are regular Army, have lots of experience, and volunteered for duty here. We're lucky to have them. A few of you might have already met them. Since most of us are here, I'd like to give them an official welcome."

Sally first led Mildred and Grace to Mary. "Lieutenant Belanger gave you a tour last evening. Time to meet again."

Both new nurses extended their hands, which Mary shook. Sally smiled and turned. "This is one of our top triage nurses, Lieutenant Julie Fellows." Julie shook Mildred's hand. Without looking directly at her commanding officer, Julie stiffly shook Grace's hand.

"To get started, Grace is going to work in triage. She'll be lucky to have someone like you to help her, Fellows."

Julie's back straightened.

After introducing the rest of the nurses, Sally's gaze scanned the tent. "Grace, why are you sleeping in that corner? I'd like you to move closer to others. That way, you'll get to know these ladies more quickly. Look, there's an available bunk. Please move when you have the time."

The senior nurse smiled at all the nurses. "I have to run. By the way, I hear there's more volleyball this afternoon." To the new nurses, "If you're into the sport, be careful of Mary. She's a tiger on the court."

Grace smiled. "This is our second warning about her volleyball skills. I can't wait to see her in action."

"Lieutenant Belanger, your reputation grows."

Sally started to head out the door when Julie called out.

"Ma'am, I like it quiet. Alright if I move to Grace's old bunk in the corner?"

Sally turned, looking directly at her. "Negative, Fellows. I like my nurses together as a team." She spun and left. No one spoke.

Late that afternoon, Mary catnapped. In the background, she heard her boss softly call her name. Sally said, "Hope I didn't wake you. It looks like we'll be off again tomorrow. Let me ask a favor. Would you like to join a few other nurses and me tomorrow at a local orphanage? One of my friends has been helping a priest, and the nuns care for a mess of kids. There are too many noncombatant casualties in war, which leaves children without parents. In addition, some kids are sick or injured and aren't receiving regular medical care. Another pair of talented hands would be welcome."

Her baby back in New Hampshire immediately came to mind. "Count me in," Mary said. "When do we leave, and what should I bring?"

"My friend is scrounging medical supplies, clothes, and donations. She got a couple of jeeps assigned. We'll have to squeeze in everything and as many nurses as possible. 1100 hours tomorrow, we'll meet in front of the mess hall and will be at the orphanage in time for lunch with the kids. After that, we'll work doing whatever we can."

"May I contribute to any financial donations you're collecting since I can't find anything I need to buy? I have the military scrip they pay us to slow down the black market. Can they use that at the orphanage?"

"Officially, no, but give me the scrip. My friend will turn it into cash for the orphanage. It's better if you don't ask how she does that. Thanks for being generous. These kids need whatever help we can give them."

Mary stood and pulled out her duffel to find the scrip. Grace came up behind Sally. "Ma'am, I heard you're looking for help at an orphanage tomorrow."

"Want to join the party?"

"I do, ma'am."

"You got it, but you can only come if you get past the ma'am and call me Sally. Say, 'Yes, Sally. I'll be there tomorrow.'"

"Yes, Sally, I'll be there tomorrow."

All three laughed.

"Good, keep it up." Sally headed out the door with Mary's donation.

With the scrip Mary kept, Grace asked, "Why are we paid in scrip and not US dollars?"

"If you've got a minute, I can explain how it works."

Grace examined the different denominations Mary showed her. "The Army knows that Korean businesses would demand dollars if we rich Americans started spending US currency here. Then the local currency would become worthless. They pay us with this scrip for use on base to avoid that. It's worthless if a local tries to use it without a military ID. One thing to watch out for is the Army changes the scrip periodically, so you must be ready to swap your old version for the new one. They do that to try and control the black market."

"It doesn't look like real money," said Grace. "And I'm not even sure how a black market works."

Ann chimed in. "I know something about it and a few secrets about getting things from the black market the Army doesn't supply."

Another nurse joined them. It heartened Mary to see the others reaching out to Grace. Julie watched and, without a word, went out.

At 1100 hours, Grace, Ginny, Ann, and Mary stood outside the mess tent. In a cloud of dust, two jeeps rolled up. From the passenger seat of the first vehicle, Sally announced, "This is Abbie. In the other jeep are Steve and Walt, our guards for the day. It turns out we got more donations than expected. Getting us all in will be tight, but we'll make it work."

She turned to the driver. "Miss Abigail, are these truly donations?"

A huge grin filled the perky brunette's face, which peeked out from under her floppy hat. "All procured on the up and up."

The nurses broke into laughter. Mary and Grace scrambled up to wedge into the back of the jeep. Off they sped. The breeze from the drive brought the slightest of relief to another warm day.

Abbie leaned back, shouting over the engine noise. "Thanks for giving up your R&R to help. When you see what the local priest is dealing with, you'll appreciate how much you're needed."

Mary shouted back. "Happy to help." She wanted to tell Abbie to keep her eyes on the road. Instead, the jeep kept speeding, as pedestrians dodged the distracted driver.

Once past the base checkpoint, congestion forced them to slow. Abbie finally maneuvered carefully through the teeming mass of humanity camped on the airbase's outskirts.

Mary was amazed. *I thought there were lots of refugees camped here when I first arrived. Now there's many more. What happens to these people if we can't hold back the North Koreans?*

In a less crowded part of Pusan, the jeep sped up again. Mary recognized the smell she'd first associated with Korea. The odor would have caused her to gag only a short time ago. As she'd been told, it was now simply unpleasant.

Abbie aggressively worked the horn as Koreans hustled out of the way. Through the teeming crowds of the poor, Mary thought about how fate dictates what life we get to live. *This place is vastly different from where I grew up. Even without war, life is challenging for anyone who lives here. There's nothing better than being born an American. What would life be for me with Cindy if this was our home? Probably begging for charity like many women here. How would I even keep the two of us alive?*

The two jeeps entered an older neighborhood, then made several turns through a warren of streets crowded with shoppers at small market stalls. Abbie pulled to a stop in front of a low set of dilapidated concrete buildings. A large group of youngsters lined the roadside. In front of the children stood a small Korean priest with a bent back and long white beard. Behind him were several nuns and a few Korean women.

Abbie leaped out to shake hands with the priest. "Father Khang, these are five of the finest nurses America has. We have clothes, medicine, and food for you. Plus, I have money here." She patted her pocket.

"God bless you, Abbie," the priest said in good English. He then stepped forward to shake hands with each nurse. "Welcome. God bless you. Thank you."

He waved to one nun, who stepped forward, bowing. In broken English, she said, "Children practice song for you. Okay?"

Abbie replied, "We would love that."

The nun raised her hands to the assembled children to lead them in a Korean song of greeting. When the singing started, Mary scanned the scruffy group. Most wore dirty rags, and more than a few had open sores. Her eyes zeroed in on the smallest, and she thought again about Cindy. *In New Hampshire, one child needs me. Here's a group of infants desperately in need of anyone.* Her eyes welling up, Mary felt Sally take her hand.

All the Americans clapped, bringing broad smiles to the children. One of the GIs stepped up. "Abbie, there's a crowd gathering. I'm worried they may start grabbing things. We're going to push them away from the jeeps. I suggest you get the donations inside the orphanage now."

Abbie turned to Father Khang. "Could we get the older children to help us carry things inside? And ladies, let's lend a hand."

With the donations safely stored, the nurses smelled the rich fragrance of Korean cooking.

Abbie said, "It's exciting for the children to have lunch with an American. Almost none speak any English, though. Do the best you can with sign language and smiles. They have set a place for each of you in a group. Remember that they've dipped into their precious supplies to make this meal for us. Enjoy the local cuisine and be thankful."

Mary said, "I see the children are organized by age. Might I eat with the youngest group?"

"That group is near the smaller building in the back. When you head that way, stick your head into the room on the left. That's where the babies live."

Mary's heart fell. Of course, there would be babies. She moved toward her luncheon group, who appeared to be between two and five years old. Through a door to her left, Mary peeked inside. A row of crude bassinets stood in a dank room with cracked walls and a concrete floor. A quick count told her there were eleven babies crowded in. Over in one corner, a Korean woman held two infants, balancing bottles while several cried. Mary wanted to run in to help the exhausted-looking woman, but her group waited.

Near the circle of toddlers, Mary scanned the layout of the orphanage. A small church and two crumbling buildings surrounded a cobblestone courtyard. The door to the church stood open, revealing piles of bedding, probably where some of the children slept. When she tried to count the children in the various groups, there were too many for her to track. Some of the older ones carried bowls of food to the different circles.

When the nurse joined them, the children in Mary's group scrambled to their feet, bowing. In front of each child lay a bowl containing beef in sauce served over rice. She noted that not one child had touched their food as they waited.

At the spot reserved for her, Mary returned the bow. After straightening, a few in the group tittered. *Obviously, a poor bow by local standards.*

In halting English, Sister Nah introduced herself. "Thank you coming. Okay, children sit?"

"Please have them sit down." A few Korean words to the children, then to the nurse. "You eat. Then children."

Would hungry American children sit with a plate of food and wait until their guest ate first? Mary sat awkwardly cross-legged on the rough cobblestones, feeling her stiff muscles resist. Finally, she reached for a bowl, observing the wide eyes staring at her. *I bet I'm the first American woman they've met.*

"Thank you, Sister, for the guidance." Mary wasted no time taking her first bite of food. Despite the hot spices that assaulted her mouth, she turned to the children, smiling and rubbing her stomach. Soft giggles came back. With custom observed, the children attacked their lunches.

The burning of Mary's palate built, quickly becoming unbearable. Her forehead openly perspiring, she anxiously searched for a beverage. Mary waved her hand to Sister Nah, pointing to her mouth, squawking, "Water, please."

The nun's eyes widened. She jumped up and ran to the kitchen. Back with several pieces of bread, Mary croaked, "No bread, water."

The nun shook her head. "Water bad. Bread good."

Desperate, Mary reached for a piece, chewing as fast as possible. Although the burning didn't completely go away, its effects eased. She bit into another piece of bread while Sister Nah took the nurse's plate away, returning with plain white rice and two more slices of bread.

The children stared at Mary. Smiling at the children, the nurse pantomimed eating, then fanning herself. The group burst into hysterics.

Abbie came over. "You're a real comedian to get these kids going without knowing Korean. What you experienced happened to me when I first learned how spicy Korean food can be."

Mary shook her head. "I've only been eating in the mess hall. Is all Korean food like this?"

"Not all, but a lot. Wait until you try the kimchee. I don't want to be around for that. By the way, the nun saved you. Water spreads the heat, while bread absorbs the spice. Besides, if you drank the local water, you'd soon suffer from dysentery, unless you already do."

Mary thanked Sister Nah again, who bowed in return. The children sat politely, staring at the Americans. Mary asked the nun, "Would the children like me to sing a song from my country?"

The nun translated the offer, eliciting immediate clapping and smiles.

With the last of the spice cleared from her throat, Mary sang the tune Cindy most responded to, "That's An Irish Lullaby." Softly serenading, Mary gazed from face to face, rapt with attention. Her heart aching, she saw innocence and need in each child's eyes.

At the end of the song, Sister Nah clapped. The children erupted.

"Besides volleyball, singing is another hidden talent," Sally said, joining the group. "I'm sure you could entertain all afternoon, but it's time to go to work."

Despite her cramped muscles, Mary managed to stand. One little girl from the other side of the circle jumped and ran to embrace Mary's leg. All the children followed into a group hug. But Sister Nah clapped her hands, and the children headed off.

"Kinda gets to you, doesn't it?" Abbie said.

"How often do you come here, and what does your commanding officer think of this?"

"Her CO is aware of this and turns a blind eye," Sally laughed. "He doesn't want to know where she gets some of the supplies. I heard that a few nurses explained the black market to Grace. When she's ready for the advanced course, Abbie teaches that one."

After a few minutes of planning, the nurses set up individual stations to examine each child. Two more nuns appeared. After introductions, Mary realized these sisters didn't speak any English.

Sister Nah said, "You teach us. We watch. I share." She then translated for the other nuns.

Each of the Americans would work with the group they ate with. Once a nurse finished her group, she would move to the babies.

Father Khang, Sister Nah, and the nuns moved from group to group to translate the medications dispensed and follow-up instructions from the examinations. When Mary got started, the line of children seemed daunting. Within minutes she became focused on the individual patient in front of her.

Several children would require more serious treatment, like one child with a cleft palate. When Mary asked Sally what should be done, the senior nurse grimaced. "Do the best you can today. I'll speak with Doctor Walsh. We'll try to get permission to bring them on base for needed care or surgery."

Back with her group, Mary tried to understand this Sally compared to the one who reacted to Bones' assault. She clearly had a good heart and was dedicated to the well-being of all patients, including these orphans. Why didn't that dedication extend to the safety of the nurses in her command? *I like the woman I see today, but what happens in the future if I bring up an issue she doesn't like?*

The hours flew by until one last child waited. *Where had the time gone? I didn't even notice the hot weather being this busy.* The girl stepped forward, quickly reaching for Mary's arm. She pulled back the nurse's sleeve to examine Mary's watch. The young girl stared wide-eyed at the device, probably the first she had seen. Another reminder of how impoverished these children were.

Back on base, the volunteers stood outside their quarters. They were exhausted but wouldn't trade the day's experience for anything. Abbie gave each nurse an embrace. "I've got to scrounge follow-up supplies and medications. Thanks again." She and the guards sped off.

Grace laughed. "Your lunch a little spicy?"

Mary said, "Oh my God, I thought I'd die. You must've felt the same way."

"It's a little warm, but we like spicy food down south. You pale New Englanders don't go for the heat."

"Did you eat it?"

"A welcome change from the mess hall."

"I've got to lie down, but I want to hear about where you grew up and how you got into the Army. Breakfast?"

"I'd like that. See ya then for Army bland."

Mary found a package on her bunk. A nurse across the aisle said, "Mail call today. I grabbed your stuff. If there are goodies, you must share."

Mary smiled, feeling newfound energy. But, more than goodies, she hoped for letters and pictures.

There were sweets in the box, and she passed around the cookies and chocolates. Everybody wanted to see pictures of the baby and cooed about Cindy being deadly cute. Mary marveled how different she appeared in such a short time.

Group envy peaked over the fur-lined L.L. Bean boots and two pairs of long underwear. Ann said, "I don't like the idea you might need these thermals since it would mean we'll be here longer than any of us want. Maybe I should've passed on the chocolates and taken one of those union suits."

"I wrote to my mom when I realized the war could continue into the winter. These boots and underwear are non-negotiable. But I agree never having to use this stuff would be wonderful."

While she nibbled on a cookie and examined the boots, Grace said, "I've seen nothing like these. Will it get that cold here? I mean, it's hot now. How bad could it be during the winter?"

Ann said, "Grace, we have serious talking to do. Let's leave Mary alone. There are letters she wants to read. We can educate our southern sister about how winter weather blows into Korea from Siberia. We want to be out of this country before that blast arrives."

MANCHESTER TIMES
NEWS BULLETIN
UN TROOPS EXPAND PUSAN PERIMETER

United Nations forces pushed back the aggressors for the first time since the North Korean Army invaded their southern neighbor. Allied elements of the UN gained fifteen miles of territory, recapturing the town of Taegu. This campaign is the first step to relieving pressure on Pusan's defensive perimeter, the principal base for UN forces.

Although optimistic about this positive development, an Army representative urged caution about expecting rapid progress. "North of Taegu is a series of mountains, and the North Koreans are already digging in. Until the Allies can assemble a much greater force, the communists will be hard to dislodge. While a difficult struggle is still ahead, this is the first step to turning this war around."

CHAPTER 12

At the mess tent, Mary looked for Grace. Over on the far side, she spied her sitting with two Negro soldiers. Mary got her food and headed that way. "Mind if I join you?"

The two men paused, checking out the new arrival. After a few seconds of silence, Grace piped up. "I wanted to catch up with these two clowns. My apologies for heading here before you. Yes, please join us." She turned to the two men. "She's fine."

Mary introduced herself to Ronnie and Fred, who shook her hand. "I don't think I've seen you two around. Are you new?"

Ronnie answered, "We stand out, don't we?"

Fred hit his buddy in the arm and said, "Yeah, we're new. We're ambulance drivers. Guess the Army needs a few smooth men to keep you nurses company."

Mary smiled. "Welcome. We have a wonderful group of people. I meant nothing by asking."

Ronnie stared at Mary until Grace said, "She's cool. Lighten up."

"My apologies, Lieutenant," Ronnie said. "Sometimes my mouth starts before my brain."

Half-smiling and picking at her food, Mary said, "I want

an apology for calling me Lieutenant. It's Mary. We're relaxed here. I bet you don't call Grace by her rank."

Fred grinned. "Oh, I like this. Another apology from Ronnie. This woman has your number, brother."

Ronnie broke into a grin. "My sincere apologies, Mary. It won't happen again."

"Did I interrupt your conversation?" Mary asked. "Please go back to what you were talking about."

Grace said, "Nothing important. Just trash-talking about the Army and how we got here. I met these two jokers last night."

"You promised to tell me about your home and ending up in the Army. Is this a good time?"

"Sure, I'll give you the basics, although Ronnie and Fred already heard this. I grew up in Natchez, Mississippi. daddy worked in the fields or did heavy labor for pay. Mama cleaned houses—laundry, domestic work, whatever. I'm the youngest of three children. We were poor, but my parents made sure they fed the kids, even though they might skip a meal. My father died when a trench he and another man were digging collapsed. Then it was my mom and us kids. My sister and brother quit school to bring money in. Since I was the smallest, the others took care of me."

Grace paused. "My brother's in jail, and my sister lives at home with my mother. Mom's done in. Now my sis does the cleaning and laundry work. My enlisting in the Army turned out to be the best thing that ever happened. It got me trained and a regular paycheck. I may do laundry here, but the pay is better, food provided, and the money I send home makes a big difference."

Mary stopped eating. "That's terrible about your father. What a horrible accident!"

Grace's eyes welled up. An angry look clouded her face, and she stared into space. "Two Blacks were working in the trench. All the white workers were up on the street. When the trench caved in, one passerby told my mama the other workers put little effort into digging."

Mary reached over and put her hand on Grace's back. "How could people be like that?"

Ronnie grew indignant. "Where are you from?"

"New Hampshire. Manchester."

"You see many brothers and sisters up there?"

Fred said, "Ronnie, be careful."

"I'm careful. This woman doesn't know what goes on outside of those lily-white states. Grace, tell Mary what it's like when you enlisted and how the local Klan reacted."

Grace wiped her eyes. "My mother and I were downtown before my high school graduation. I didn't have plans but wanted something different. The poster at the Army Recruitment Office of a nurse looked interesting, so I asked mama if I could go in. The sergeant started talking about how the Army would train me. That sounded fine, and mama got excited for me to get a good job. Here I am."

She smiled. "When it got to a few days before my time to report, that sergeant came to our house saying they were having problems safely getting Blacks out of town. It seems the Klan didn't like the idea of colored getting uppity. On the day I was to leave, the sergeant said he would pick me up at one in the morning in an unmarked car. He'd dress in his civilian clothes and drive me to Atlanta. That way, there would be less chance for an incident."

The others were watching Mary, who had stopped eating. She stammered, "I didn't know things were that bad down south."

Fred said, "I'm from Chicago. It might be different circumstances, but life is harder when you have skin like ours. If I moved to Manchester, I bet they'd roll out the unwelcome wagon for me." The three Blacks laughed.

Grace put her hand on Mary's back. "That's the way this world works. Maybe one day it'll be different. I appreciate what you've done for me already. I know you talked to Sally, and most of the nurses have been nice, except Julie and a few others. But I don't worry about them. I've had it a lot worse."

On her way back to quarters, Mary couldn't get Grace's story out of her mind. Ronnie and Fred also shared some experiences in the officially desegregated Army that still offered limited assignments for minorities. For the first time, Mary realized minorities made up the majority of ambulance drivers.

"Guess this is a job they think we can handle," Ronnie had explained.

Mary remembered seeing minorities growing up in New Hampshire. When she asked her father why there weren't more, he'd said, "It's too cold here."

When she shared this comment with Fred, he doubled over in laughter. "Yep, much too cold. I bet my parents thought that during nights without heat in Chicago."

These stories left Mary unsettled. Her parents raised her in a sheltered world, and getting this glimpse into the experiences of Blacks made her nervous. *How do I fit into this? What's the right thing to do?*

Back in the nurses' tent, Sally was organizing a work crew. "Perfect timing, Belanger. I need one more pair of hands to help me with a shipment of supplies. Our break may be coming to an end. There's an all-unit meeting at 1300 hours if you didn't see the notice. All right, ladies, let's go."

In a cavernous airplane hangar, the unit sat in one corner. Behind the meeting area, several jets were being serviced. The continuous air operations made it hard to hear because of the open door. The whole unit sitting together showed Mary how much it took to support the doctors and nurses. There were a few new faces and lots of introductions. Among the doctors, she spied two new arrivals.

The three senior officers stepped to the riser. Major Phillips picked up a microphone, and everyone jumped to attention. "At ease," Phillips ordered. "Please take your seats. We'll have to put up with the background noise. Welcome to the personnel joining us. Over the next few days, please introduce yourselves to our newcomers. I want you to know how proud I am of this unit and how each of you performed in Taegu and during the withdrawal. We've needed this break, but all good things do come to an end. It'll soon be our turn to return to action."

A collective groan escaped the group.

A scrambling of fighter jets reverberated through the hangar. Once the outside noise level dropped again, the commanding officer went on. "The nature of a MASH mission is to be right behind the front lines. In our next assignment, we'll be even closer to the action. Over the next few days, we're going through training to prepare us for the possibility of working under live fire. They rushed our unit here after the invasion, and we didn't have the opportunity for training. I'm sure some of you will think what will occur is chicken shit and a waste of time, but HQ has dictated a program, and we'll follow it. The next couple of days will be full. Dress in fatigues. You'll get dirty. Make sure you drink lots. I mean water, not what many of you are thinking."

A ripple of light laughter went through the group. "All right, that's all I have. Captain Walsh and Lieutenant Bates, anything to add?"

Both gestured no.

"All right, questions?"

An orderly in the front row asked, "Are we headed back to

Taegu or elsewhere?"

"No comment on where we're going. I'm happy to report that not only have our lines stabilized, but we've also pushed the North Koreans back in a couple of places."

A resounding hurrah filled the hanger.

"It's a small start, but hopefully, the beginning of turning this war around. What else?"

There were no additional questions.

"All right, report to your officers, who will explain the next few days' activities. Dismissed."

In a Quonset hut, the nurses queued up for new equipment. After hearing what they needed, the exasperated sergeant admonished the nurses about missing vests and gas masks. The women explained how they had evacuated from Taegu, and the sergeant calmed down. He reluctantly issued replacement equipment, repeatedly complaining about the shortage of everything. Mary felt thankful to get away from his grousing.

Later that morning, at a remote part of the base, the nurses stood in line for calisthenics. Jumping jacks, a few pushups, then a short run. Even in this cooler morning temperature, soon, everyone was soaked. One nurse offered, "They let us sit around recovering for days and then want us to run our butts off. I hope this doesn't become a daily routine."

Someone called back, "If there was beer at the end of the run, you'd move your ass."

Once the laughter quieted, off to the left, Mary watched the ambulance drivers at target practice. Amidst much teasing and joking, they were holding a vigorous competition. Since some of those men had never regularly fired a rifle, it appeared the bulk of the training focused on loading and positioning. Maybe a few had hunting or training experience since they regularly hit the targets.

Because of a current shortage of weapons, there would be a central arms store for medical personnel in emergencies. If a situation developed where nurses might need weapons, Mary hoped to be at the back of that line. She was glad not being trained with weapons, but it made her worry what could be ahead.

The nurses bounced in the back of a truck to the next training exercise. By now, everyone agreed it looked like there was a serious mission ahead. The truck stopped next to a wooden wall that looked to be over twenty-five feet high. Heavy rope netting covered one side. Over to the right, Mary noticed an obstacle course.

A stubby sergeant with a loud voice called the nurses to assemble around him. "Ladies, I'm Sergeant Borson, and I'll be your trainer this afternoon. Please come closer to hear me better." The nurses squeezed together.

"There will be two exercises. First, scaling the wall, and then a bit of fun with an obstacle course. I know you already did some running this morning. Now you can loosen those muscles and get a bit more exercise in. The major challenge with the obstacle course is the final stage, where you'll crawl on your bellies under a series of barbed wire barriers. If you keep your heads and butts down, nobody gets snagged. One more thing. While you're crawling, there'll be live fire going over you. You could be hit if you lift any part of your body."

Several of the nurses looked nervously at each other.

"I see a few of you are concerned about getting hurt. Not one person ever got injured in all my time with this training. The purpose is that in actual combat, you'll know what to expect and how to protect yourselves. If anyone experiences a problem on the course, signal and help will come. Before that, we're going to do a little climbing. Ladies, please fall in behind me. Let's hit the wall."

With the women assembled behind the wooden structure, ladders stood leading to a platform just below the top. The sergeant explained, "There are four ladders. When instructed, you'll ascend to the platform. Those four individuals will wait and, on command, step over the top of the wall using the rope netting to come down the other side. It's easy. I've got several of my finest climbers who will now demonstrate this for you."

Four enlisted men in the background stepped forward, scurrying up the ladders. Mary doubted she'd be climbing up that fast. She did not like heights. Even the live-fire exercise sounded more appealing.

"Ladies, please follow me to the front side of the wall, where these talented Americans will show you what you missed in high school gym class." There were a few nervous laughs from the group.

"Gentlemen, commence your descent."

The four men swung their legs over the top of the wall, placing their feet in the netting. When the men climbed down, Sergeant Borson called out instructions. "Watch how they get their feet set first before moving their hands—got that? Move your feet first. Also, see how carefully they move. No need for speed. Get your footing set, then move your hands." Within a minute, the four soldiers were on the ground.

"See how easy it is? Fellas, get up there and do it again on my command. Let's have the ladies observe one more time."

After the men descended again, Borson asked for questions. Again, the nurses stayed quiet until one nurse asked, "Why are we doing this?"

"At ease, Lieutenant," Sally barked. "When the time is right, you'll know what you need to know."

Sally turned to the sergeant. "I believe we're ready. May we proceed?"

"Yes, Lieutenant. One more thing. Everyone does this twice. If someone has a problem on either of their climbs, we'll have them do it a few more times. It's essential everyone is proficient at this."

Sally called, "Ladies, time for some more exercise."

Near the ladders, Grace caught up to Mary. "Don't do it right, and you do it until you get it right. I'm motivated. Besides, I'm going to pretend a Klansman is chasing me. Watch me fly down."

Grace scrambled onto the bouncing ladder showing what good shape she was in. Mary stood speechless.

The exercise proved more demanding than Mary expected. Climbing up the shaky ladder, she moved slowly because of her fear of heights. On the platform, she tightly gripped the top of the wall and tried not to look down. When the order came to descend, it took all her nerve to swing her leg over the top. The netting felt loose, and with the others also climbing on the ropes, it affected Mary's balance. In the end, she got down on trembling legs, all her muscles aching. All too soon, the order came for a second climb. Thankfully, this time it went more quickly. When a few nurses needed to climb a third time, Mary felt relief not being called.

Most nurses sat by the truck, waiting for the others to complete their climbing. Ginny leaned forward and said softly, "Did you hear what the guy at the bottom of the wall mentioned to me? He said if you think this is hard, wait until you're doing this going from one ship to another in choppy seas." The group went silent.

"What did he say again?" one nurse asked.

Ginny repeated what she'd heard. "Looks like we're going on a ship." Everyone spoke at once, wondering what that could mean. The group fell silent when Sally approached.

The senior nurse recognized guilty faces. "What were you talking about?"

"Nothing," one nurse quickly said. "Only a bad joke."

With a skeptical look, Sally called, "Sergeant, we're ready for the next exercise."

The nurses returned to the truck after the obstacle course, although Sally did not join them. Despite being covered with dirt from their crawling, they all celebrated having the day's training over with. Grace wondered aloud if they weren't actually firing blanks on the obstacle course. "The instructor said there's an ammunition shortage. Why would they waste real bullets for training and possibly injure someone? I've heard real bullets before, and things sounded different today." Shrugs and nods met her remark.

The discussion shifted back to Ginny's news about climbing down from a boat. As their truck left the training area, the nurses watched troops climbing down the same wall and netting in full battledress with equipment. Something big was up. Everyone agreed not to mention what they heard to their boss. She'd already barked when asked why they were doing the wall. Sally knew where they were going but wasn't going to explain.

Back in quarters, the nurses found a shower announcement for 1600 hours. A cheerful voice called, "Someone figured out there should be showers after crawling in the dirt. Who says the Army doesn't occasionally plan well?"

Resting on her cot, Mary hoped there might be really hot water instead of tepid or cold. Today she planned to wear panties in the shower. Recently, there had been an occasional man or two showing up. If co-ed showering happened, she wanted some coverage. After her struggle with Bones, whenever that happened, she felt sick. Hopefully, today would be women only.

In the open shower area, hot water flowed. Lively chatter

flew between the women as they passed soap and shampoo. The wooden floor felt slippery, but the women luxuriated in this simple pleasure. Too soon, from the door, Mary heard male voices. *Damn, not again.* She fought to take a deep breath to calm down.

After apologizing for their mistake, the men agreed to get in and out fast.

Mary stayed quiet and kept her back to the showers with the men. Almost done washing, she heard a familiar voice. "Mary, is that you?"

There stood Ben. Mary's arms flew up to cover her breasts. "Ben, what a surprise."

Everyone around them cracked up.

Mary silently cursed and grabbed her towel, hustling to the shower door. Over her shoulder, she called, "I'll see you later." The laughter grew, along with comments and jokes.

Ann dried off next to her. "How do you know that guy?"

"He was the medical officer where I got my physical at Fort Devens. Now, he's the head of the Eighth MASH. What are the odds something like this could happen?"

"You won't hear the end of this for a while. Given how embarrassed you were, I don't know how much of a look you got. But that guy naked, va va voom! Did you say his name's Ben? If you don't want him, sister, do me the honors of an introduction."

Mary grimaced. "I didn't get a good look." With her robe on, she hustled back to quarters.

Later, on her cot writing a letter home, Mary heard a male voice by the tent door.

Ann came over and said, "Your naked friend is here. From what I remember, he looks as good in uniform as he did without."

Trying to ignore the knot in her stomach, Mary turned to a small mirror to arrange her hair. Ann leaned close. "Don't bother with that. Get him back in the shower. If not for your benefit, then for the rest of us."

Mary gave her a friendly push. *I've got to figure out why I keep reacting like this.*

Once outside, Mary spoke softly. "Nice to see you again, Major, especially in uniform."

Ben blushed. "I want to apologize for this afternoon. We didn't understand the shower schedule, and that's unacceptable. When I saw you, I shouldn't have called out your name. I'm sure you're getting guff you shouldn't have to put up with."

"Well, we are the subject of discussion."

Ben looked uncomfortable. Mary then dropped her guard and smiled. "It's good to see you here. I thought the Eighth moved forward when our guys pushed the enemy back."

"That's right. We're back in Taegu, still reconstructing the hospital that your unit had to evacuate. The North Koreans did a lot of damage there. I had to come down for meetings. Since your unit's been off, you might not have heard about the encephalitis outbreak among US troops. Cases are growing, and we're trying to figure out how to deal with it. I'm heading to another session on that topic, but I wanted to swing by and see if you might be interested in dinner together."

"I'd like that. How about we meet at the mess hall? What would be a good time?"

"1830 work for you?"

She nodded.

"All right, it's a date. See you then."

Mary went back into the tent and found five nurses huddled on the other side of the door. The group stepped back, smiling.

Ginny said, "First, a naked shower, then a dinner date. We're totally jealous."

Mary kept quiet while the banter went back and forth.

Back at her bunk, she thought of Rob and felt a wave of guilt. *Why should I feel guilty? Rob cheated on me. Might still be, for all I know. Ben's a nice guy, and I can trust him. This is nothing more than flirting. Are we flirting? I've got to calm down. They're teasing me because they like me.*

Ben and Mary leaned across a table in the empty mess tent, sharing all that transpired over the past months. Pleased that Ben had asked about Cindy immediately, she felt embarrassed when he inquired about her husband. Shame about her marriage kept her response to the bare minimum.

Ben described his selection to head the Eighth MASH shortly after Mary had shipped out. It proved an exciting and intense assignment to muster staff and resources. His unit had the advantage of time in Japan to train and study reports from the 100th.

He described recent discussions with Major Phillips, who spoke effusively about how Mary had grown into her position in the OR. "Not only did he say you're working with the senior surgeon, but your head nurse is also complimentary. You should feel good about how you're doing."

Interesting that Sally said good things. I wonder if Phillips knew about my complaint about Bones. Does Ben know about that?

"Thanks for the kind words. I must admit I was initially scared that I wouldn't measure up, but Dave and Sally have been great."

Outside after dinner, Ben said, "I've got the evening free before I go back in the morning. Want to get a cup of coffee or maybe something stronger?"

"I could do with the stronger, but not too much."

"There's a bottle stashed in my guest quarters. Let me grab it."

Ben retrieved the liquor and a couple of cups. Mary led him to a quiet part of the camp near the volleyball area. The cooling September temperature felt perfect as the two settled on an old log. Even the bugs seemed off-duty tonight. Under a clear sky, stars twinkled, and the two toasted running into each other.

"I regret not having a wider selection of spirits, Lieutenant, and I seem to have forgotten the ice. Hopefully, neat works."

"One must learn to put up with shortages in a war zone, Major. Neat will be the smallest sacrifice I've yet to bear here."

They sipped their drinks. Mary asked whether transitioning to administration from day-to-day medical care had been difficult.

"I miss the hands-on care of patients." He paused. "I know you're getting a lot of teasing about the shower snafu, and want to apologize again for not being more discreet. When I saw you, I got excited and didn't think. I can be such a social moron."

Mary smiled and touched his arm. "Don't worry about it. I've been getting a lot of guff, but being part of a group that cares about me enough to tease is enjoyable. You're not the first man who's stumbled into our showers. And several nurses say they wouldn't mind if you made a return visit."

Ben chuckled. "Okay, chapter closed. There's one more thing I want to say. I'm disappointed fate's taking you away again. This time with you is wonderful. I wish it were longer."

"Where am I going?"

Ben bit his lip. "I shouldn't have said that."

"Maybe on a ship?"

Ben's eyes widened. "Where did you hear that?"

"Rumor mills are full-time operations here. I won't repeat what you said. The nurses put one and one together and figure we're going someplace by sea."

"Whatever you think might come, keep it under your hat. All I can say is the 100th has a big job ahead. That means I won't be seeing you again anytime soon."

"That's disappointing, but who knows? While we're both in Korea, it might happen. In the meantime, could you spare another tiny splash of your finest?"

Ben poured them both a generous amount.

"Whoa, whoa, there. That's too much for me." Mary poured most of the whiskey into his cup. "This is my first drink since my incident."

Ben looked down at his full cup. "Your incident? That sounds intriguing. What happened?"

"Now it's my turn that I shouldn't have said anything. I just learned I have to be careful around this stuff. With all the misery here, drinking can be an escape. And now, it looks like more suffering is coming my way." Mary took a sip, making a face as the whiskey burned. "Ben, there's one thing about you that impresses me."

"What might that be? My promotion?"

"No," Mary chuckled. "Although congratulations again. Since we met, you've always asked about my situation with the baby. The Army doesn't give a rat's ass about my having to leave Cindy. Your interest tells me you're a good man."

"With all that's come your way, I'd like to be a friend when you need support."

A warm glow filled Mary. "My, oh my. That's enough hooch for me." She spilled the rest on the ground, then leaned back, starting to slip off the log.

Ben reached over to keep her from falling. "Got ya. You okay?"

Embarrassed but enjoying the feel of his hand, Mary thought how gentle this man was compared to Bones. Without thinking, she shifted closer to Ben. "Another thing that impresses me is you even ask about my terrible husband. He wrote me a letter apologizing and saying he'd been bad but would mend his ways. His sister recently died, and he needs our marriage to adopt the baby. There's nothing in his letters regretting that he hurt me, only that I'm needed to make sure the baby stays in the family. Why did I ever decide to marry that weasel?"

Mary could see Ben struggling with how to respond. She went on, "This news came in a recent letter. Then my best friend wrote Rob hasn't changed and is still cheating on me."

"I'm sorry to hear that."

Mary waited for Ben to say something more, but he stayed quiet. While she silently started to weep, he pulled her closer. "I'm sorry to bother you with my problems," she whispered.

Ben took Mary in his arms. Her head dropped to his chest while he softly stroked her hair. "I said I wanted to be your friend. You're a good woman who deserves better. Tell me what I can do to help."

"Thanks for saying that," Mary said into his chest. After a moment, she sat up, gazed into his eyes, leaned forward, and kissed him. Shyly at first, then long and hard.

CHAPTER 13

Early the next day, Mary and Grace went to Sally's tent and found her packing. "We've been looking for you," Mary announced.

"What can I do for you two?"

"How about we track down Abbie to make another run to the orphanage?" Mary said. "Even if she doesn't have more supplies, checking on the challenging cases would be good. What do you think?"

Sally stopped her packing and shook her head. "Us going back to the orphanage won't work. Great idea, though." After another pause, "If you went to the base gate, you'd discover they've sealed our post. No one in or out, meaning there can't be any excursions."

The two nurses looked at the items spread on the bed.

Grace said, "I get it. We're on our way. You don't need to say anything, ma'am, but how should we pack if we want to get ahead of things?"

"Small packs like this should soon be on your bunks. Your larger duffels will catch up with us down the road. Pack personal items, extra underwear, medications, and other essentials. We'll be mustering late this afternoon."

Back at quarters, several nurses were already packing.

Then, a cry came from outside. "Mail call."

Taking her pack of letters, Mary skipped the packing and sat down to read. Heart thumping, she dreaded more bad news. One positive—there was no letter from Rob. Instead, she found the most recent postmarks, ripping open one from her mother.

Dear Mary,

I'm happy you are getting a break over there. Your news helps me relax as I worry about your safety.

There's been a bit of excitement here. First, Sharon's funeral went well, with lots of people and flowers. At the reception, everyone asked about you. You're the hometown hero. It made me proud to talk about your important work, although I would trade all that for you being here.

Richard and Rob suffered during the ceremony. Your husband is having difficulty dealing with the loss of his sister. The other night I found him crying on the front porch. He admitted he's been taking risks with his drinking and playing around. Sharon's death made him realize he must stop. Since that night, I've seen him showing interest in Cindy and, for the first time, getting involved with her care.

Rob's father is acting like a madman. Remember how he never visited the baby? Out of the blue, he decided Linda and I were not good enough to take care of the baby with you away. Without asking, he hired professional nurses without even a thank you to us. Richard said he wanted the best for the baby now that Sharon is dead.

Thank goodness Rob stood up to his father, maybe for the first time in his life. He sent the nurses away, but what a fight between those two. Richard threatened not to give Rob a job, and Rob said fine. Since he's still unemployed, we're keeping Rob busy on the home front.

Richard then showed up one morning with his attorney to lecture us that a married couple would have to adopt Cindy under state law. If you decide to leave Rob, he could not get custody.

Honey, I hate to write with this difficult news, but you should know what is going on. In the meantime, the most important thing is you staying safe and resting away from the fighting.

All my love, Mom

PS—The baby is fine.

Away from the fighting, but for how long? She reached for Linda's letter.

Dear Maar,

When I think it cannot get crazier here, it does. I read your mother's letter before she sealed the envelope and won't repeat what she wrote.

Your husband has not had a drink since the funeral. That's a step in the right direction. Whether he is still seeing Mona, I'm not sure. He hasn't been able to find another job and told me he might have to beg his father for work no matter what he said in the big blowout.

Richard has not been back since he came with his attorney. (I'm praying he stays away.) Like your mom wrote, the attorney's message is you must remain married to adopt Cindy. What are you thinking about divorce?

On the baby front, your mom, Rob, and I are caring for her. Cindy's sleeping better at night.

Look, I have to run. I promised Stan a rare dinner at home. So take good care of yourself, and be sure to fill me in on any and all cute doctor interactions.

Love, Lin

Mary sighed. At least things didn't appear to be any worse than before. If Rob cleaned up his act, nothing would be wrong with that. The issue with Mona seemed to be a question. Even if he ended the affair, what about his history of lying? Cindy was still in the care of her mother and Linda. That was good. Richard bringing in professional nurses—typical of him. Rob standing up to his father—that was the shocker.

Both letters brought up the adoption issue. *All I want is to curl up under a blanket and think this out.*

She stuffed the letters into her pocket with the growing bustle of packing around her. Angrily shoving things into her pack, she heard Sally's voice. "They found more mail. I said I'd run these over. Belanger, here's one more for you."

This one came from Linda, which she'd mailed the day after the one Mary just read.

Dear Maar,

This letter will be brief because all hell is breaking loose here. Last night, the New Hampshire Child Services Protection people showed up with a court order to investigate our care of Cindy. It turns out someone filed a complaint that the baby is being abused. They even had a police officer with them to ensure they got inside the house.

After their visit, they found nothing wrong but said there would be additional surprise inspections. If they find anything wrong, they may take the baby away. The State Inspector said she wants a plan about who will adopt the baby with the mother deceased. That brought Richard back. Rob is walking around with a sick look on his face. He shared your last letter where you told him not to write anymore.

We are wondering who filed the complaint. Stan thinks it's Mona trying to get even with Rob for dumping her (if he ended things). That makes sense.

One more thing. The state people said they would send you and your commanding officers a series of questions about your marital status. They refused to give copies to Rob, saying they were confidential. Richard's attorney is trying to figure out what they asked.

I wanted to get this out before the mailman comes today. You don't deserve any of this shit.

Love, Lin

At 1630 hours, the nurses assembled. It'd been a rush. Dinner happened early to allow the mess crew to break down their equipment.

With everyone wearing helmets and carrying gas masks on their packs, the seriousness of what lay ahead hit the entire unit. Sally's lack of specifics about their mission put the nurses on edge and fueled a vibrant rumor mill.

A convoy of trucks arrived to load the unit up. The first were loaded with a variety of equipment. Staff loaded into the back of the last four trucks. This sultry day had several looking forward to being on a ship with fresh sea air.

Sally stood up when the nurses had all found seats on the trucks' benches. "It's hard not knowing where we're going, but you figured out there's a ship involved. Onboard tomorrow, you'll get a full briefing. We'll be at sea for a few days. If anyone knows they're subject to seasickness, I'll get you medication. I cannot say more now. The next days will be relaxing at sea before going back to work. See you onboard."

The nurses were quiet. Then one called out, "I took my honeymoon on a cruise. I hope this one turns out better."

Laughter erupted.

Mary laughed, but not for long. *I doubt this trip is anything I'll want to repeat.*

After a short ride, the personnel climbed down while the equipment trucks moved toward the ship for unloading. People and equipment moving filled the dock area. The personnel of the 100th MASH mustered well away from two ships loading a stream of fighting men in battledress. Cranes swung piles of supplies up to the decks. Hundreds of troops stood in a long line by the ships.

While the medical staff milled around taking in the scene, Major Phillips stopped and shouted for everyone's attention. With his unit crowded around him, he announced, "When it's our turn to load, I'll be back. How about we form some sort of marching order to make things look a little military? I know we haven't practiced this but try it. Humor me. There might be a general watching." The CO then moved quickly to a ship's boarding ramp.

After looking at each other for a minute, the individual groups of the 100th organized. Many off-color comments flew about looking military if a general might be paying attention. Suddenly Phillips returned. "We're next for loading. Follow me."

Mary tried to keep in step with her fellow nurses, who Sally was leading. Despite the effort to stay in formation, it was ragtag. The closer she came to the ship, she breathed deeply the fresh salt air. The sun sparkled off the water. In this second week of September, the warm days were giving way to cooler nights. Once at sea, maybe the unrelenting heat would be done.

As they approached the ship, Mary marveled at how high it towered over the dock. Craning her neck to look up, she saw the decks crawling with sailors directing the soldiers coming on board. Other crew members manhandled the mountain of supplies from the dock. From inside the ship, loud metallic banging could be heard. Bedlam looked like the rule, but Mary assumed a plan must be in place to get everyone and all the equipment in the proper places—like their bug-out from Taegu.

Mary worried about how much rust ran along the side of the old vessel. Further down the quay, another ship looked a lot newer. She spent a second wishing the 100th could be on that vessel. Then the first nurses moved to the long ramp leading up to the main deck. *Until a few months ago, I'd never been on a plane. Today, another first—heading out to sea.*

On the steep wooden gangway, she grabbed the railing to pull herself up. The pack on her back felt heavier with each step. It took effort with so many moving on the bouncing ramp. Finally, she reached the loading officer, who was counting bodies at the top. Major Phillips stood close by, instructing each nurse how to find their quarters. Behind her, she glanced down at the dock. With her fear of heights, her head spun with how high she was.

More than a few sailors stopped work as Mary and the other nurses moved toward the ship's bow. One called, "Welcome aboard, ladies." Another offered, "Party on the stern later tonight. All nurses are required to attend." A few of the women gave a thumbs-up.

Once her column turned left, she ducked down through a narrow hatch. The low interior lighting made it hard to maneuver her pack, which caught on the steep, narrow metal stairway. She concentrated on not slipping on the slick metal steps. The strong, musty smell and odor of diesel fuel made her want to get topside again for fresh air. Two MPs wearing helmets stood with sidearms flanking a door marked "Women Only."

Inside quarters and carefully maneuvering through the narrow walkways, Sally assigned individuals to the three-tiered bunks. Mary felt lucky to get a mid-level row since the top one looked challenging to get in and out of. With her pack on the bunk, the thought of rolling onto the metal deck during rough seas suddenly occurred. *Maybe I should get seasickness medicine, just in case.*

Sally called for quiet, gathering her nurses around her. "You saw where the facilities are as we passed. The mess hall is on this level. We have a schedule for eating. Be sure to check the chart on the door for our slot. There are lots of men on board. Conduct yourselves properly."

She smiled. "Everyone is wondering what this is about. There will be a full briefing tomorrow. Now that we're quarantined on board, I can tell you we are part of an invasion force being put behind enemy lines. General MacArthur wants to surprise the North Koreans and cut them off from their supplies and reinforcements. It'll be a few days before we reach the landing zone. I'm sure you have lots of questions. Please save them for tomorrow."

The nurses nodded.

Sally spoke again. "We've got a few jobs on board, like packing our supplies, but you should have plenty of time to write letters and relax over the next days. Try not to do much unpacking since you can see how crowded it is here. That's more than I should've said. There will be a lifeboat drill after we cast off. Our unit gathers on the bow, where I'll take roll. There's a life jacket on each of your bunks. Be aware of where it is at all times. Prepare the small bag tied to your lifebelt with personal items, including medications you need in an emergency. See you at the drill."

A deafening blast from the ship's horn found most of the nurses gathered by the railing, watching the lines cast off. A strong breeze freshened the air as the troop carrier edged away from the dock. Mary's hair fluttered in the wind; her hand shaded her eyes from the bright sun. *This would be enjoyable if not for the mission ahead.*

Gracefully, the bow slowly swung toward the open sea, with another vessel maneuvering behind for loading.

A sailor came up. "See those ships out there? That's where we're going. We'll join them until the entire convoy forms. Then we'll head up the coast. You'll see a lot of tin cans around us for protection, and you may have noticed plenty of air cover."

The nurses could see the outline of many ships in the distance and heard the far-off scream of streaking jets. Ann asked, "What's a tin can?"

"Destroyers, ma'am. They're positioned with the flyboys to protect the convoy from submarine attack."

"Do the North Koreans have submarines?"

"They have a few. Not as good as ours, but you can see we're taking no chances. The US Navy wants to take care of you nurses."

"That seems like a damn good priority," Ann said.

A loudspeaker crackled to life, followed by a piercing whistle. "Now hear this. Now hear this. This is the captain speaking. The alarm will ring next for lifeboat stations. This is a drill. When you hear the alarm, put on your life preserver and report to your station. Repeat; this is only a drill."

A shrill alarm rang, and troops started rushing about the ship. "Damn, I left my vest on my bunk," said Mary. She and Ann hurried to the hatch to return to quarters. They had to push and bump against the traffic to get to their life preservers. They scrambled back to the deck through the empty corridors.

At the assembly point, Sally and the other nurses stood waiting. In a non-too-friendly tone, Sally announced, "There you are. Glad you could join us. Okay, we're all here. Do you all have your life preservers? Belanger, don't carry the vest. Could you put it on and learn how to secure it? Someone give her a hand."

A naval officer appeared. "Are all your people accounted for, ma'am?"

"All present."

He turned to the group. "That's too slow. If this were an actual emergency, you would need to move faster. That lifeboat to your right would be where you load. The two sailors standing there will crew the boat. Let's hope we don't have to do that. I expect we'll run at least one drill daily, if not more. Please stay at this station until the captain releases you." With that, he moved along to the next group.

Submarines, lifeboats. Know where your vest is at all times. Isn't this supposed to be the relaxing part?

Gathered with the rest of the 100th on the stern the following day, the nurses enjoyed the bracing ocean breezes. Everyone enjoyed the welcome change of having to wear jackets after the oppressive weather back on land. Ships filled the horizon. The smoking stacks of the naval destroyers moved around the convoy. Overhead was a continual roar of Air Force jets.

Mary was tired. The previous night had been tough, and she'd developed a throbbing headache. Besides the pungent odor of diesel fuel and too many people in close quarters, the temperature below deck grew uncomfortably warm. Incessant noise from the constant thumping of engines and metallic groans made it sound like the ship was coming apart. She woke repeatedly.

A couple more nights of this, and how am I supposed to be at my best when we go into action? After this briefing, I'll look for aspirin. I should learn to carry some at all times.

Before crawling into her bunk last night, Mary had chased down Sally to give her a heads-up about the State of New Hampshire sending questions.

Sally looked annoyed. "I regret what you're going through, but your news couldn't come at a worse time. We've got the biggest challenge in front of us and need you one hundred percent present and focused. I wish I'd known about this before we got on board. Then, we could have left you behind. I need a commitment that personal problems will not get in the way of your professional responsibilities."

The nurses knew Sally could be all military, but this harsh response to a simple heads-up made Mary bristle. "Ma'am, I wanted to inform you in case letters arrive where you need background. Nothing will be less than my absolute best, and I'm offended you question my commitment. You've seen the work I do. Previously you've said I'm one of the best."

The two nurses stood toe to toe. After a moment of staring, Sally shrugged. "All right. I need to know you're not distracted. If I get those questions, I'll look for your input before responding. Do you want me to mention this matter to Major Phillips if he receives inquiries?"

Her exasperation growing, Mary bit her tongue. "Yes, ma'am, that would be fine. I'm sorry I bothered you."

Sally took a deep breath. "No bother, Belanger. My apologies. You did the right thing in giving me the heads-up. I guess I'm not managing the stress well. It scares me someone might be injured or killed, and there's much more I need to do."

Sympathy now tempered Mary's anger. She said, "We're all scared about what's ahead, ma'am. Being our CO, I'm sure it's worse for you. If there's anything we can do to help, we're here for you."

Sally straightened up. "I'll be fine. Go get yourself some rest." She turned and hustled away.

Maybe it's not me you should be worried about, Sally. It looks like you're the one we should be concerned about.

In the bright morning light and brisk wind, Major Phillips and a Marine officer arrived, taking positions in front of the

100ᵗʰ, who stood shoulder to shoulder in a small area. All around, the flotilla filled the horizon. Another Marine worked his way to the front carrying a large easel with a map of Korea.

Phillips spoke first. "At ease. We'll keep this brief since we're all packed in here. First, I want to introduce Colonel Knox of the Marines, one of the key leaders of this mission. He'll fill you in regarding what we're about to do to the North Koreans. Colonel Knox."

"Thank you, Major, and let me welcome everyone on board. I want to show everyone what will happen now that you're part of Operation Chromite. Please don't ask me why that title, but it's a name we'll remember for the rest of our lives." The Marine with the large easel stepped closer, placing the map beside the colonel.

"Although Marines will lead the initial phase, we're thankful your MASH unit is with us on this historic mission. There's often competition between the Army and Marines, but we all fight for Uncle Sam. Many Army units will take part, but Marines will be first ashore, given our experience with amphibious landings in the Pacific during the last war. It gives all Marines confidence to know your expert medical care will be with us. I've read about the heroic service you provided in Taegu. Major Phillips tells me you're the best, and your service record confirms that."

Using his pointer, "What is Operation Chromite? Since the North Koreans invaded, we have been pinned down in the Pusan area. Once we got sufficient forces and equipment in theater, we stabilized lines and pushed the communist forces back. With the resources sent under the United Nations' flag, we're getting stronger daily. But since the North Koreans fell back into the mountains north of Taegu, they've been difficult to dislodge."

He paused and looked at the assembled group. "General MacArthur decided we'll do an end-run around them and land at Inchon." He pointed to the map. "The Third Marine

Battalion is on this and other ships and raring to fight. We have tanks and the necessary equipment to make this a successful operation. The ships of our Allied nations will deliver the first blow with one of the biggest bombardments in history. We already have a surveillance unit established on an island outside Inchon Harbor."

He again pointed to the map. "That scout unit has informed us that the North Korean defenders do not show that anything is out of the ordinary. On the other side of the Korean Peninsula, there's a large diversionary movement to distract the enemy. Our intelligence tells us that Inchon Harbor is lightly guarded. The coming naval bombardment, supported by massive air power, will soften the enemy's defenses. Marines will hit the beach at dawn on September 15, weather permitting. The meteorologists predict we'll have fine weather to deliver the blow that turns this war around."

Colonel Knox smiled, then turned serious. "One issue we face at Inchon is the tides. Significant high and low tides in that bay vary by as much as thirty-two feet. We'll be limited to the highest tides to land people and equipment. That means we can't be continuously putting troops and supplies ashore. The logistics are challenging, but it should work because we expect light resistance."

Mary grew more unnerved the more she heard. *I'll be part of an actual invasion. What did he say? It should work?* Her head throbbed.

The Colonel began to speak again. "The first assault wave will go ashore at dawn in three days. When the tides are again high that afternoon, we'll send in another wave of people and equipment. Your unit will be part of that second landing."

The Marine's eyes swept over his silent audience. "I'll not sugarcoat it, ladies and gentlemen. Your hospital might be the closest to actual combat we've ever placed a MASH unit. There will be casualties from the invasion, and you know better than anyone the importance of prompt medical attention in saving lives. You may be under enemy fire, but we Marines will do our damnedest to prevent that from happening. One of our first assignments will be establishing a strong protective ring around where you'll be located."

The Marine flipped the page over to display an enlarged map of Inchon Harbor. "These arrows show the four landing zones. Your landing area is called Green Beach, and the medical facility will be in a building close to the water where you see the M. We'll deploy your unit only if we make the expected progress with the first assault and have security in place. If we're not satisfied with conditions on the beach by that afternoon, you'll go in the third wave the following morning."

"Ladies and gentlemen, this is a bold operation. Once we secure Inchon and move inland, that will trap a good portion of the North Korean Army. A short drive north will free Seoul, the capital of South Korea. General MacArthur, who proved brilliant in commanding the Pacific War against Japan, conceived this end run. This military maneuver will go down in history as one of the greatest of all wars. Thank you for your service; again, we're fortunate to have you. Major Phillips, back to you."

"Colonel Knox is right. You're the best. That's why the brass selected us for this mission. That's all I want to say. I'm turning you over to your senior officers for more on landing assignments and duties ashore. You know how hard the work will be once we're on the beach. Get rest over the next days. Dismissed."

Shipboard life passed quietly. After reviewing, counting, and repacking medical supplies for the third time, even Sally concluded that the nurses were as prepared as possible. The only training for the nurses centered on treating encephalitis. Like Ben mentioned, the contagion was multiplying into an epidemic concern. Limited treatment options for the infected existed, with the essential being to move the patient's limbs and joints aggressively to keep them from locking up.

The discussion of how contagious the disease was worried the nurses since manual therapy would be their responsibility.

"How are we going to be able to handle the time this will take?" asked Julie.

"The 100th has yet to see a single infection. Pray it stays that way," said Sally.

The work details were soon completed, but unfortunately, the ship had limited entertainment options since the convoy operated in blackout. Even stepping on deck to smoke at night was prohibited. "There are only so many games of cards we can play before we're back to worrying about what's coming," Ann complained to Mary.

More details on the invasion plans came from Major Phillips. The 100th would put personnel ashore in two groups, ensuring that at least a portion of the unit would land if one of the boats experienced a problem or took enemy fire.

Mary could feel the tension around these risks growing in the group. Sally had reminded them to write letters now as they might not have an opportunity once they landed. So Mary settled down to put her thoughts on paper.

Dear Mom,

By the time you read this, the invasion force I'm a part of will have completed our mission. Newspapers will report whether we were successful. I'm on a troop transport to a place called Inchon. We'll go ashore to treat the wounded in a couple of days. I don't want to scare you, but I fear what lies ahead. Our MASH unit will be closer to the front lines than ever before.

The odds are I'll be okay, but if I'm wounded, know I love you. You and dad were the best parents ever, and I wouldn't be doing this important job without the values you gave me.

After this mission, I'll wrestle with what to do about staying married and adopting Cindy. I'm torn because of how Rob hurt me, but he seems to have altered his ways from what you and Linda have written. Has he changed enough for me to stay with him? What do you think?

Time to get this letter in the mail sack.

Your loving daughter and, with all love possible, Mary

Dear Lin,

I'm thankful to have a friend like you who will tell me the truth about what's happening. Sometimes it's difficult to read, but I need to know the latest.

I won't repeat what is happening here. My mother will share that from her letter. I want to ask that if anything happens to me, could you please help my mom deal with the fallout? Thanks, although I'm sure you'd do that anyway.

It makes sense that Mona might file a complaint about the state starting an investigation to get revenge. If she has taken that step, I hope Rob truly broke up with her.

I spoke with my commanding officer about the questionnaire she might receive from New Hampshire. She promised if a letter showed up, she wouldn't respond without talking to me first. I can't ask for anything more.

Time to wrap this up. You and Stan might consider taking the baby if anything should happen to me. I hope I'm not being presumptuous, but I know you two would make great parents. Thanks for being the best friend ever.

Love, Maar

P.S. Maybe I shouldn't share this, and you must promise not to tell anyone, but you brought it up. I kissed a handsome doctor, and he kissed back—a whole lot of kissing, but nothing more. He's not in my outfit, meaning I have space to figure out my feelings. What you lightheartedly asked is another complication for me.

The convoy sailed through calm seas and clear skies. On the main deck, Mary searched the ship for Father Phil, finally discovering him in the corner of a dining area, hearing confessions. Once the last soldier left, she asked for a few moments, and they sat down at a table with coffee.

"Father Phil, I'm concerned about Grace. Julie is still pretty cold to her and sometimes insulting. I don't know what more to do. I've asked Grace how she puts up with it. All she says is this is the way the world works sometimes. For me, it's just not right. Maybe you could talk to Grace about how she's dealing with this."

The priest nodded. "I'll try, but Grace may have a bias against a Catholic priest, given some of the religious beliefs in the south. Prejudice can be about anything different, whether skin color or religion. I know you're doing as much as possible, and I agree with Sally that change takes time. Thanks for caring."

He looked at her with some concern. "How are you doing? You have an important mission ahead and must be nervous."

"I'm well beyond nervous. I'm terrified of what we might experience. When we go ashore, I hope I'm able to function. All our boys will be counting on me, but all I want is to be back home."

Phil patted her hand. "If I lined up every person on this tub who wished they were elsewhere, this would be a ghost ship.

It's natural what you're feeling. I'm sure you'll rise to the occasion. Try to get some sleep tonight, and I'll say a special prayer for you. After the first wave has gone ashore, I'll say mass on the fantail tomorrow morning. Confession will be just before the service. No better way to go ashore than in God's hands."

"Better say two prayers for me, Father."

"I will. How are things on the home front? I've heard you got more bad news."

"My neighbor keeps writing that things cannot get crazier, then they do. So let me give you the latest."

After bringing the chaplain up to speed, Mary let her frustration out. "How can divorce not be an option in the Catholic Church? What have I done wrong? I have a cheating husband who continues to lie, meaning I'm stuck with him for life? Come on, Phil, where's the compassion in that?"

The priest pursed his lips. "You're in a terrible situation with church law regarding divorce." He thought for a long moment. "Since you have no children with your husband, there's a small possibility you could dissolve your marriage."

Mary caught her breath. "What do you mean?"

"Have you heard of an annulment of marriage for specific situations? Occasionally it's granted. With no children of your own, you might qualify. But, it's rarely allowed, and you shouldn't count on it. I'm even reluctant to mention it."

"I understand it might be a long shot, but I'm all ears. Tell me more."

Later that afternoon, Mary wandered the deck alone, watching the ships in convoy. In the distant skies, fighters circled the vessels. Clusters of Marines sat on the deck cleaning weapons, issuing more than an occasional whistle when she strolled by.

Word passed that the ship was close to Inchon. She

replayed her conversation with Father Phil. Still unsure what she wanted, the annulment option could create a way out.

Today's perfect weather had struck Mary as a stark contrast to what tomorrow would bring. Her mind drifted to images of Dave and Ben. Both played a growing part in her life. *Why should I feel guilty about being attracted to other men? What's wrong with that? Haven't I been a loyal wife? What's that gotten me? Why shouldn't a woman be able to stand up for herself when she's wronged? It's 1950, damn it, not the Middle Ages.*

Her thoughts returned to those two men and how similar they were. *Each man a dedicated doctor. Attractive and nothing but kind. Ben's easy to talk to and interested in the baby. He's great, but something about Dave stirs me. It might be the stress we face together. Maybe it's something more.*

At the foredeck, Mary spied Grace sitting with a group of Black soldiers, laughing. Ronnie and Fred were part of the group, along with several Marines. Grace looked to be running the gathering.

Mary walked over to say hi. Ronnie lit up, jumping up to give her a big hug. Fred announced to the gathering, "Fellas, meet Mary. She's alright."

After a round of introductions, Grace said, "This lady cares for me. She pushed the Catholic chaplain on this Baptist girl. I told him I'm fine as long as the Pope stays away."

Mary blushed amidst the burst of laughter.

Grace ordered them to hush up. "She asked the priest to check on me because she cares. I didn't know they grew such nice people up north. Sit yourself down, girl, if you can stand these mutton chops."

Once settled into the group, Mary said, "Not everyone from New Hampshire is nice—more than a few creeps there."

Fred shook his head. "There are bad eggs everywhere."

Grace said, "One of those rotten eggs is Mary's husband. Sister, since you shared those letters from home, I hope you don't mind a bit of advice." Without waiting for a response from Mary, she went on. "Back in New Hampshire, this wonderful lady cared for her sister-in-law's abandoned baby. At the same time, her hubby's out screwing around. Brother and sister in that family think only of themselves while Mary is doing the right thing."

Embarrassment washed over Mary as her problems were put out there for the group. Grace reached over to hold her hand. "I don't share this to hurt you, but you're too good of a person to put up with that shit. It's time you take care of number one."

"Not right," Ronnie muttered. "Who's caring for the baby since the Army got you?"

"My mother and a neighbor."

Ronnie nodded. "We see where Mary gets her niceness. You've got a giving mama."

Fred spoke up. "Once you get away from this place, are you going back to that asshole?"

She was shocked to hear her husband labeled that way. "I'm not sure."

Grace now leaned closer, putting her arm around Mary. "Fellas, we need to tell Mary what to do with that cheat when she gets home. How she should throw his ass out the door and find herself a good man who'll treat her right."

Around the corner came Julie, who stopped and stared. After looking hard at Mary and Grace, she spun on her heels and disappeared.

"That the one you mentioned, Grace?" Ronnie asked.

"That's the one."

"She looks like trouble."

In the distance, big guns suddenly erupted. Everyone jumped up. The troopship was approaching Inchon, and the naval bombardment was underway. As they steamed closer, they could see a number of warships firing volley after volley. Smoke from the firing slowly settled over the fleet. On land, the explosions were constant, obliterating the view of the shore. This deafening shelling would continue until the first landing boats reached the beach.

Fear consumed Mary. *How could anyone survive this bombardment and still be able to fight? They told us many of the enemy would. Tomorrow I'll be where shells are now landing. Almost everyone on this ship will be there. How many of us will die?*

For the nurses, it was another sleepless night. Anxiety filled their quarters. The barrage of gunfire only grew louder and more intense while the troopship maneuvered closer for the assault. With so many thoughts filling her head, it didn't surprise Mary that she couldn't sleep. Then, around 0300, she heard the sounds of Marines preparing. She decided to check out the activity and headed to one of the dining areas.

Marines packed the tables, where they were being served a hearty breakfast. Instead of the usual boisterous banter, this morning's conversations were subdued. To her left, she heard a voice say, "Ma'am, there's an empty seat here."

Mary looked down at a blond-haired leatherneck. He managed a small smile, but clearly, he looked terrified. She sat down. All the Marines at the table stopped eating and looked her way. After an awkward silence, Mary said, "That looks like the best food I've seen since I got on this tub. Steak and eggs, wow."

A young man down the table said, "This is what they serve condemned men, ma'am."

Everyone stayed silent. Not knowing what to say, Mary gave a small smile. The young Marine next to her said, "I'm not hungry, ma'am. I can't eat anything right now. You can have mine. I haven't touched it. I could go get clean utensils for you."

Flooded with emotion for the men struggling with what they were about to face, Mary fought to control her emotions. *What should I say? Some of these guys may soon be dead. Say something.* "I'm not hungry either, but thanks for the offer. Where are all of you from?"

"Arkansas, ma'am."

"Nashville, Tennessee."

"Missouri."

"Franconia Notch. That's in New Hampshire."

"The Notch," Mary smiled. "I know where that is, and I've been there. Manchester's my home, although it's not as pretty as The Notch."

Everyone started talking.

Keep it light. What's going on here is as crucial as surgery right now.

The wind whipped off the white-capped waves in the predawn darkness. Mary pulled her jacket tighter. She repositioned her earplugs to protect against the unrelenting artillery barrage. The thunderous sounds made it impossible to speak unless someone was right next to you. In the distance, the first rays of sunlight revealed a red-streaked sky—a beautiful sunrise in spite of the violent bombardment.

The Marines started to go over the side and into the stream of landing craft surrounding the ship. Mary studied how fast these men scrambled down, filling each boat in minutes. Another assault boat immediately took its place. These precise maneuvers were impressive.

She thought back to the training wall. None of the nurses moved nearly that quickly. A new fear hit her. *The wall was one thing. It looks entirely different with the water pushing the landing craft around. I think this is higher than the wall. Am I going to be able do this?*

Once all the landing craft were loaded, the flotilla of assault boats turned in unison. The heavy guns from Navy ships kept firing but shifted to targets away from the beach. The landing craft, too many to count, raced toward their targets.

Mary thought she'd never seen a more magnificent and awful sight. She fingered the rosary in her pocket. With the first bead, she prayed for the Marines she'd met this morning, "Our Father, who art in heaven . . ."

Early afternoon. Standing up from communion, Mary slipped on her helmet, tightening the strap. An overflow crowd had lined up for Father Phil. Before mass, Phil had stopped hearing individual confessions because of the many lined up. He gathered those waiting in a circle around him. "Please think of the sins you were planning to confess." After a moment of silence, the chaplain said, "I absolve all of you in the name of the Father, the Son, and the Holy Ghost. Each of you say one Hail Mary for penance. Let's get mass going."

Reports from the beach indicated although the North Koreans were putting up stiff resistance, the initial objectives were secured. Wounded, currently attended by medics, waited for needed treatment. The 100th would go ashore on schedule. Mary's heavy pack was suddenly tugged. This was the third time Sally had done this with each nurse. "Keep your pack and shoelaces loose in case you end up in the water. You don't want to drown before we get to the beach," she called.

I bet someone just told her these instructions, or we would have heard it repeatedly before this. Everyone is unlacing their boots. I'd better get down and do that. How might loose boots affect being on the ropes? Shit. Maybe we should have practiced this.

The ship's loudspeakers crackled, calling the first groups to board their landing craft. The 100th stood to the back while fighting units went over the side. Far too fast for Mary, the call came. "On deck, 100th MASH."

Mary's unit edged forward. Heart pounding, she worried it might explode. On shaking legs, she edged closer to the railing. Staring down at the deck, she feared making eye contact with anyone, convinced they would see how petrified she felt. At the railing, she raised her eyes to look over the side. A small landing craft approached, bouncing on the waves.

How am I going to do this? I can barely stand. Please God, let me just get down the netting.

The landing officer barked, "MASH Group One, go, go, go!" Several of the unit's orderlies were first over the railing and quickly out of sight. Doctors followed. Mary and the nurses were next. Straight down, the half-filled craft rose and fell in the waves, banging against the ship's side.

How in the hell am I going to do this?

"Nurses, over the side." Mary and several others swung their legs over the railing to settle on the netting. She concentrated on the training exercise. *Find a secure foothold. Then release the opposite hand to reach down. Don't move until your footing is secure.*

"Ladies, you need to move faster," came the command from above. "Boats are stacking up. You sailors, when a nurse gets close, grab her and get them in the boat. I don't care if it's a rough dismount."

Mary tried to move more quickly but didn't want to fall. Almost down, she looked up and saw the last two nurses starting on the netting. Strong hands gripped her waist. "Let go, ma'am. I've got you." Relief washed over her.

"Everybody stay seated. No standing," came the cry from the coxswain in the stern of the rolling boat. One nurse remained on the cargo netting—that was Julie. She'd stopped a little over halfway down, locked in fear.

The frozen nurse became the target of screaming from above and below. Mary doubted much could be registering with Julie. The landing officer dropped his clipboard and bull-horn, swung a leg over the side, and started to climb down. Grace sprang from her seat, scrambling up the netting. She reached Julie first, leaned over, said something, then placed her hand on Julie's. The two nurses edged their way down.

The landing officer scrambled back up, ordering, "When you can reach those two, grab 'em and move that boat out pronto."

In a few seconds, crew members reached for both nurses. Simultaneously, the landing craft spun away at high speed, causing both sailors to lose their balance and fall into the boat. Julie and her sailor fell on top of several doctors and orderlies, but the crew member who held Grace lost his grip. The nurse fell away, hitting the bottom of the speeding boat hard. She did not move.

Doctor Anderson reached Grace first and turned her over. The small boat banged through the waves, making everyone reach for something to hold onto. Blood was running down Grace's face, coming from a forehead gash.

"Grab me a first aid kit," the surgeon called. Sally joined him and opened her pack to get bandages and antiseptic. Dave knelt behind those two, yelling for everyone to stay in their place and prepare to hit the beach.

Grace's eyes popped open, watching Anderson treat her wound. "Are you okay, Grace? Can you speak?"

With a deep breath, she said, "I'm okay. Got the wind knocked out of me. How bad is the bleeding?"

"It's a surface wound. You know how a forehead can leak a lot. So it should be easy to close." The surgeon looked up. "Captain, do you want to take over?"

Dave said, "No, you're fine. When you get that finished, do a concussion protocol."

Grace started to sit up. "I'm fine, sir."

"Lie down, Thomas," Sally barked. "We need to get you bandaged. If you pass the protocol, then you'll be back on full duty."

At the other end of the boat, Mary held a sobbing Julie. "It's okay. You made it. We'll soon be on land. Then we need to work. You've got to pull yourself together."

Julie lifted her face and looked at Grace, then slipped out of Mary's arms to move toward the injured nurse. She reached past Sally and gripped Grace's hand. "Thank you. You saved me."

"Fellows, get back to your seat," Sally snapped.

Julie returned by Mary, wiping her tears. Mary turned to look over the side to see the beach straight ahead. She could now hear the crackle of small weapons over the grinding sound of the engine and smell of burning gasoline. The waves slammed against the boat, pitching it up and down. Combat and the unknown lay right in front of her.

CHAPTER 14

With the boat bouncing, sheets of spray came over the top, soaking everyone who fought to stay seated on the hard wooden benches. Mary's team members were quiet, consumed with personal thoughts. To get a perspective on what was ahead, she stood, grasping the side of the boat, wanting to take in everything around her.

Their amphibious boat closed in toward the beach. In front she could see other landing craft beaching and delivering troops. Several were unloading tanks. Past the high tide line, a mountain of supplies grew. Strewn about lay burned-out equipment from the original assault. The crackle of gunfire grew louder—enemy soldiers could not be far away. Further up the shoreline, Mary could see other landing areas where more troops and equipment were going ashore. The magnitude of the operation astounded her.

"Belanger, get your ass down," came the cry from her CO. "Are you trying to get shot?"

Sheepishly, Mary sat. She looked over at Grace, who was sitting up with her forehead heavily bandaged. She wanted to go and check on the injured nurse but stayed put, knowing that moving would draw another rebuke. Close by with their heads together were Julie and Sally. Sally was doing all the talking. Julie's head was down and nodding.

"Three minutes to the beach. Prepare to disembark," came the cry from the coxswain over the loudspeaker. Everyone assembled their gear. The boat slowed, riding high on a wave. Explosions from combat filled the air. Mary forced herself to breathe deeply, trying to settle her nerves.

When the boat gave a shudder and came to a sudden stop, everyone slid forward. The front landing craft ramp started to lower. "Welcome to Inchon," a crew member yelled. "Be careful out there."

The personnel at the bow moved down the ramp, stepping into thigh-high surf. Mary followed, dropping into the icy water, gasping at the cold. One foot stepped into a hole, pitching her forward and almost under. Someone steadied her. Regaining her balance, she waded past abandoned packs left by Marines. Each step through the surf and soft sand took effort.

What happened to the guys who carried that gear? They might be dead or wounded. Damn, this water is cold.

Once on the shore, her boots were heavy and water-logged, making it hard to walk through the sand. Kneeling down, she hurridly tied her laces. She couldn't see any fighting in the ruined terrain ahead, but not far away, combat reverberated. *Should I get my ass down?* Suddenly, a jeep with Major Phillips at the wheel rolled up to her left.

"Dave, Mary, Roger, Chet, and Judy, get in. I'll take you to our site. Wounded are waiting. Sally, you lead the rest over to where we're setting up shop."

Mary jumped into the back of the jeep with the others. Phillips floored the engine, and the jeep bucked through the sand. Mary got thrown to the side and was about to fall out, when a hand pulled her back. She turned and Chet smiled. "No getting out of this assignment, Belanger."

Mary hung on with a death grip on the back of the seat in front of her. The rough ride didn't let up. Within minutes, the jeep climbed out of the sand to race along a dirt road. The smell of cordite, burning vehicles, and the sounds of gunfire filled the air.

On the right, Mary caught sight of a row of enemy bodies. Up ahead, two slow-moving tanks blocked the road, causing Phillips to swerve back onto the sand to get past. Ahead lay an old maintenance facility. Outside on the ground lay stretchers with the wounded tended by medics. A little further away lay several US body bags.

How did this building not get leveled in the bombardment? The Navy must have purposely spared this area.

Phillips braked hard, causing Mary to fall into the front seat against Dave. The 100th CO barked orders. "Get upstairs where we have your equipment located. Gas for anesthesia should be there. Once you're ready, let the medics know to bring them in. I'm going back to see if the others need help."

The team sprang from the jeep, sprinting toward the building. At that moment, a heavy whoosh filled the air. A tremendous explosion shook the ground to the right, sending a column of dirt into the air. A blast of flying sand hit Mary. The concussion knocked Dave, Mary, and Judy off their feet. They struggled to get up, as Roger and Chet stepped over to help. Phillips returned to make sure no one had been hit.

Mary fought to regain her equilibrium, her head and ears ringing. *That's too close. Will we be able to operate if the enemy is targeting us?*

Chet, who was supporting her, spoke. But with the ringing in her ears, nothing came through. Still dazed, she let Chet help her into the building. Fortunately, there were no follow-up mortar shells. The team stumbled up dirty, narrow stairs to the second floor, where two orderlies were setting up portable operating tables.

How did they get ashore before us? I still can't hear anything, but I can stand and work.

Mary bent at the waist, shaking her head. When Chet tried

to ask about her condition, Mary heard nothing, but faked it with a thumbs-up. The anesthesiologist moved off.

After shaking her head hard again, a faint voice from an orderly said, "There's no water and soap yet. Prep with the alcohol we put out. Gowns and gloves are in a box next to the alcohol. We should be ready to go here in a few minutes. No lights yet. Daylight and flashlights will have to do. A generator for lights will be in by dusk."

My hearing is coming back, thank goodness. The ringing is terrible, but I should be able to make out what Dave is saying.

Mary joined the other doctors and nurse scrubbing hands and arms as thoroughly as possible with the alcohol. Once done prepping, she said, "I'm heading in."

Chet followed her and said, "Roger, since we're in separate rooms, I'll be with you as soon as I get Dave's first patient knocked out."

Mary found an equipment trunk next to the operating table and took out several trays of instruments. Unlike standard procedures, she covered each tray with a clean cloth. No sooner was she done when another mortar shell exploded nearby. The building shook, raining down dust and plaster. Mary fell to one knee. Then, with a deep breath, she stood and looked at the dust and dirt on the coverings. *Thank goodness all of the instruments stayed clean. I don't know what made me cover them. Where are the Marines that are supposed to be protecting this place?*

As Mary wiped the dust from the operating table, Dave stepped in. "That's close. I hope the North Koreans keep up their lousy aim and our guys knock out those mortars. Our first patient is on his way. Chet, you ready to go?"

"Yep. I don't know how Phillips got these two orderlies here so quickly, but they did a great job organizing things."

With clean linens down, the orderlies placed the first wounded Marine on the table. Mary saw that one leg was missing below the knee. The other hung mangled. The man's hollow eyes looked up, catching Mary's. Behind her surgical mask, she smiled. "Hey there, leatherneck, you're first for us today. You've got the best surgeon the US offers. Time for you to nap so we can fix you up."

Chet placed the mask over the young man's nose and mouth.

The anesthesiologist gave Dave a thumbs-up, then headed out the door to assist the other surgical team. Another mortar shell exploded nearby.

Please let that be the last one.

Dave looked over. "Let's work on the left leg. Get me bandage scissors. Best surgeon America offers. I'll have to put that on my resume."

Mary reached under the cover on the tray and found the correct instrument. She would keep everything covered even if it meant nicking herself to reach for tools.

"If you're going to own the best surgeon title, I might as well claim the best surgical nurse. That seem fair?"

Dave started cutting. "Yeah, we're a good team. If we could only find a better place to work."

The hours ahead would be grueling. With the stress of the amphibious landing past, she could already feel her adrenaline level drop. With her head still ringing, she fought this first wave of fatigue. One thought stayed with her. *He thinks we're a good team.*

Later that night, Sally put on a mask and stepped close to the table where Dave and Mary labored.

"How's it going out there?" Dave asked. "Many waiting?"

"It's not too bad. Better than we expected. Reports are that a few North Korean units are still putting up resistance, but they're being pushed back. It's been hours since any shells fell in this area. So they must have gotten that mortar targeting us."

"That first shell that hit when we got here was too close for comfort. Is your hearing better, Mary?"

"There's a slight ringing in my ears, but it's almost back to normal."

"You still haven't said how many are waiting, Sally."

"There's maybe twenty out there—many fewer than expected. It looks like MacArthur outwitted the enemy. The question is if and when North Korean reinforcements will arrive."

Not lifting his eyes from his work, Dave said, "Keep us posted if anything changes."

Sally turned to go, then came back. "One quick story. You'll both enjoy this. When we were setting up shop, they moved the wounded into a trench in case one of those mortar shells hit that area. Grace got to one wounded Marine who needed a transfusion and sent Julie to grab plasma. Once she got back, Grace had the IV ready to go. With it in, Grace spied a Marine standing guard. She called him over to hold the bottle up. The Marine didn't react—just stared at Grace. Julie climbed out of the trench and got right in the face of that Marine. 'You heard the Lieutenant. That's an order. Get your ass down there and keep your buddy alive.' Fastest moving Marine I ever saw."

Dave and Mary nodded with smiling eyes. While the surgeon made his next cut, "Grace okay after her tumble?"

At the door, Sally said, "Grace appears to be fine, and I think maybe things will be better with Julie."

Close to midnight, the flow of casualties slowed to a trickle, allowing the surgical teams to take breaks. Dave offered to go last, much to Mary's annoyance at not being consulted. She felt dead on her feet.

Besides wounded Americans, injured prisoners also needed treatment. Mary had mixed feelings about those patients. She empathized with the civilians caught in fighting, especially women and children. But, on the other hand, with each North Korean soldier brought in, she struggled to treat them the same as any American. After all, these were human beings doing their duty for their country. Intellectually, she knew that was right, but each prisoner triggered thoughts that none of this suffering would happen without North Korea's aggression.

Word spread quickly about a troubling incident in recovery. After waking from surgery, a North Korean soldier ripped the tubes out of his body. He then attacked other wounded prisoners. After a struggle, guards and nurses subdued and sedated him. Then they tied down the enemy soldier and moved him away from the others.

A translator explained that North Korean leaders taught their soldiers that if US doctors treated them, the Americans would use them for medical experiments. To avoid a painful death, the prisoners should resist medical care.

When she heard this, Mary wondered if she would ever stop being disgusted by the awful things in war. How terrible of North Korean officers to mislead their troops rather than let them receive treatment.

She hoped American prisoners needing medical care were receiving treatment. He shook his head when she asked the translator if that was the case. "Many North Korean units have no medical support. They shoot most Americans captured." Mary was deeply grieved by this and continued her struggle to give the best possible treatment to any prisoner, although not enthusiastically.

When another surgery finished, Mary reached for the next tray of instruments when her knees buckled. The stress of the invasion, so many surgeries, and lack of sleep hit her hard.

Every one of us must feel the way I do. Somehow, I've got to get through this.

Sally appeared, pulling on a surgical gown. "Belanger, I've been watching.You need a break. Things are slowing down. I'm sending you to get chow and rest. Besides, I want you to stop spoiling Dave by making him look good. Time for him to remember the good old days when I worked with him."

"I'm fine, ma'am. I don't need a break. We're all exhausted."

"You're not fine. None of us are. I'm giving you a direct order to go eat and catch a few winks. Now!"

Mary stepped away from the table while the senior nurse took her place. "Thank you, ma'am."

Dave said, "Great job, partner. We'll be right behind you since we're almost done here."

Outside of the close confines of surgery, Mary gulped in the cool, fresh air. The ferocity of combat had dramatically dropped. The rumble of fighting continued but was now distant. Her watch read 0300. No boats were being unloaded on the low-tide beach, although other activity continued under rigged-up lights. Soldiers moved supplies inland. Out in the harbor, the myriad of ships blazed with light while landing boats waited for the next high tide. *This would be a pretty picture if it weren't for the sporadic firing in the distance.* Another image from an amazing day she would never forget.

Mary staggered a few steps in exhaustion and plopped herself down. An abandoned life vest rested on the ground, which she put next to a jeep and leaned back. The relief to her aching feet from the hours of standing in wet boots felt immense. Her shoes and socks off, the evening air provided relief. A satisfying feeling grew within her. *I did it. I met standards in Taegu and now here. Even got down that damn netting. People have confidence in how I work. I'm a darn good nurse and part of a fantastic team.*

She surveyed the beach with its burned-out vehicles and two North Korean corpses still needing removal. *I'm doing what's needed, but why do things like this happen? The suffering on both sides is awful.*

To her left, she spotted a small flowering bush that had somehow survived the bombardment of the past days. In the middle of this mess, these might be the prettiest flowers she'd ever seen—pinkish petals and a dark magenta center. *Things like this should be what life is about—not kill or be killed or prisoners trying to hurt other prisoners. How many Korean families and children played on this beach before the war? When this is over, what then? Will Korea recover from this killing?* A sense of futility filled her.

Out of the darkness, Julie appeared. "You okay? Gosh, you look exhausted. I must look the same."

Mary took her fellow nurse's hand, stood, and smiled tiredly. "Thanks for helping me up since I'm not sure I could have done it alone. I'm going to skip food. Is there a place for us to sleep?"

"There's a tent next to the big one with supplies. Let's hit the rack."

The two walked arm in arm. Julie leaned close. "I learned something today," looking Mary in the eye. "Grace is a helluva nurse—one of the best. She worked rings around the rest of us."

Mary hoped this might end her friend's racism, but the following words dashed that hope.

"I've seen that back home. Find what a Negro is good at, and they can sometimes do as well as us. Grace is that kind. We're lucky to have her in the unit."

Mary's head spun. *Is this progress? Maybe of sorts, I guess. She's still down on Grace. I can't deal with this now.* The two silently made their way to quarters.

MANCHESTER TIMES
NEWS BULLETIN
MACARTHUR LAUNCHES SUPRISE
INVASION
BEHIND ENEMY LINES

In a bold move to turn the course of the war in Korea, Supreme Commander General Douglas MacArthur ordered an amphibious invasion behind North Korean lines at Inchon. Located on the east coast of Korea, Inchon is twenty miles south of Seoul, the Republic of South Korea's capital.

The largest flotilla since D-Day in World War II has been putting troops and equipment ashore since dawn yesterday. Initial resistance was overcome when elements of the US Marines established a beachhead. Because of secrecy, there is no specific information on the number of ships or troops involved.

General MacArthur's representative expressed optimism at the initial progress but stated that Allied Forces were preparing for a North Korean counterattack.

CHAPTER 15

The following two days flew by as the North Koreans chose not to mount a serious counter-attack. With 70,000 troops ashore, the Allies now outnumbered the enemy. Although casualties stayed relatively low, a steady flow of injured needing surgery and care kept the 100th busy. Whenever a patient died, Mary prayed for their soul, grieving that they couldn't have done more.

With the danger of the invasion past, MacArthur predicted the war would be over by Christmas. That seemed like a wonderful possibility, but the holidays remained months away.

Word came the 100th would soon move out. Seoul lay only twenty miles away, and the liberation of South Korea's capital would be next. If enemy resistance to that city remained light, Mary hoped to get a break in Seoul. She thought that she might even grab dinner at a local restaurant. Anything other than the mess tent's repetitive fare sounded appealing, even if her first experience with the local cuisine had been disastrous.

The announcement of mail surprised everyone. Given the priority of unloading troops and equipment, no one thought there would be letters. Mary's heart sank when she discovered only a letter from her husband. Might their messages have passed in transit? No. Linda had mentioned that Rob knew Mary didn't want to hear from him. Could Rob be ignoring her request not to write? Determined to get the annoyance out of the way, she ripped open the envelope.

Dear Mary,

Please excuse that I'm writing after you said not to. But there has been a development with the state investigation that will affect both of us. Your mother said she told you about the inquiry. My dad's attorney insists I write since it's crucial for Cindy's welfare.

Our attorney said my dad and your mother are too old for guardianship. Under current regulations, I won't be eligible as a single man to have custody if we are not married. You could apply, but you aren't a blood relative of the baby.

The best adoption route is for us to file together. I know I hurt you in the past. All I can do is hope you will give me a second chance. I've stopped drinking and promise never to get involved with another woman again.

There's one more thing the attorney told me to ask. New Hampshire sent you and your commanding officers a series of questions. We don't know what they requested. If and when you get those documents, the attorney requests that you share what they ask and how you respond. That would help our planning.

That's a lot to ask, but this is critical to my sister's baby, whom we both treasure.

Love, Rob

Mary gritted her teeth. *There's nothing here about a husband caring about his wife. Or what I'm going through. Not even a real apology. He only needs me to keep the baby. By the way, give us a heads-up on what you're planning to say. This mess is all because of Rob's selfishness. He's not changing. Damn that man.*

CHAPTER 16

The day before they moved out of Inchon, Mary went looking for Sally, anticipating the worst about how her boss would react to this latest news. She found her in the administration tent. "I'm sure you're busy, but I wonder if you might have a few moments, ma'am?"

"I can spare the time. Before we get to what you need, listen to these figures. The casualty count totaled only 566 Allied troops killed and 2,713 treated in the last three days. That doesn't include prisoners and civilians."

The numbers surprised Mary. That so many UN troops died despite the light resistance struck her as still far too many. She nodded. There was nothing to say.

"What's on your mind, Belanger?"

"Is there a place we might talk alone?"

"I saw an unoccupied table outside. Let's see if it's still available."

Someone had left part of a meal at a folding table next to the admin tent. Sally looked disgusted and swept her arm across the table, throwing the debris on the ground. "Always satisfying to do a little bit of housekeeping."

Mary took a deep breath, wondering which Sally she was about to get. "I don't know how to begin or request what I want. Please bear with me. I'm quite nervous."

After summarizing the latest letter from home, Mary described the pressure from her husband to stay married and adopt the baby. When she paused, Sally reached across to touch Mary's arm. "Gosh, on top of everything here, that pressure from your husband is awful.."

"On the ship you questioned my commitment to our mission. I hope you saw that I gave nothing less than 100 percent. Now I'm asking whether I might get leave to go home to see if I can get my situation straightened out. I understand my tour is nine months, then get a month off. If I could take time now, I'd be willing to commit that I don't take that month. Do you see any way I might make this happen?"

"I was hard on you, and you've more than proven yourself. This job's stress sometimes gets to me, and people like you get it. My apologies for what I said. As far as your request, it's a long shot. If I might ask, what are your thoughts on whether you'll stay with your husband?"

"I'm not sure. One moment I don't want anything to do with the bastard, but if getting a divorce means losing the baby, that tears my heart out. If I could get home and talk to my family, maybe I can figure it out."

"I'll do my best to see if leave is possible. However, it's unlikely given what's happening here. So don't get your hopes up."

Mary was relieved that she'd gotten the supportive Sally today. "Thanks, I'd appreciate anything you could do."

"Since we have this time together, let me ask a sensitive question. Are you getting involved with Dave? Is there anything going on between you two?"

Dumbfounded, "No. Why do you ask? Have I done something?"

"There's nothing specific, but we all have eyes. The way you look at him in surgery and how you two interact. You could only be close friends, but it's part of my job to ensure relationships don't get out of hand and affect the unit."

"Look, he's a great guy and certainly a friend. I'd do anything for him and believe he'd do the same for me. But we're professionals. Besides, Dave considers himself engaged, and I'm married. The more I think about your question, I'm offended you're asking me such a thing. I've done nothing wrong. Does this have anything to do with my complaining about Dr. Wright's assault?"

"I regret if I'm off target, but I felt I had to ask. Apology accepted?"

Mary's blood boiled as she stood up. *Damn! When my boss looks like she's finally on my side, then something like this. Sally said she'd try for the leave. Better keep my mouth shut.* "Sure, apology accepted. Well, I need to get moving."

Major Phillips came out of the tent holding a large envelope. "Just the two I need to see. This envelope just arrived through official Army channels and not standard mail. There's a letter to each of us. I've read mine. Mary, it deals with New Hampshire's investigation of your family situation. Sally mentioned it to me earlier."

"Yes, sir. We were just discussing this issue."

Phillips handed each nurse a sealed envelope. "If the two of you would like to read this alone, we can talk later."

With her envelope already opened, Mary read while the Major continued to speak. Several questions addressed her commitment to the Army and when Mary might be released from duty. The last inquiry seemed key. "Given past marital issues with your husband, do you plan to stay married to him? If yes, then are you committed to filing for formal adoption of Cynthia Anne Belanger with your spouse?"

Mary lifted her head and saw the other two comparing their correspondences. "What do your letters say?" she asked.

Sally replied, "We both received the same questions. New Hampshire wants any information regarding whether you told us if you plan to stay married or seek a divorce and when your tour will end."

Unconsciously, Mary crumbled the letter, tightened her jaw, and shook her head in frustration. *Damn my husband and his philandering. Our dirty laundry now involves my commanding officers. I'd better get out of here before I say something I'll regret.*

Major Phillips read the frustrated nurse's reaction. "Let's meet later to discuss this. It would be best if you had time to process this. Let me say one thing. I've no intention of discussing any of my people's personal issues unless you request that. If you want me to respond to these questions, we'll discuss beforehand what I write. Sally, I'm sure you feel the same way."

"I do, sir."

"And, Mary, there's a war going on. Lots of letters and documents get lost. It might even happen to these. I'm not even sure this envelope ever arrived. Maybe none of us got the questionnaires."

Mary felt a tear escape down her cheek. Without another word, she hustled back to quarters.

Expectations of a quick military thrust to Seoul bogged down. The North Koreans moved troops into defensive positions instead of attacking the Allied invasion. With a series of hills on the way to Seoul, fighting settled into mile after painful mile of combat. The 100th joined a slow-moving caravan following the front.

A sign of progress came in an almost daily parade of North Korean prisoners marching south to confinement. It disturbed Mary to see many of the captured men paraded naked. Why were the North Koreans humiliated in this manner?

When she asked a wounded patient about this, he snarled, "Do you know the enemy doesn't take many prisoners? I cannot tell you how many dead Americans I've come across with their hands tied behind their backs and a bullet hole behind their ear. Besides, no clothes allow better security for the guards since prisoners might be hiding a knife or other weapon. I'd love nothing more than to shoot every one of them myself."

She patted the angry man's arm and thought about an Allied unit that had recently executed enemy captives and been disciplined. Then she remembered the violence she'd observed in Inchon City before the 100th pulled out. The South Korean Police, who were brought in to take over from the Allied troops, rounded up civilians identified as North Korean sympathizers. Without trials, the police executed many in public ceremonies. This tit-for-tat violence turned her stomach.

Abuse and vengeance killings probably occur in every war. I still feel we're on the right side of the fight since the North Koreans started the war. But no one side is above criticism when atrocities occur. This is the worst of humanity. Let's see how Father Phil explains this one.

Casualties continued to stream in despite having to move camp almost daily. Mary marveled at the efficiency of relocation. Their entire operation could get packed up and moved within hours, with treatments almost uninterrupted. Despite the steady progress to Seoul, the constant packing and unpacking wore on the nurses.

Although the buildings in Taegu and Inchon had been far from desirable, life under canvas proved harder. The tent where surgeries took place was the best of the lot, but it also had dirt floors and wooden platforms on which the medical staff stood. With colder temperatures setting in, the nurses' quarters grew more uncomfortable. There were never enough blankets, and that early gift from home of long underwear became Mary's pajamas. The nurses celebrated when a potbelly stove arrived, but cynicism reigned when they discovered that missing pieces made it useless. Rumors flew that high-quality sleeping bags were on the way, but given the Army's track record, betting favored delivery in spring. This quick shift from unbearable heat to never getting the chill off their bones made them all unhappy.

Many nights, if a generator was unavailable, the nurses' quarters lacked electricity. As a result, candles and kerosene lamps became the norm, further adding to the gloom. Rats and other vermin appeared the minute the unit set up at a new location. The scurrying and squeaks from rodents disrupted sleep. Mary learned to leave nothing of value on the ground after discovering a mouse in her boot one morning.

The worst were the times when only slit trenches were available as toilets. Everyone dreaded relieving themselves in the open, especially amidst the various creatures attracted to those pits. Several nurses refused to visit the trench without someone to keep watch.

A growing need was sanitary pads. Mary had brought a supply from home, but all the nurses had run out. No matter how many supply requisitions the nurses submitted, this necessity somehow never appeared. The ladies created a fund to buy as many as possible if they discovered a source. In the meantime, they washed and reused rags.

Colder weather also brought rain. On the way to Seoul, the heavens opened. Boot-sucking mud replaced the incessant dust. Tent leaks became a problem. The nurses often had to move bunks in the middle of the night because of sudden drips.

With the ground soaked, tanks and trucks regularly bogged down, causing traffic backups. In one camp move, the 100th got caught in gridlock, trapping nurses and patients in the back of trucks for hours. With everyone huddling to stay dry, Ann remarked, "The weather in this place goes from bad to worse, and it's not even real winter yet."

Into this general malaise, Sally delivered Mary a setback. "I pushed for emergency leave. While the brass was sympathetic, they said that things are too dicey to lose a nurse unless someone is dying back home. Major Phillips offered to set up an emergency call for you, but you'd have to coordinate to ensure the right people were there when the connection went through. The major said we're available when you're ready to discuss the inquiries from New Hampshire."

Thanking her boss for trying, Mary thought about the offer of a call. After Sally left, Mary sat on her bunk with her head in her hands, shoulders sagging. *Would a radio call home do any good? A call would have to be relatively short, and coordinating things complicated. Why even try? Others in the unit who had attempted that type of call talked about how poor the communication sounded. Would a call possibly make things worse compared to sitting face-to-face?*

She thought too of the state inquiry. Perhaps the best option would be to ignore it. She didn't feel she knew enough to decide about her marriage. As far as Rob's request for an update, any communication with him might turn into a rat hole. But Linda also wanted to hear what the state asked. Should she respect what her friend requested? If that information went to Linda, might it eventually make it to Rob? Her head throbbed.

Mary wished Ben were available to talk things through, but his unit was chasing the enemy on the other side of the Korean peninsula. What if instead of calling home, she asked for a call with Ben? How likely would it be for the Army to approve that request, and what reaction would Sally have? If her CO might be concerned about a relationship with Dave, what can of worms would a call to Ben create?

She fell back, aggravated by a new puddle in the middle of her bunk. *Not another tent leak!* Tears of hopelessness swelled. Mary ignored the seeping dampness on her backside and pulled a blanket over her head. She wanted to shut out everything in her life and ignore the chill in her bones that wouldn't go away.

United Nations forces battled up to Seoul's outskirts, where the level of fighting reached a new ferocity. The North Koreans adopted a defense of fighting house to house. Casualties skyrocketed.

There was a brief pause in the fighting the first night near Seoul. For once, the nurses enjoyed a quiet evening with most in quarters. The repaired potbelly stove glowed warmly, and for a change, an electrical generator hummed in the background. With no rain, the nurses relaxed, listening to Armed Forces Radio. The news led with General MacArthur announcing that Seoul was fully liberated and under UN control.

Everyone looked at each another in surprise. "When MacArthur, sitting back in Japan, decides he's liberated a city," Julie said, "the hell with reality."

Tent gossip shifted focus to Ellen and Chet and how they were getting involved. Ellen talked freely about it and shared a recent argument with Sally. "I don't care if Mother Nurse thinks it's her job to monitor my life. There's nothing in the regulations against us spending time together since I don't report to Chet. I told her to mind her own business. Guess I'll be getting a lot of the dirty jobs for a while."

Several nurses congratulated Ellen on pushing back. Mary thought about being quizzed about Dave. It looked like everyone experienced Sally's prying. The discussion with Ellen about her romance made Mary realize how she longed for a close relationship. Before her recall, sharing with Rob had become rare, let alone sexual intimacy. Some nights when she drifted off, fantasies arose of being with Ben or Dave. Although those were tempting thoughts, she promised herself never to stray while married. She would not lower herself to what Rob had done.

Ann said, "I'm tired of that same old crap on Armed Forces Radio. Let's go to the crazy stuff. Turn on Seoul City Sue. She plays better music, and I love her outrageous claims about the war."

While one nurse objected to listening to communist propaganda, the majority voted to change the station. In a minute, they were listening to the North Korean announcer introducing Frank Sinatra and "I Only Have Eyes for You."

Seoul City Sue was the daughter of American missionaries who worked in North Korea before the war. Raised in the north, she fell in love with and married a local man. Sympathetic to the communist cause, Sue hosted an evening radio program. Unlike other announcers who spoke English with heavy accents, her American dialect smoothly pitched the benefits of Marxism and why UN soldiers should defect.

Occasionally, Sue got the names of individuals serving in Allied units and spoke to them directly. When she came back on, it shocked the nurses to hear their outfit addressed.

"My greetings to the gallant nurses of the 100th MASH. We complement your service, providing medical treatment for your troops who carry out atrocities. Your job is not to determine what crimes American troops commit, but to save lives. You have much in common with the medical service of the brave North Korean Army."

"There are many nurses I want to recognize tonight. Sally Bates is the head nurse and works very hard. Ginny Gomes and Mary Belanger, who help with the operations. There are too many nurses to mention. I cannot honor them all."

The nurses crowded around the radio, chattering until Julie shushed them.

"Tonight, I want to highlight one special nurse, Grace Thomas. Grace is the only Negro nurse in the 100th MASH. We in the north know the prejudice she experiences. The US Army may say there is no discrimination, but let's be honest. Grace, you've experienced prejudice every day of your life. We salute you for putting your life on the line for a country that cares so little for you. When you return home and have to sit in the back of the bus or find yourself excluded from white-only restrooms, you'll see your sacrifice has been in vain. Will the nurses who work with you today stand up and say, please come into this segregated restaurant? Will they insist your children go to the same schools with theirs? We know the answer to that, don't we? Your friends today will not even look at you."

The nurses in the tent were silent, averting their eyes from Grace.

Sue went on. "That type of discrimination doesn't happen in North Korea, Grace. Why don't you slip away and enjoy a truly free and equal society? If you do, bring some of your fellow nurses. We'll be happy to teach true equality to them. Until we meet, Grace, let me play a special song for you. Here's Duke Ellington's, 'Don't Get around Much Anymore'."

Grace reached over, snapping off the radio. "How does that bitch get our names? What is wrong with this Army that they can't keep our identities confidential?"

Ginny moved over to embrace Grace. "Don't listen to her. I speak for all of us. You're equal to everyone here and one of the best nurses. None of us would ignore you back in the States."

Several nurses said much the same thing and joined in comforting Grace.

Julie stayed seated. "Grace, I know it's hard for you sometimes, but you should understand that we think you're a helluva nurse. The Army is lucky to have you."

Ginny gave Julie a withering stare, then faced the group. "As far as Sue goes, I hope our troops get that so-called missionary."

The nurses wandered back to their bunks when a voice rang out, "Next person who suggests we listen to Sue gets extra laundry duty."

An uneasy quiet settled with each nurse sitting alone with their thoughts. More than one realized the truth in what Sue said. In the face of community pressure, how many would stand up for Grace or other minorities back home?

Grace opened the latest copy of the *Stars and Stripes Army Newspaper*, pretending to read. She knew Sue hit the nail squarely on the head.

MANCHESTER TIMES
NEWS BULLETIN
SUPREME COMMANDER MACARTHUR
ANNOUNCES LIBERATION OF SEOUL

With the North Korean Army driven out of Seoul, General MacArthur reinstalled the South Korean government led by President Syngman Rhee. The capture of Seoul directly results from MacArthur's invasion of Inchon several weeks ago.

In a related development, the US Eighth Army continues to push up the Korean Peninsula's western side, driving enemy forces back. The offensive action on both sides of Korea shows initiative from the Allies as United Nations troops close in on the 38th Parallel, the boundary between the two countries. General MacArthur clarified that UN attacks would not stop at the former border but would continue northward to destroy North Korea's capability to wage war.

CHAPTER 17

Four days after MacArthur announced Seoul's liberation, UN Forces secured most of the city. Occasional firefights or sniper action continued. Some noted that MacArthur chose not to march into a liberated Seoul like he waded ashore in the Philippines during World War II. There would be no staged photographs by his public relations team this time.

While Allied forces regrouped in Seoul, the focus for the 100th shifted to medical treatment for thousands of injured civilians. Given the city's almost complete destruction, the UN needed to set up a food distribution network and rebuild the city's infrastructure. Once Mary took in the utter devastation, she laughed at herself for thinking she might go to a restaurant.

In line for morning chow, Sally approached. "Belanger, I know you enjoyed it when we went to that orphanage in Pusan. Today we're splitting the unit, with some of us heading into the city to work at the local hospital. Are you interested in going, or do you want to work here?"

"Count me in for heading into the city. When do we leave?"

"0800 muster. We have docs joining us. You'll be working with Dave." Sally hurried away to finalize assignments.

Under a cloudless sky, two trucks with over thirty staff

headed to the main city hospital. Several jeeps of heavily armed guards accompanied the medical team. A new addition was a dentist with a portable chair. Soldiers with wounds to the mouth would benefit with immediate treatment.

Surrounded by strong security, the caravan drove cautiously through the city. The ruined capital lay all around them. Smoke filled the air from fires still needing to be extinguished. Rubble littered the road, sometimes requiring the vehicles to backtrack to find a passable route. Almost every building was surrounded by broken glass or riddled with bullet marks. Dead bodies still littered the streets, fouling the air. The stench of raw sewage made cholera a worry. The local population slowly emerged from shelters. Most wore stunned expressions.

The procession of vehicles stopped in front of a shell of a building displaying a large red cross. Poking her head out of the back, Mary realized this was all that remained of the city's hospital. One entire wall was gone with shattered concrete rubble blocking the entrance. The guards deployed into a security cordon. Only then did the medical teams step out in front of what seemed to be an abandoned building. Down the rubble-strewn road, two children combed through garbage, shoving whatever food scraps they found into their mouths.

From within the shattered building came the crinkle of broken glass being swept and rubble being removed. A low-level smell of natural gas filled the air. Out stepped a smallish Korean man, his full head of hair caked with dust. Once past the pile of debris, he introduced himself as the head doctor. In perfect English, this stooped man explained what remained of his staff were working to recover what they could of the building and equipment. They planned to move patients inside once it was habitable.

Puzzled, Dave stepped forward. "Where are the patients if they're not inside?"

The Korean doctor indicated they were being treated back

of the hospital in the open air.

Dave turned to his team. "Orderlies, get in there and help with the cleanup. Figure out how to deal with the gas problem. We need to get the injured out of the weather. Sergeant, determine how many guards you can reassign to help with the cleaning. Doctor, please lead us to where you have patients. We can then determine how best to help."

The medical staff grabbed their bags, following the Korean doctor and laboring over piles of rubble. When they turned a corner, the Americans took in a stunning scene. Endless rows of injured lay on the bare ground, most without blankets. Only a few doctors and nurses were delivering treatments. Open wounds and soaked bandages were visible.

Mary flashed back to the scene in *Gone with the Wind* where, after a battle, the wounded filled the screen as far as the eye could see. Never did she imagine being a part of such an actual disaster. It took her breath away. *Where will we even start?*

Dave, Sally, and the Korean doctor huddled. After a few minutes, the senior nurse came to her people. "All right, ladies, here's what we're going to do."

The darkening interior in the unheated hospital signaled to Mary that it was growing late. An evening chill washed over her while she pushed back a strand of troublesome hair. The most critically injured now rested inside, but most patients would spend at least another night outdoors. She heard a supply truck crunching through the rubble to deliver more blankets. There were still not enough to go around. It would take days to work through the patient load.

A few flickering candles and too few flashlights battled the fading light in the cavernous room. The smell of dinner underway by the cook staff was one positive sign. A long line of adults and children from the neighborhood waited patiently outside with empty bowls. The earlier American lunch had been many locals' first meal in days. In the background, the sound of more trucks arriving gave Mary hope for needed supplies. She pushed her uncooperative hair back again, holding a flashlight while Dave worked.

Ginny came running up, grasping a fistful of US currency. "Dave, I need to borrow Mary for a moment."

The doctor never looked up, giving a nod. After handing the flashlight to her partner, the two nurses stepped away. "Ginny, what's up? Why do you have all that money?"

"Remember when we said we should load up if we found a source for sanitary pads? A black-market dealer is operating nearby. That guy has a bunch but will only deal in dollars. I have the money we chipped in. Do you have any additional cash?"

"I have a few bucks back on base but nothing here."

"What about Dave? Ask him if he has any money we could borrow."

"I can't tell him what we're buying. That's too personal."

"Then don't tell him what it's for. Instead, say we need money, and we'll pay him back. Besides, he's a doctor and knows we need this."

Mary returned to her surgical partner, "Got any dollars we can borrow? There's something we want to buy at a shop nearby, but they only take American currency."

"I carry a twenty in case some liquor is available. Might you be sharing what you buy?"

"No sharing. This is strictly for nurses. We'll pay you back."

Dave pulled out his wallet, handing a well-folded bill to Mary. "Sure you can't share?"

"No sharing. Thanks."

"Keep it."

Mary smiled, realizing Dave knew what the money would buy. She passed the worn money to Ginny, who scurried away.

Back at work, Mary and Dave wiped the sweat off their brows, preparing for their next patient. A young girl, all alone, limped toward the two, looking petrified. The surgeon smiled and tickled the youngster under her chin, eliciting a smile. Mary gently stroked the girl's hand, then started to remove filthy bandages from her legs. From the door, a familiar voice rang out.

"The 100th thinks they can have all the action. Well, the Eighth MASH is now in town. People, you've had a long day. It's time we take over."

Nurses and doctors carrying more supplies streamed in behind Ben. The Korean doctor and Sally rushed over to greet and brief the arriving team. Sally told Ben, "You're a sight for sore eyes. We've been here all day and wondered if we're even making a dent. There are more patients outside that we'll be unable to get inside tonight. We stopped a gas leak, but there's no heat here." She stopped, realizing that she was babbling with fatigue.

Ben scanned the darkening building. "We've brought additional supplies, including tents and a portable generator. I'll have one of my mechanical guys look at the gas system. How about we do a transition? You match my teams with your folks. Then, after the handoff, your unit heads back to base. Later, we can figure out how to coordinate coverage for the coming days. Will that work?"

"That would be fine, Major."

Ben turned to his people. "Follow the instructions from Lieutenant Bates. Let's get these tired people on their way home." With the roar of a generator firing up, the dingy building partially lit up.

"Major," Dave yelled. "Get over here."

Ben joined them. "Good to see you, Captain." He turned to Mary, smiling. "Lieutenant."

Ben reached into his pocket and handed the young patient a candy bar. Her eyes lit up as she ripped open the wrapper.

Behind her mask, Mary's eyes sparkled. *What a surprise! Can't let Dave see how excited I am. What are they doing here? I thought his unit was assigned to the other side of Korea.*

Dave asked the same question. "I thought you were supporting the campaign away from here. What brings you to Seoul?"

"We were relieved by a new MASH unit, the First. The brass sent us here for a little R&R. Some genius must have figured, send them to Seoul for the nightlife."

"What your people are doing doesn't look like R&R, but we're thankful. Now is the second time your outfit has bailed us out."

"Volunteers were easy to find. I had to order a couple of nurses to stay behind since I knew they needed rest."

Ben looked over at Mary. "How are you, Lieutenant Belanger?"

She brushed back the hair from her face, realizing she couldn't hide the fatigue and grime. Ben looked so clean. "Good to see you, Major. How long are you in town for?"

Before Ben could answer, Sally stepped in. "Dave and Mary, meet Jerry and Susan. They're your relief. Give them an overview after you're finished with that patient, then muster outside."

Ben smiled. "I'll leave you to your hand-off." Ben looked back when he turned to go, giving Mary a wink.

After showing the new team the routine, Mary and Dave pulled off gloves and gowns, heading for the door. Over in a corner, Ginny worked the arriving nurses to get more cash.

Outside in the darkness, members of the 100th wearily loaded into trucks. Sally leaned close to Dave, showing him a list of supplies that would be needed the next day. Since several serious surgeries were scheduled, they planned to ferry those patients back to the MASH facilities. A soldier walked by helping an elderly Korean priest with a gangrenous foot into the back of a truck. When Dave had attempted to treat the priest earlier, the man resisted, saying the Americans must serve all the other patients first.

Mary turned to her surgical partner. "How'd you convince him to get treatment? I thought for sure he wouldn't leave the hospital."

"I said he needed to fill out paperwork for us to treat more patients tomorrow. Once back on base, I'll knock him out with medication and treat that leg before he wakes. We can save the foot, but it'll be too late in a few more days."

"You're a devious surgeon. If you need someone to gown up, I can assist."

"Although I suspect Sally will spend most of the night chasing down items on that list, she offered to help. Tomorrow will be busy again. Get some rest. One question. Grace told me she's eager to get back in the OR. She started surgical training before transferring here. I want to give her a chance to assist with this priest since Sally will be there. This could be a way to develop another OR nurse. What do you think?"

"I think Grace will be steady. Look how well she does with other assignments."

Out of the corner of her eye, Mary saw Ben at the hospital entrance waving his hand to meet around the corner. Mary dropped her bag. "I'll be right back."

Once she stepped around the edge of the building, without warning, Ben pulled her close. Fully against him, they found each other's lips. Ben whispered, "When we got to Seoul, I went looking for you. I should've known you'd be here."

Mary grabbed the lapels of Ben's jacket. "I want to talk with you about the latest from back home. It keeps getting worse. I need a level head to help me sort things out."

"When you kiss me, I don't feel level-headed." He grinned at her before another long kiss. "I've got a full schedule and bet you'll be back here tomorrow. How about dinner tomorrow night? I need to be with my people tonight."

"That would be terrific. Do you think you can get away?"

She heard insistent honking from the truck. Without waiting for an answer, Mary gave Ben a quick peck on the lips, then ran.

CHAPTER 18

Dear Mom,
Please forgive me for writing about how scared I was before the Inchon invasion. They didn't tell us where we were going until we were at sea. But, in the end, it all worked out.
All is back to normal if there is a normal in war. Being part of the invasion proved to be the adventure of my life. But I never want to experience anything like that again. We are currently in Seoul. The enemy is on the run. Word is we will move out in a day or two to continue pushing north.
In Seoul, my unit worked for days at a local hospital. You must laugh since I keep finding people to treat besides our fighting men. Like I've written before, those who suffer most in war are the innocents. Although exhausting, similar to my time at the orphanage in Pusan, it made me feel valued.
Over these past months, I've learned a lot about myself, including how I enjoy helping people. Although no job is perfect, being part of a team that saves lives is rewarding. The people that make up my unit I like and admire. With any group, there are a few creeps

and challenging people. One individual I struggle with is my commanding officer. I can't figure her out. One minute she is supportive and has a heart of gold; then the next, she's biting my head off. I suppose part of that might be the stress of her responsibilities. It makes me wonder what I would do in her position. On the other hand, I know the head surgeon I partner with believes in me. Dave is the most talented doctor I've ever worked with, and he thinks I do great work.

I could go on about the other people in our unit. It's impressive how we've come from different parts of the country and formed a tight group. Someone told me that when people are thrown together in extreme conditions, they grow close since they must rely on each other. Whatever the reason, I've never felt more valued and committed. I want to say the little girl you and dad did such a good job raising is now a confident and darn good Army combat nurse. Thanks for help- ing me become who I am today.

Let's hope MacArthur is correct this war will be over before Christmas. I'm still wrestling with what to do regarding Rob and the baby. Maybe I'll be home around the holidays to figure things out. Have to run.

Love, Mary

P.S. Please share this letter with Linda since I don't have time to write her too.

Two days north of Seoul, Marine and the Army units ad- vanced. The nurses learned that the renewed drive would be challenging because their respite in Seoul allowed the en- emy to reinforce defensive positions. UN forces would soon cross into North Korea. Everyone expected the intensity of the fighting to increase when the North Koreans fought to protect their native soil and families.

The weather grew steadily colder, resulting in changes to the nurses' quarters. New reinforced and insulated tents arrived. A rearranged camp configuration placed the female quarters further away from other tents, allowing greater privacy. Late one night, a joker nailed a sign over their door that read "The Boudoir."

Thin mattresses were next, significantly improving cot comfort. Unfortunately, because of the deteriorating weather, keeping the tents as closed as possible to retain heat made the interiors gloomier. Mary told the others, "I doubt I'll ever get used to this goddamn musty smell. Thank goodness we finally got those mattresses. When will the promised down sleeping bags show up?"

At 0300 and slightly south of the 38th parallel, Dave and Mary worked at their surgery table. Because of a recent rare North Korean counterattack, the casualty numbers were up. Without enough sleep, Mary asked for another cup of strong coffee. Within minutes, an orderly returned with her third of the evening.

Dave closed the patient on the table while Mary thought about how automatic much of her performance had become. Even the rat who just ran across her boot during the last surgery no longer threw her off. Still, she wished to never again have to deposit a severed limb into a pile for burial.

While waiting for the next patient, she reflected on last night's dinner with Ben. He'd arrived late from meetings. The Eighth would ship out in twenty-four hours, so tonight would be their only chance to visit. Once together, Mary launched into describing events back home and her struggles with how to respond. When she paused, Ben asked, "Do you want to answer the state of New Hampshire questionnaire?"

Mary sighed. "No."

"Do you want either of your bosses to answer their letters?"

"No."

"Then take their generous offer to burn the documents. Let New Hampshire wait for an answer about what you'll do when you return. Since home inspections show all is well, it's unlikely that agency would take a baby away when the primary caregiver is serving her country. If the state agency proposes action, getting a lawyer to intervene for more time should be easy."

She nodded, leaning her head on his shoulder.

He went on. "When you think of your husband, do you feel confident he's changed enough that you want to commit to a life together?"

Mary paused for a long moment. "No."

"Do you feel that obligated to the baby that you're willing to live with him?"

A longer pause. "I'm not sure. I do know I don't want a relationship with Rob."

"Looks like the answer is no. The baby isn't enough of a motivating factor to stay in the relationship."

"It sounds easier when you put it that way, but I feel guilty since I love Cindy and want what's best for her. I wish I didn't have to choose."

"Didn't you tell me you suggested to your neighbor that she consider adopting the baby if anything happened to you at Inchon?"

"Yes."

"If the neighbors were a possibility before, why can't they still be a viable option? I know I'm blunt, but maybe they would be better parents for a child than you and Rob could ever be."

Mary silently processed this last statement. "One more thing," Ben said. "You've said how much you've enjoyed becoming an excellent OR nurse. Have you thought about staying in the service? If you went back to being a housewife in Manchester, would you be resentful that you'd missed an opportunity to discover how good a professional you might become?"

Mary bit her lip. "That's something I haven't considered. I do like our mission and have to think about that. Now I have a question for you. How much of what you're saying about my marriage is because we are attracted to each other? Let me put it another way. Are you saying this because you want me to leave my husband?"

Fingers now clicked in front of her. "Hey, daydreamer," Dave said. "We have a new patient. Whatever you're thinking about had you far from here. It's easy to go automatic when finishing a procedure like the last one. It's time to focus."

"Sorry, my mind wandered to what I should do when I get home."

"I wish that could be tomorrow. Unfortunately, several people need our full attention now. An emergency tracheotomy is in place because of the severe damage to his mouth and teeth. I'll pull a few molars and let our oral surgeon take over. There's a piece of shrapnel sticking out of his skull. Maybe it didn't penetrate through the bone. We'll have to be careful. Let's get the other injuries out of the way first. Bandage, scissors, please."

Fifteen minutes later, only the piece of shrapnel needed attention. Without warning, a loud crackle of gunfire erupted. Mary looked toward the surgery door but could not see what was happening. The fighting outside grew more intense and closer, including the sound of a machine gun. The entire staff in the OR stopped. Something was up, and it was close.

Dave yelled, "Keep your focus on the patients! Walter, get out there and figure out what's going on."

The orderly sprinted out. In the meantime, outside gunfire and yelling grew more heated.

Dave shouted to make himself heard above the shooting. "Finish up as fast as possible and move the patients to the ground. Then get your asses down there with them."

Major Phillips burst into the OR, wearing his helmet and carrying a carbine. "Partisan attack. They caught our sentries by surprise. We're mounting a defense. Get the patients and yourselves down as soon as possible. When you're done, doctors and orderlies, crawl to the supply tent to get a rifle. Nurses, stand by in case we need to move you." He headed out.

Desperately wanting to get down like others, Mary said, "Shouldn't we leave the shrapnel in for now? We need to get this guy on the ground?"

Dave took a deep breath. "There's a risk to moving him with that shrapnel still in. Give me a medium forceps. I'm going for it."

He took the instrument from her. "Get ahold of the top and bottom of this guy's head. I'm going to see if I can yank it out."

She wanted to ignore him but reluctantly handed him the forceps. Automatic weapon fire suddenly tore into the tent. The lighting over the empty operating table beside them exploded, raining down a shower of sparks and glass. Mary and Dave dropped to their knees as debris flew.

Then there was no more firing into the OR. Dave looked at Mary through the table legs. "Grab the emergency flashlight. Let's stand up and do this. I know I'm taking a big chance, but it'd be a mistake not to finish. You hold the light, and I'll pin his head down when I pull. Got it?"

No! This is crazy. Shit, Dave's already up.

With her head bent down, Mary crouched and switched on the emergency light. Dave moved to the head of the operating table, placed his left hand on the man's head, and gave a quick tug, which freed the shrapnel. He threw the forceps to the ground and grabbed the flashlight from Mary. The surgeon leaned close, spreading the forehead skin apart.

Already down on one knee, Mary cried, "What are you doing?"

"I'm making sure the brain isn't pierced. The skull looks partially cracked. This guy's lucky the shrapnel didn't penetrate further. We'll get some X-rays later to make sure I'm right."

Mary gritted her teeth, wanting to scream for him to stop. *We need to get back on the ground.* But Dave needed her help. She stood, and the two lifted the GI to the ground while the fighting outside continued.

"Get that wound cleaned and bandaged. I'm going to join the others to see if they need more hands."

Kneeling next to the wounded man, Mary reached up to bring supplies to the ground. Quickly washing and closing the wound, she heard American voices yelling to follow Phillips and pursue the partisans. Mary's hands began to shake, and soon her whole body trembled.

The next thing she felt was Ginny touching her shoulder. "Take it easy, gal. It looks like the worst is over. I couldn't believe how long you two stayed standing. You were the last ones up." Ginny gasped and cried out. "I need help over here! Oh my God, look at her back. Mary's been hit."

CHAPTER 19

Her head felt stuck to the stretcher. Slowly opening her eyes and blinking to clear the fog, Mary saw a bottle and its tube leading into her arm. *Why am I getting an IV?*

When she tried to move, Ann's gentle hand settled on her. "Stay on your side. You just came out of surgery to remove glass shards from your back. Take it easy. Let me get this blood pressure cuff on you."

The monitor pumped up, pinching her arm. Mary breathed deeply, trying to clear her sick stomach. Her tongue stuck to the dry roof of her mouth, making it impossible to speak.

Ann read the blood pressure numbers as Dave leaned down. "You feeling okay? That attack rattled us all, especially after you got hit by that flying glass. Your pulse and other numbers look good. Try to get some sleep."

"I don't understand," Mary said, her voice a rough croak.

"You were wounded during the partisan attack. Remember when the lights exploded above the table behind you? A couple of shards went deep into your back. We had to put you out to clean it up. Did you even know you got hit?"

Mary shook her head.

"You were so focused, somehow, you never felt being hit. By the way, congratulations on your first medal—a Purple

Heart. This story will sound better than if you got injured playing volleyball." He grinned. "For the next few days, lots of rest. You'll start feeling uncomfortable from the stitches. That's why we have to keep you on your side. Enjoy getting spoiled."

Dave stepped away, allowing Father Phil to move close. "Doctor's orders are to rest, but can I get you anything?"

"Could you please find my rosary? It should be in my pocket. I'd like to hold it."

Phil brought the beads to her. "Good to see your faith is helping."

It would take too much effort, and Mary didn't want to debate. Instead, she was just glad to feel a familiar comfort in her hand. As she drifted to sleep, she wondered how the soldier with the head wound had fared.

Now the object of attention, Mary wondered how she could possibly rest with the constant parade of well-wishers. From visitors, she learned how the partisan attack proved more dangerous than anyone first thought.

One North Korean strategy was to arm sympathizers or leave troops behind Allied lines for surprise raids. The attack on the 100th caught two guards unaware, resulting in their deaths. One of the guards got a few shots off, which allowed the others to react. Since only two raiders made it to the camp center before being killed, things could have ended much worse. One of those two partisans had fired the shots into the OR tent that injured Mary.

Eventually, the Americans drove off the raiders, but there were casualties. Ronnie lay wounded a couple of stretchers over from Mary's screened area. Four members of the 100th died—the two guards first attacked, Ronnie's friend Fred, and Walter, the orderly, who ran out to get information.

When Grace visited, she said Ronnie felt inconsolable at losing his close friend. His wounds were severe, including losing two fingers. The war was over for him.

Mary also learned that the four deceased were being moved soon. She wanted to attend the service that Father Phil was leading. When she attempted to stand, Julie argued about the wisdom of Mary moving around. Finally, Mary's stubbornness won out. Julie and Ginny took an arm and walked Mary to where the 100th had gathered. *This wind is awful. I better not complain about the cold, or they'll take me inside.*

An orderly ran up with a chair, allowing Mary to sit. Aware of the stitches in her back, she continually shifted her weight, searching for a comfortable position. Julie brought blankets. The unit pushed together to protect each other from the gusting wind. Under a damp, overcast sky, four body bags lay on stretchers in front of an ambulance. Major Phillips and Father Phil moved to the front of the unit. The purple stole of the priest almost blew away in the wind, forcing Phil to pin it inside his jacket.

Phillips announced that the service would be brief as more wounded would soon arrive. Often now, helicopters delivered the most seriously injured. While this development was another tool to increase patient survival, it also meant less time for the 100th to prepare.

All too quickly, Father Phil sprinkled holy water, and the ambulance carrying their fallen comrades departed. Almost on cue, chopper blades resounded, forcing staff to scramble to the landing area. Deflated that those close comrades could not have a full memorial, Mary realized that the war waited for no one.

Dave and Chet carried her back to bed in the chair. Along the way, Dave complained, "First, she humiliates me on the volleyball court. Now I'm lugging her around like a princess. Where did I go wrong, Chet?"

"It's a long list of your sins, Dave. We should be celebrating that she's not more seriously wounded. Otherwise, people would learn how many of our mistakes she covers up."

Mary's spirits lifted at their teasing, while she bit her lip to hide the pain of being carried. Once back in bed, she reached out to take Dave's hand. "I wish they could have said more about Walter and the others. He was a good orderly with a wonderful personality."

Dave knelt next to the cot. "I feel guilty about ordering him out to assess the situation."

"I didn't say that to make you feel badly. It's no one's fault."

He squeezed her hand. "You're kind to say that. But it'll be some time before I can be in the OR and not think of Walt." He sighed. "Well, those arriving patients might be waiting. I need to run. You rest and get better. Sally's covering for you, but I need you back when you feel better."

Dave hurried out. Mary fingered her rosary, praying for four Americans who would never see their families again.

The next day, Mary was resting when Grace came by with letters. "Mailman arrived. Here's a bunch for you. I know you need to read them, but whenever letters arrive, you get depressed. Maybe these will contain good news for a change."

Dread filled Mary while she sorted the envelopes and started with the most recent from her mother.

Dear Mary,

It made me feel better to get your letter that you're safe after that invasion. Your message from the ship had me worried. If MacArthur's strategy results in getting you home sooner, it will have been worth what you went through.

The good news is the state dropped its investigation. Like Linda suspected from day one, Rob's girlfriend filed false charges when he dropped her. There is still the need for a plan of who will adopt Cindy, but you already know that.

You asked me what you should do, given your issues with Rob. Unfortunately, I can't offer advice. It has to be your decision as to what's best for you. We can work out arrangements with the baby no matter what you choose. Don't feel pressured to stay in a relationship that isn't right.

I'm pleased to hear you enjoy working with people in your unit. You're growing professionally and as a woman, but I still want you out of that war as quickly as possible.

Right on schedule, I hear our little one. Time to go.

All my love, Mom

Mary smiled, then turned to Linda's letter for the real lowdown.

Dear Maar,

Never a dull moment here, although I'm sure what you're going through takes the cake. Here's the latest.

Mona withdrew her complaint to the state, meaning the state investigator stopped the home visits. (At least we don't have to clean the toilets so often.) It's incredible how some money can solve things. That's right, Richard paid off Mona. I'm not sure how much it cost, but we're thankful for something he did this time.

The agency's notification letter wants an answer regarding whether you and Rob will adopt. Have you seen the questions the state sent? If yes, what have you said in response? I promise not to share that information unless you want me to.

On the domestic front, Rob continues to improve.

He's staying away from alcohol, is more engaged with caring for the baby, and working for his father. We'll see how long that all lasts. With the death of Sharon, father and son seem to have mellowed. Maybe there is hope for those two. Rob repeatedly asks whether I think you'll take him back based on what you write. I tell him I don't know and refuse to let him read any of your letters. (Your mother said she's also not sharing anything you write with Rob.)

Your mom is thriving. I believe taking care of Cindy has added years to her life.

One more thing. The adoption agency approved Stan and me for a baby. I've shared how frustrating it's been for the two of us not to conceive. Cindy showed us how much we want a child. With this final approval, we are in line when an infant comes available. Even if we get a child while you're away, I promise not to stop helping your mom. Heck, what's better than one baby? You guessed it. Don't worry about anything here. Please focus on being safe.

Next letter I promise pictures of Cindy. I'll get my camera out this afternoon.

All my love, Lin

Mary felt a tear slip down her cheek. For once, the news lifted her spirits. Happy for her friend to be approved to adopt, but would that prevent Linda and Stan from taking Cindy if Mary opted for divorce?

CHAPTER 20

In less than a week, Mary insisted on returning to the OR. Although her back remained uncomfortable, the workload never let up with the front moving north.

After morning surgeries, Mary finished a late breakfast. This morning's menu included soggy pancakes without real New Hampshire maple syrup. *I prefer instant eggs. Someday they'll surprise us with fresh fruit and serious coffee.*

Outside the dining tent, Dave bumped into her. "Oops, sorry about that. How's your energy holding up? It's good to have you back in the OR."

"I'll feel perkier when I sleep on my back again. Having to sleep on my side hasn't been easy."

"I want to apologize again for keeping us standing during the attack. It's my fault the glass hit you. We should've gotten down sooner."

"Forget it. We went to ground when the shooting hit those lights. The way it happened, I got hit in the back rather than my face. You should stop feeling guilty. Most importantly, the patient survived."

"Thanks for saying that. Fate favored me when you arrived and ended up at my table."

"I feel the same way. When I think back to how scared I

was when I got here, it reminds me how much I've learned being part of our team. Everyone has been supportive. Well, there is one person I'd prefer to go away."

Mindful of her attraction to Dave, she thought momentarily before stepping over to embrace him. "Another thing I've learned about myself is I'm a hugger. I hope you don't mind since I plan on doing it more."

"I don't mind at all."

Dave went inside to get his meal.

Mary felt a pang. *How long before Sally confronts me over that hug? Damn it. I don't care anymore what she thinks.*

Napping inside her newly arrived winter sleeping bag, Mary relished the warmth. On a wintry day like this, snuggling into down allowed her a few hours of getting the chill out of her bones. The weather had changed for good in the mountains of North Korea. While her eyes grew heavy, Ginny and Ann entered the tent, chatting away.

"I tell you, Chet said this is the fourth Chinese soldier he's treated," Ginny said.

"How can he be sure they're Chinese?"

"Chet dated a Chinese woman back in the States and learned a little of the language."

"MacArthur said there's no way China would get involved. If Chet is sure, has he reported what he's seeing? What does the Major say?"

Ginny shook her head. "Phillips ran it up the chain of command. They're telling him his doctor must be wrong, and the major needs to keep his eye on his guy. I heard Phillips went bonkers. He told the colonel that Chet knew a bit of Chinese, and HQ needed to stop being in denial about what's going on."

"I read in *Stars and Stripes* where MacArthur committed to not crossing the Yalu River into China. We're still a fair distance from there."

"If the Chinese attack, this war won't be over by Christmas. We could be here for a long time."

The nurses saw Mary looking up at them. "Oops, we didn't see you there. Hope we didn't disturb your sleep."

Mary sat up. "That's okay. Fill me in."

In a meeting with her commanding officers, Mary finalized her decision to destroy the state questionnaires. The three joked about how the letters must have gotten lost somewhere over the Pacific. When Mary started to leave, Major Philips asked about scheduling an emergency call home. She stopped and explained that a brief radio call wouldn't do much. To herself, she prayed for an end to the war in order to get home in a couple of months.

She pulled her knit cap and collar close in the biting wind on the way back to quarters. Mary wondered about whether to skip a shower. The last two times, there had been no hot water. A shower in this frigid weather was not the least bit appealing. But since she needed to wash her healing back, she resigned herself to a bracing experience.

Once she had her personal effects and headed to the showers, Mary noticed a new mobile trailer. Next to it, Julie was talking to an unfamiliar officer. She decided to see what Julie was up to.

Doctor Wilson introduced himself as the new optometrist assigned to the 100th. His mobile lab would allow faster eye treatment, explaining how many soldiers damaged or lost their glasses in the field. Those needing replacements had to be sent to Pusan, removing them from the front lines for up to a week. With this new trailer, repairs would be available in hours. Although Mary found this interesting, she could see the optometrist was more focused on Julie.

"Slick," both nurses said. With a wave, they headed to the showers.

Julie gushed about how she found the new arrival attractive. Mary smiled and said, "Now we have an oral surgeon, psychologist, physical therapist, and eye specialist. The 100th is turning into a full hospital. I wonder when they'll add a gynecologist."

Her fellow nurse punched her in the arm. "Get real. This is the US Army. They can't even get sanitary pads, and you want a gynecologist."

"Guess I'm getting crazy. By the way, you're right. The new guy is cute. Go for it."

In surgery that night, Mary fought to ignore the frigid conditions. At least the shower water had been tepid. Since then, no matter how much coffee or extra clothes she put on, Mary felt cold. With these bitter temperatures, she wondered if her fingers would have enough feeling for the fine work of surgery. And it wasn't even November yet.

For the first time, steam escaped from a patient's body when Dave opened it. Because the surgery tent was warmer than quarters, off-duty nurses chose to sit along the sides for the second night in a row.

One positive had come—a letter from Ben. Word had gotten to him that Mary had been wounded. He expressed frustration in not being with her to ensure she cared for herself. His letter released a flood of emotion. She still wrestled with being a married woman as Ben grew more open with his feelings. He made her feel appreciated and desirable. Were his growing feelings another complication she'd have to deal with?

Sally came into the OR. "More wounded in triage are reporting they're battling Chinese troops. The fighting is more intense than we've seen for some time. Pace yourselves since we've got a long stretch in front of us."

The surgical teams went quiet. The implications of this development hung heavy over everyone. "Why would the Chinese attack?" one orderly asked. "We're far from their border."

Chet explained, "Perhaps China feels threatened about losing a communist ally in North Korea and doesn't want an enemy like the US anywhere near their border."

With the thunder of artillery and gunfire growing closer, Mary felt disgusted that political considerations might mean more unnecessary loss of life. A terrible battle was now taking place. She was cold. More wounded were piling up. Hopes for Christmas in New Hampshire were going up in smoke.

Only a few moments later, Major Phillips entered. "Finish up what you're doing, and no new surgeries. We're bugging out of here in two hours. Headquarters says that over 100,000 Chinese troops are attacking. How they got that many here without HQ knowing will have somebody's head rolling. Our lines are reeling. We've got to move fast."

"What about the wounded in triage?" Dave asked.

"We'll take as many as possible, but we may have to leave black tags behind since we don't have enough transports. Remember, two hours."

Dave spoke to the whole OR. "Take your time, and finish what you're doing the right way." Then, returning his attention to the patient on the table, Mary heard him say under his breath, "Damn, damn, damn."

MANCHESTER TIMES
NEWS BULLETIN
TENSION BETWEEN WHITE HOUSE AND MACARTHUR GROWS

With China's intervention in the Korean conflict, President Truman expressed frustration with the leader of the United Nations forces, General Douglas MacArthur. The general assured the President and leaders of the UN Allies that his offensive would not cross the Yalu River dividing North Korea and China. While UN forces stopped short of that border, China sent over 100,000 troops to attack.

Allied units fell back under the Chinese Army's on-slaught. MacArthur is calling for additional troops and the potential use of atomic weapons on the battlefield. General Chiang Kai-shek, President of Nationalist China on Taiwan, offered to send his soldiers to Korea to aid the UN. President Truman quickly precluded either involvement by the Nationalist Chinese or the use of atomic weapons. The President stated his desire to limit this conflict to the regional level and not involve the Soviet Union. A few commentators are calling for the President to dismiss MacArthur and appoint a new commander of the UN forces.

CHAPTER 21

The rain pounded down, soaking through the truck's canvas cover. Constant drips added to the misery of the wounded. Heavy, wheezing breaths escaped more than one man. Huddled in the back, Mary and Ann did what they could with patients almost stacked on top of each other. Despite the challenging conditions, all viable cases were evacuated. Mary understood the reality of not having enough space for the wounded likely to die, but the thought of leaving anyone alive ate at her. She prayed death would visit them quickly and peacefully.

Mary blew uselessly on her gloved hands to try and get feeling back in her fingers, then reached for the canvas top to stretch her aching back. She knew much more bending would be required before this ordeal was over. With the cramped conditions, she found no relief. Her stomach knotted when the truck stopped yet again. Since this muddy road was only wide enough for a single traffic lane, reinforcements rushing forward pushed the evacuating medical transports to the side.

"Nurse," a weak call came from the furthest corner of the truck. "The pain is getting worse. Is there anything you can give me?"

"I got this one, Ann. You stay put." Mary carefully stepped over several men.

"That you, soldier?"

"Yes, ma'am. I'm sorry to bother you, but it keeps getting worse."

Mary focused her flashlight on the wounded GI, lifting the wet blanket to see bloody bandages soaked through. "Ann, throw over the bag. I need to get a tourniquet on this guy and give him a shot."

With the supply satchel in hand, she looked down at the now wide eyes staring at her. "Ma'am, my name is Bobby Feinstein from Hoboken. Will you tell my mother I love her?"

Ann arrived to help Mary with the tourniquet. By the time Mary leaned down, the young boy was dead.

Mary felt Ann grip her arm.

Next to his deceased comrade, a soldier said, "I'm sure he's glad he could say that to you."

Mary forced her eyes shut, shaking and fighting tears, afraid to speak for fear of breaking down.

From the other side of the truck, "Nurse, my mouth is really dry. Is there any water?"

"On my way," Ann said. With a lurch, the truck moved, sliding through the mud and throwing the nurses onto each other.

After reaching their new site, staff worked to get the wounded out of the weather. Like a zombie on fumes, Mary wondered how long she could keep going. Slowly moving to help with the next patient, she looked off into the distance at the wind-blown, snow-capped mountains. *That would be beautiful back home. Here, it's another sign of worse to come.*

Sally came up. "I hate to do this, but we need to get a couple of tables going. Head to the admin tent and lie down for a little while. There's food there. You and Dave will start as soon as we get the OR set up."

Mary nodded, reflexively wondering how effective she'd be in surgery. Her fingers were numb. She felt shaky on her feet and nauseous from exhaustion. *How can I perform? What if I make a mistake that costs someone's life?*

Inside the admin tent, Mary spied a couple of cots close to where Phil stood. "Ah, Phil, I'm taking a bit of a break before heading into surgery. I need a favor."

"What might that be?"

"A young man died in the truck. His name was Bobby Feinstein from Hoboken. He asked that I get a message to his mother with his last words, 'Tell my mother I love her.' Could you help me do that? I feel like I'm going to lose it."

Phil wrote a note to himself.

Mary lowered herself onto a cot, turning away from the others.

The priest looked at the exhausted nurse. "Are you okay?"

"I'm not. Are you okay?"

"None of us are. I'll say a prayer for you, Mary."

"Good, because I'm out of prayers, Phil."

The potbelly stove in the OR blasted heat, making Mary thankful she and Dave were closest to it. The heat was the only positive experience in a while. Several cups of coffee and un-expected adrenaline gave Mary hope she could cope. Besides the backlog of patients from the withdrawal, newly wounded kept coming.

Major Phillips announced a rotation schedule for the ex-hausted surgical teams. With the intensity of the attack, sur-geries would be around the clock. The rumble from combat continued, adding to the gloom.

Dave volunteered that he and Mary would go on the last

rotation. After he announced that, she wanted to scream, "Please stop being selfless. I need rest." Tears of exhaustion filled her eyes, but she bit her tongue. Sally would gown up and order Mary to a break if she complained. *Others are hanging in. I'll have to find a way.*

Not until the next day did the flow of wounded slow. Only then did all the surgical teams get a break. When Mary finished cleaning up, she watched her boss start to resupply the OR. Although she wanted to help, Mary couldn't do anything more. Even Sally looked defeated, unsteady on her feet.

Mary knew she should eat, but food sounded disgusting. Back in quarters, off-duty nurses were asleep. She removed her boots but didn't remove her jacket before crawling into her sleeping bag. Instantly, she slept.

The following days brought little letup. The Allies were fighting an overwhelming enemy, and the sixty-bed capacity held almost three times that number. Allied defenses hung by a thread. This dire situation brought more and more patients wearing what one doctor called the "thousand-yard stare." These men were suffering from shock and often didn't respond to questions. Several mentioned how the Chinese blew bugles at all hours to keep their enemy on edge. "Please, no more bugles," one young man cried while rocking back and forth uncontrollably.

This critical battle in the war created the worst conditions for treating the men with shock. Earlier in the war, if an individual's mental health had been affected, a psychiatrist would typically order that person to the rear for one or two weeks of rest before returning to active duty. Now, fighting men with the same symptoms might get a warm meal, be put in a cot for two hours, then sent back to the front.

Everyone was aghast to hear how the Chinese Army dealt with prisoners. When they captured an American, the enemy removed anything of value, such as watches. Especially treasured were US Army boots since Chinese soldiers only wore thin canvas shoes. They then released the captured, so the attacking enemy didn't have to deal with prisoners. If barefoot personnel made it back to Allied lines, they likely faced frostbite amputations.

A dreaded job for the 100th continued to be disposing of removed limbs and burying the dead. That assignment became more challenging with the growing list of deaths, a shortage of body bags, and digging in the frozen soil. Mary now heard explosions on the edge of camp intended to break through the frozen ground for graves. No matter how awful the conditions were, Father Phil led all internments.

When it looked like things couldn't get worse, another storm hit. Mary remembered how she looked forward to New Hampshire's first snowfall. There were no magical feelings here—only howling winds, plummeting temperatures, and more complications operating vehicles. Tents needed continuous removal of ice. She wondered how to get another coat over the layers she already wore. The frigid air burned her lungs.

The awful call came mid-afternoon. Allied lines were falling back again. Camp staff went into their all-too-familiar drill of packing up. Like the last evacuation, taking all patients could not happen because there weren't enough vehicles. This time, besides black tags, additional patients would have to be left.

Dave found Mary. "I'm going to help an orderly who volunteered to remain with the wounded. He'll be captured with the patients we leave. Would you stay with me so we can help him for as long as possible? Before the enemy arrives, we'll jump in a jeep to catch up with the rest of the unit. Grace also volunteered to help."

Mary didn't think twice. "I can do that. Which orderly volunteered to stay, and how will you determine which patients to leave?"

"Charlie Keyser. The guy is nothing but selfless. Patients not well enough to move will remain."

"What do I need to do?"

"Go throw your things together and put them on the truck. Then report back here, and we'll get things prepared. Thanks. If nothing else, we'll have a fast ride in the Korean mountains when we bug out."

CHAPTER 22

The sides of the tent flapped in the growing wind. Riding in a cold jeep would not be pleasant on this stormy night. Mary tucked in a blanket for a shivering patient. *How can I be thinking of myself with what these guys have in front of them?* Another gust made it feel like the whole tent would come down.

The main body of the 100th had already left. Charlie, the remaining orderly, moved among the patients, checking if anyone needed last-minute medical attention before Dave, Mary, and Grace left too. The two nurses had supplied him with all the morphine they could gather. Mary saw deep fear in Charlie's eyes, anticipating becoming a prisoner of war.

Sally stepped into the tent. "Okay, this is it. Ginny and I are riding in the last ambulance. Father Phil, time for you to join us. Dave, there's a jeep left for you three. Follow us in no more than fifteen minutes."

Dave nodded and went on changing bandages.

"I'm serious, Dave, only fifteen minutes. The enemy will be here soon. Many of our front-line troops have already withdrawn past us."

"Got it—fifteen minutes."

Phil stepped over to Charlie, hugged him, and quickly

blessed him. Then Sally and the priest were gone.

"Grace, could you give me a hand over here?" Dave asked. "And bring a vial of morphine."

Mary and Grace looked at each other. Each suspected they wouldn't be leaving on time. And they were right. It was nearly ninety minutes before Dave and the two nurses loaded into the jeep.

When Mary gave her last hug to Charlie, her heart felt like it would fall out on the frozen ground. These helpless men, who could do nothing for themselves, would shortly be in the hands of the enemy. And this wonderful orderly, what would be his fate? For all she knew, they might be dead in the next hour.

Feeling sick, she climbed into the jeep's shotgun seat and leaned forward, grasping the door handle while the jeep sped and skidded over the icy road.

With daylight gone, Dave wrestled the steering wheel back and forth to keep the jeep moving forward. The heavy vehicles that had gone before left deep ruts, which the jeep fishtailed in and out of. He insisted on driving without headlights to avoid enemy detection. The vehicle had downlights, which Dave also wouldn't use. In the pitch-black conditions, he fought to keep the jeep moving. Thick snow started falling, cutting visibility even further.

Mary worried since she could barely see ahead. Twice she argued with Dave about turning on the headlights for a second to check where they were going. But he refused, saying even a flash of light could betray them. Mary looked back at Grace. The nurses exchanged concerned looks.

A few minutes later, the jeep shifted viciously to the right and tumbled on its side, sliding down a ravine. Mary screamed as they bounced down, metal screeching as it dragged over rocks. All three fell violently against the passenger side. Finally, the jeep slid to a stop. Dave lay on top of Mary. The jeep rested on its side at the bottom of a muddy ravine; a small stream ran through the lower part of the vehicle.

"Everyone okay?" Dave asked.

Grace said, "I'm alright. A little banged-up. Mary?"

Mary could barely hear their voices. Her head smashed against the side panel, water slowly filled her mouth. *Something is on top of me.* She tried to swallow, then choked and coughed, unable to lift her head out of the stream.

Grace screamed, "Dave, get off Mary. Her face is in the water. She could drown."

Reaching up for the steering wheel, Dave strained to pull himself up. Grace grabbed Mary by the collar to lift her head out of the water. Spitting and coughing, Mary gasped for air.

Dave raised himself more toward the driver's side door, which faced the cloudy sky. With a couple of hard bangs, he pushed the door open. Sitting on the side of the jeep, he called down. "See if you can pull Mary up. Then I can grab her."

Grace felt the frigid water soak through her boots as she tried to get a better grip. "Mary, can you hear me? Try to stand?"

Voices. What are they saying? Someone is pulling on me. Cold. I'm so cold. Why are they yelling? I can't move.

"Mary, pull your legs out. Bend them. We need to get you up."

With all her strength, Mary gave a push. She felt herself suddenly moving upward. A second pair of hands grabbed the top of her jacket. At the open door, the howling wind bit into her wet uniform. She cried out. Dave pulled her close.

"Do you have her?" Grace asked.

"I've got her, but I think she's seriously injured. Can you get out?"

"I need to crawl your way. Can you get her on the ground? I'll be right behind you."

In a few minutes, , the three stood in the ravine next to the jeep. Dave lowered Mary to the ground, then knelt over her head to keep her sheltered from the wind and falling snow.

Grace leaned under the surgeon, using a handkerchief to clot a wound on Mary's temple. It didn't appear deep. Dave held their one flashlight while Grace cleaned and bandaged Mary.

Semi-conscious, Mary tried to open her eyes. Could someone be touching her head? She couldn't be sure. A sudden blinding pain behind her eyes made her vomit.

"Oh, baby. Let me wipe that up. That's the best I can do," Grace said. "I see no other wounds but don't think we should start taking off clothes to check. We'll have to hope she's not bleeding elsewhere. Honey, can you hear me?"

"Ummmmf," Mary croaked. She forced her eyelids open. A face seemed to float above her.

"Her eyes are open, Dave. Hey sister, are you with us? Can you say anything?"

Every part of Mary hurt. Her efforts to move made it worse. She squinted, concentrating on focusing her eyes. Slowly, she recognized Grace. "What happened?"

"The jeep slid into a creek. We're okay, although you got the worst of it. How's your vision? Can you see me clearly?"

"Yeah, I can see you." Mary twisted her face to the side, wincing.

Dave asked, "Mary, how many fingers of mine do you see?"

In the flickering light of the small flashlight, "One."

"Probably a concussion," Dave said. "Hopefully, it's not too bad. Mary, raise your left leg."

The injured nurse could not sort left from right, lifting a leg.

"Raise your other leg. Next, your arms. Can you move your head?"

With great effort and pain, Mary managed those maneuvers.

"All right, let's get you standing. Then we can get out of here."

Once Mary was on her feet, she was dead weight. Without support, she would collapse.

Dave said, "Let's move Mary out of the way. I want to tip

the jeep over and see if it will start. Even if we can't get it started, we can use it to get out of the weather."

"Got it," Grace said.

They moved the injured nurse down the ravine through the snow and slippery mud. While Mary leaned heavily against Grace, Dave tried to right the vehicle. With the jeep wedged against a couple of rocks, he gave up and returned to the nurses.

Grace asked, "What if we lay Mary down and both push on the jeep?"

"It's really stuck. Besides, she's already wet. Let's try to keep her off the ground."

Dave removed his jacket, then wrestled Mary's soaked coat off, substituting his own. "This might help a bit. Help me get my gloves on her."

Grace worried that Dave now had no protection from the cold, but she recognized that there wasn't an alternative.

Dave pointed up the snowy bank of the ravine. "It doesn't look too steep. Let me see how hard it is to get up there. Hang onto Mary." He disappeared into the darkness.

In a fog, Mary tried to focus. "What happened?"

"Dave drove us off the road. He should've listened to you and used those damn headlights. The jeep is wrecked. He's off to see how to get out of here."

The snow stopped falling, but the wind picked up. "I'm cold," Mary said. Her body shivered against Grace.

"Me too, honey. Here, let me block the wind for you."

Dave reappeared. "If we walk a little down the ravine, there are bushes to grab onto where I think we can scramble up. How are you doing, Mary?"

"What happened?"

Before Dave could speak, Grace explained, "I've answered that question twice. It's a concussion. Let's get moving. She's losing body heat, and I'm cold."

Dave nodded, suddenly lifting Mary over his shoulder. He

walked down the ravine, carefully picking his way over the slippery, uneven ground. Grace followed. Mary found breathing difficult, her stomach bouncing up and down on the surgeon's shoulder.

"Grace, here's the spot. You come up behind me. If I slip, you can catch us."

"I've got a better idea. You don't fall. Look at the size of me, As if I could ever stop the two of you."

"Fair enough."

After several slips, Dave managed to reach the muddy road. He stood Mary up, fighting to catch his breath. Grace joined them.

Mary said, "I'm feeling a little better. I think I can walk some."

"Good," Dave said. "We've got to find shelter. If we get moving, that'll help warm us up. Ready?"

"I don't see what choice we have," Grace said. "Let's put Mary in the middle. Then we can each hold an arm. Do you have a compass? That way, we can be sure which way to walk."

"No compass, but I think it's this way." The three took their first steps, leaning into the cutting wind.

Each step took more and more effort as the trio slipped in and out of the deep tracks. Wind gusts blew them back at times. When they tried to get out of the ruts by walking on the side of the road, ice, and snow on the downward pitch proved more difficult. With each step, Mary became more of a burden.

Despite wearing Dave's jacket, her shivering grew worse. The wind went right through her. No matter how much she concentrated on putting one foot in front of the other, her limbs wouldn't cooperate. Through her fuzziness, she realized hypothermia was setting in. For the first time, she asked herself if she should tell her companions to leave her and save themselves. Instantly, she forced herself more upright, realizing how much she wanted to live.

After an hour, Grace lifted her head and looked to the left. Silhouetted against broken clouds and faint moonlight stood a shack. "Dave, there's a hut up on that hill. Let's head there and see if we can get warm."

"Good find. I had my head down in this wind and would have walked right by. Look, Mary, shelter."

The three stumbled off the road and up the rise toward the small building.

What if Chinese troops are in there? Please, God, if there are troops there, let them be ours.

Close to the hut, Dave said, "You two stay here. Let me check it out."

Mary and Grace knelt in the snow. Dave hunched down to move forward. After circling the shack, he pushed the door open, then hurried back to the nurses. "Looks like a peasant's summer shelter. There's even wood and a chimney. Let's go."

Inside was a bare wood sleeping platform. Grace and Dave laid the injured nurse onto it. "Grace, lie next to Mary to get her warm. We've got to keep her awake because of the concussion."

"Will do." Grace moved Mary over, wrapping her arms around her friend, telling her to fight sleep.

Dave looked for a way to light a fire. None of the three had a lighter, and the jeep's first aid kit's emergency matches were missing. He picked a couple of rocks to strike together, attempting to create a spark. After a frustrating time of rubbing stones together, he gave up, throwing them in disgust against the wall.

"Damn it. That won't work." He looked apologetically at the two nurses. "I screwed this up by staying with the patients too long. Then I refused to use the headlights. Now, I can't even get a fire going. I've got you two in a real mess."

Grace pulled Mary closer. "Forget it. We are where we are and need to figure out how to get back to our lines. Mary, you doing okay?"

Mary didn't respond, already asleep.

"Damn it," said Dave. "We've got to keep her awake."

In an exasperated tone, Grace said, "I'm doing the best I can. She must have nodded off. Come on, honey. Wake up. It's for your own good."

Mary awoke but couldn't understand any of what was being said.

A couple of hours later, Grace had nodded off. Dave shook the two women, whispering, "Someone's heading this way. They may be Chinese or North Korean."

Grace bolted up. Mary tried to understand his words. Slowly she grasped what Dave had said. Fear somewhat cleared her thinking.

If this is a North Korean patrol, will they execute us? Maybe that wouldn't be the worst thing. I've heard rumors in camp about what the enemy did to American women.

"Listen, I'm going to head out and get some distance from this shack, then make noise," Dave said. "That should get their attention. After I draw them away, duck out and head to the back of the hut. There are hills behind us. That would be the best place to hide. There might even be our troops dug in up there. It's a long shot but the best I can think of. Mary, do you think you can run?"

"Help me up," she stammered. Pain shot from her head down the back of her leg. She tried to hold her head up, but it was a struggle. "I'll do the best I can."

Grace grabbed Dave's arm. "You don't have to do this. Maybe it'd be best if we get taken together."

"I think you might escape. That's better than waiting to see what an enemy patrol might do."

By the door, the two nurses hugged Dave. With one last look, he said, "Good luck, you two."

Dave kept low, scrambling away from the shelter. About fifty yards down the hill, he stood up and walked. Although he wanted the enemy to catch sight of him, the patrol must have been focused elsewhere. In desperation, he threw a couple of stones. Someone shouted foreign words. Rifle shots erupted.

The nurses could no longer see Dave and assumed the patrol must be chasing him. Grace whispered, "Let's go."

The two nurses crept out, staying close to the hut. In the distance, the crackle of gunfire continued. "Stay down, Mary. Let's move toward those boulders. Once we're behind them, I think we'll have enough cover to run."

The two inched into the darkness. Mary leaned forward and clung to the back of Grace's jacket to avoid falling. Behind the boulders, they knelt in the snow, struggling to catch their breath. In the distance, the only sound was the howling wind. They couldn't hear any more firing or voices.

Mary said, "I wonder what happened to Dave."

"We can't think about that now. We need to move to that ridge ahead of us. Ready? Hold my arm. Here we go."

The nurses moved as fast as they could, slipping through the snow in the darkness. Mary's head reverberated with each step. More than once, she fell. Grace struggled to get her back up. Onward they scrambled.

After several hundred yards, Mary gasped, "I need to stop." She fell out of Grace's grip, collapsing to the ground.

Grace stood up, staring behind them. "I can't see anyone coming. We have to keep walking."

I can't move. I need rest. "Give me a minute. I can't feel my feet."

"That's enough of a break. We have to go."

Grace dragged Mary to her feet and half-carried her forward as best she could. But in only a few steps, Mary grew heavier. More than once, Grace repositioned her to move a few more steps.

More and more nauseated, Mary suddenly stopped shivering, no longer cold. Through the buzzing in her head and with eyes that could no longer see, she said, "I feel warm and need to take my jacket off."

Grace knew this meant the final stage of hypothermia. "Hey there, New Hampshire, don't quit on me. It's one foot in front of the other. You think about that baby waiting for you back home. You're walking to Cindy. Put that in your mind and keep that jacket on."

"Yes. Cindy." They struggled forward.

A short time later, Mary stopped again. "I can't do it anymore. Leave me and save yourself."

"Oh no, you—"

A machine gun burst erupted. Both dove to the ground. Several boulders around them splintered. Bits of broken stone hit the women. The firing stopped as quickly as it began, followed by an eerie silence.

Grace leaned close to Mary. "I think I heard a voice that sounded American." She heaved a sigh of despair. "It's time to take a chance. Even if they're not our guys, they're right in front of us. Either way, we're stuck. So I'm going to call out."

Mary's eyes were blank.

"Hold your fire," Grace screamed out. "We're American nurses who got separated from our unit. We're injured and need help."

The women could hear distant voices. One boomed out, "Who does Ted Williams play for?"

Another voice shouted. "You idiot, those are women and probably don't follow sports. Hey nurses, what's the name of the President's wife?"

"Bess," Grace yelled. "Bess Truman. And Ted Williams plays for the Red Sox."

"Sanders, take two men and get down there. Find those nurses. No telling who might be tracking them."

In a minute, an American soldier appeared above the two crouching women. "I found 'em, Sarge. Over here."

Two more GIs appeared. The first soldier said, "You riflemen, take positions behind those rocks and keep your eyes open. Maybe these ladies are being followed. Sarge, we need a stretcher here. One of them looks to be in bad shape."

Stretcher-bearers arrived and got Mary loaded. At the same time, a medic asked about bleeding and injuries.

Grace answered, "I believe she has a concussion and hypothermia. I'm not sure about internal injuries. I can walk from here. We're so lucky we found you."

With the injured nurse on the stretcher, the medic said, "Let's get back up where I can take a better look at you both."

Behind the American line, Grace briefed the sergeant about Dave leading the enemy patrol away. "We heard firing a while ago." He paused. "I'm afraid he's captured by now or . . ."

"Can you send out a patrol to see if you can find him?"

"This area is crawling with Chinese, and we're stretched thin, Lieutenant. We can't afford to send anyone. Your officer is gone. Be glad he saved your lives with that stunt of his."

The sergeant spoke to the stretcher-bearers. "Get these ladies back to the ambulance pickup point. Then double-time back here. If there's an enemy patrol around, they may soon be here since we've exposed our position. Ma'am, I assume you can walk. Is that right?"

"Yes."

"Okay then, move out."

The bearers picked up the stretcher when Mary weakly waved the medic over.

"Hold on a moment," the medic ordered.

When he bent down, she said, "All the GIs tell me I look

like an angel when I treat them. Today, you guys are the true angels."

The medic smiled and patted Mary on the shoulder. "You're a much better-looking angel than any of us mugs, ma'am. Let's go."

The ambulance bounced over the rough road, as Grace cradled Mary's head in her lap. The driver radioed ahead the identities of the nurses.

With that news, the entire 100th gathered. When the back of the ambulance opened, Grace stepped out, lost her balance, and fell into the arms of Major Phillips.

After the CO caught her, he said, "I'm glad to see you, too. How are you? I heard Mary's badly injured."

"She suffered the worst. I'm okay. Forgive my clumsiness, sir."

Grace felt the smothering embrace of Sally, who was openly crying. "Thank God you're back. We have lots to discuss. First, let me go check on our Mary."

Corpsmen already had Mary's stretcher out. Nurses immediately surrounded her. Sally had to push through. "Give her breathing room," she said. "Get her out of this weather and warmed up."

Major Phillips asked Grace, "Any news or sign of Dave?"

She shook her head, deciding to say nothing of the sergeant's speculation about Dave's fate. "They said there were too many Chinese in the area to send out a search party."

Phillips sighed. "Get in there and get checked out. Mary wouldn't be here without you. Well done, Thomas. When you're feeling better, see me. I need more details for my report. How injured is she?"

"She got the worst when our jeep went off the road. Honestly, I don't know how she stood up, never mind ran when we had to."

The team's exam showed Mary was suffering from the latter stages of hypothermia. She also had a cracked collarbone, concussion, and numerous bruises and abrasions. Grace had fared better, with only early signs of exposure and significant bruising, but was otherwise well.

Mary would be helicoptered to a nearby hospital ship at the earliest light. To prepare for the flight, they made her as warm as possible. In the meantime, she slipped in and out of consciousness.

After her exam, Grace went over to Julie, who was sitting next to Mary. "When it gets time to take her to the helicopter, I'd like to be there. Could you come get me since I have to meet with the major?"

"I'll find you before we load her. Thanks for taking good care of our friend."

"I couldn't have made it without her. We needed each other."

Julie choked back tears. "Everyone is relieved you two are back. We're praying for Dave." She stood and took her fellow nurse in an embrace. Not sure how to respond to her long-time nemesis, Grace said nothing, wondering what this might mean for the future.

When Grace headed to the admin tent to debrief with Major Philips, she couldn't walk by anyone without getting another hug. Surprised that no one asked about Dave, she realized people already assumed he was lost.

Sally was sitting across from the major. As Grace entered, she heard the senior nurse say, "I can't do this job anymore. Almost losing two nurses has put me over the edge. I feel like I'm cracking up."

Seeing Grace, Major Phillips stood. "We need a minute."

Sally turned and her tear-stained, haggard face shocked Grace. Without another word, Sally jumped and ran out.

"If you want to talk to Sally, sir, I understand and can return later."

"I need to attend to her. I assume you heard what she said. Please keep that in confidence. She's a good woman who has given her all for this place. The stress of the last hours has been too much. But HQ wants information right away about what happened. Come on in, and I'll find Lieutenant Bates later. Since you're injured, and Lieutenant Belanger is out of commission, we can't afford to lose Sally too. There's a crush of wounded."

"I'm okay and ready to return to full duty once I get some sleep."

Major Phillips nodded. "We'll see. Tell me what happened."

Grace started with staying too long with the wounded, leaving out none of the details.

Major Phillips shook his head. "Damn, why didn't Dave get you out of there earlier? At least then you'd have been driving in daylight. Seems pretty straightforward that his delay led to losing the jeep. I hope to sit with him one day and discuss how he could have done better, but I fear he's made the ultimate sacrifice to allow you two to escape. That's the story we must emphasize, not his leaving too late."

"I agree."

"I dread having to notify Dave's parents and his fiancé. There are parts of this job I'll never get used to." He paused. "I hear a chopper. Let's see Mary off. Then you can get some well-deserved rest."

A good portion of the camp was waiting by the helicopter pad. Once the chopper set down, they brought Mary out and strapped her into a long pontoon. Orderlies locked it onto the outside skid.

Father Phil leaned over to give the nurse his blessing. Behind him came Grace, who kissed Mary's cheek before they closed the patient carrier. The two stepped back to join the rest of the 100th as the copter powered up. Grace was not the only person crying when the aircraft lifted, spun around, and dipped toward the sea.

CHAPTER 23

A fter the helicopter settled onto the deck of the *Consolation*, a medical team scrambled to unload Mary. She was still unconscious as they moved her into a screening area for evaluation and a review of the MASH records. On deck, the chopper lifted off for its next mission of mercy.

The Navy medical team found no additional issues. An orderly wheeled Mary through the pristine corridors into the women's ward. The staff was briefed that one of their own had barely escaped from behind enemy lines. They were also aware a doctor was missing in action. The attending team knew their patient would need emotional support besides treatment for her physical injuries.

Senior Navy Nurse Cathy Walters joined the attending nurse. A groan escaped Mary's lips as she tried to move her head.

Cathy leaned down. "Hey there, take it easy. They sedated you slightly for the helicopter ride. Now you're on the *Consolation*. Do you understand what I'm saying?"

After a pause, Mary whispered, "Yes."

"You have several injuries, including hypothermia. We've packed you with heating pads. Are you warm enough?"

"Yes."

"Are you too warm?"

"No."

"Good girl. Get some rest. Is there anything I can get you?"

Mary's eyes flew open. "Dave. What happened to him? And Grace? She was there." She fought to push herself up. "Dave and Grace. We were together. I need to know. We crashed. I felt cold. Where are they?"

Cathy and the attending nurse gently pushed Mary back down, tucking in the blankets. "I don't know what happened to them. Let me try and find out. I'll notify the chaplain on call. When we have news, we'll get back to you. But now, you need to rest."

Mary met with Father Gallagher the next day, who explained what he had learned about her ordeal. His account released a flood of tears that left her feeling empty. "Dave is a good man—a dedicated doctor and amazing surgeon. I'm his partner in OR. He taught me how to deal with this place."

"He must be a talented doctor. I hope he's a prisoner, and we'll see him again."

Mary became silent.

Gallagher reached into his pocket. "When they got you here, and out of your uniform, they found these."

The priest handed over the rosary Linda had given her. "I'll be saying prayers today for everyone we've talked about. I'm sure you will too."

The priest took a step to leave, then turned back. "If you want to talk or receive the sacrament before heading to Japan, alert a nurse. You're scheduled to leave tomorrow. If I don't see you again, we're glad you made it back, Lieutenant. God bless you."

After air transport to Pusan, orderlies loaded Mary onto a medical evacuation plane. Wounded service members filled the four tiers of stretchers. The loading process took a long time since only two nurses had to prepare every injured patient for the flight. With the door open for loading, Mary felt chilled even though she had two blankets.

Despite an ongoing headache, Mary felt more alert. She scanned the crowded plane, depressed by this latest example of the unending carnage of war. Only a few months before, she might have been staffing this flight. *Considering what happened, an air transport assignment might have been a safer option. But would I have become the nurse I am today without being in the 100th?*

A soldier on the stretcher across the aisle cried out in pain. "My IV's twisted around my arm."

Mary pushed herself up. "I'll help you."

"Stop that," a familiar voice commanded. "Patients must learn to stay on their stretchers and not go roaming, even you, Mary Belanger."

There stood Kelly Henderson. After sorting out the tangled IV line, she turned to Mary. "I heard about you gallivanting behind enemy lines. The minute I met you in California, I knew you were a girl out for adventure." She smiled. "Seriously, we're relieved you're okay and sorry to hear about your missing doctor. Right now, we're busy getting ready for takeoff. I'll be back during the flight. In the meantime, you're confined to your stretcher for the duration. Don't give me any trouble." She smiled again, snapping Mary's safety belts into place before moving on to other patients.

Once they were in the air, Kelly returned. "The pilot said we should have a smooth flight. When they called my name for air transport, I thought I'd die, but have come to like it. It's hard work, especially when we get emergencies. You and the others are behaving yourselves today, making this one of our easier trips. How are you feeling? Anything you need?"

"No, thank you. I'm fine."

"What happened to you? How did you end up behind enemy lines?"

For the first time, Mary told the story, leaving out Dave's waiting too long and driving into the ditch. From now on, she would not mention Dave's mistakes. Instead, the focus would be on his heroic actions and how Grace saved the two of them. Without either, she wouldn't be here.

After another long sleep, bright sunshine filled the ward in Osaka. Mary padded down the hall to the bathroom. The warmth felt wonderful. Something as simple as going to a western bathroom by herself was a pleasure. Plus, the food tasted amazing. Last night, she had another juicy hamburger, and the ice cream was a treat.

Back in bed, she appreciated how pristine and peaceful the conditions in this hospital were. The crisp linens and quiet atmosphere were such a stark contrast to frontline conditions. A week before, she'd shivered in a crowded tent with dirt floors, constantly interrupted by the sounds of war. It was a relief not to hear the rumble of artillery or cries to scramble for an incoming helicopter.

The day before, Mary wrote her fellow nurses in the 100th, sharing how well things were going. She also penned a separate letter to Grace, thanking her for saving her life. Mary hoped their paths would cross soon so she could show her appreciation in person.

The most challenging letter was to Dave's fiancé. Because

Mary felt guilty about being partly responsible for his disappearance, more than once, she tore up her attempt. Finally concluding there was no perfect way to say what was in her heart, she poured out her emotions in the closing paragraph.

No one can appreciate what you are feeling about losing the special man you planned to share your life with. I also feel a hole in my heart since he taught me so much and sacrificed himself for me. There is hope they may yet find him since they have listed him as missing in action. His not being with us today makes each day darker.

This letter to Allison caused Mary to reflect on her faith given recent events. The hospital chaplains kept saying the same thing. God works in mysterious ways; we must have faith. But, after all she had been through, that didn't seem enough. Life at times like this would be unbearable without hope that sprang in part from faith.

After much thought, *Everyone says God's will is a mystery, but the suffering of innocent children and the loss of a good man like Dave is too much. I know now God doesn't have to have all the answers. I'll just have to do my best every day to commit myself to helping those who are suffering. That's all I can do.*

A day later, Mary picked up a letter from Ben and reread it.

Mary,

I felt awful when I heard what happened. News that you survived, although injured, was such a relief. But the news about Dave is devastating. I'm optimistic that they could have captured him and that he is alive. With the lack of medical support in many enemy units, a captured American doctor may be valued to treat their troops.

It's also good news that Grace is well. Major Phillips said that she proved critical to your making it to Allied lines. I promise to give her a big hug when I see her.

Troops on this front are in a series of controlled withdrawals. The overwhelming numbers of the Chinese Army continue to be too much. It's not clear if we'll be able to stop their advance. In the meantime, the casualties keep coming. You know the routine, and it's discouraging.

By the time this letter catches up with you, you'll be recovering in Japan. I'm relieved you're safe and getting better.

Sharing what is in my heart has never been easy, but here goes. For some time, I've been aware that I love you. There, I got it out. I want to figure out how we can be together once this war is over. I pray each night you feel the same way.

It's time for me to run since we're short a surgeon, which means I'm back in the OR. All my best for Thanksgiving, and if we don't communicate before then, Merry Christmas.

LOVE, Ben

Mary finally took up her pen.

Dear Ben,

Thanks for your letter, which did reach me in Japan. I'm feeling much better, although my strength isn't all back yet. My prognosis is for a full recovery and return to active duty in the not-too-distant future. I'll keep you posted when that happens.

The situation with the Chinese pushing on all fronts is disheartening. Unfortunately, our hope for the war to be over by Christmas is no longer possible. Instead, there will be more suffering on all sides for months, maybe years, to come.

Like you, I'm devastated about the loss of Dave. In my head, I believe they probably killed him since I heard gunfire from his direction. But your idea about the value of American doctors to the enemy gives me hope. I'm wearing out my rosary, praying for him.

Thank you for the kindest words anyone has ever spoken to me. Although our time together has been brief, you have a special place in my heart. But I'm still married and cannot commit to anything until my situation resolves. Although you may find this disappointing, I hope you understand. I don't want to hurt you, but this is me. Once my life gets sorted out, we can talk about the future.

I pray things get better for you and your people. Please be as safe as you can.

Love, Mary

Mary watched Doctor Fischer pull the privacy curtain closed. "Hope I didn't wake you. I heard you'd been up and about. How are you feeling?"

"Each day is better. The main thing I need is to get my stamina back."

The doctor smiled. "I think you're ready for more, but take it slow. You're recovering from a serious concussion. I assume no more headache or dizziness?"

"My head is feeling much better."

"Your collarbone is healing well. Here's the deal. We'll keep you to build strength for four or five more days. After that, I'll discharge you for two weeks of R&R in Japan. Following that break, I'll reassess you. If your progress continues, you'll go back to your unit. That acceptable?"

"Yes. It'll be good to get out of here."

"One thing for today. This afternoon, you must be in uniform. A general is coming to give out medals. You're on the list."

"Why would I get a medal? The people who saved me deserve the recognition."

"You're a bit of a legend around here. Not leaving the wounded until the last minute and escaping an enemy patrol after being injured is impressive. I see you were also previously wounded in action during a partisan attack. The newspapers are eating it up. See you at the ceremony."

In the hospital auditorium, Mary stood at attention, along with several soldiers. The others being honored leaned on crutches or sat in wheelchairs. Staff and patients filled every seat. Reporters and photographers occupied the front row. After the senior general described each honoree's actions, he awarded medals.

Butterflies filled her belly when she heard her name announced and a description of her accomplishments. At rigid attention, she scanned the faces of the audience, knowing full well the citation didn't tell the whole story. After the general pinned the medal on her, Mary said, "Permission to address the audience, sir."

He looked surprised but stood aside and waved her to the microphone.

Her hand shook as she leaned on the podium. More butterflies. In a shaky voice that grew stronger, she spoke. "Thank you, General, for this recognition. I feel inadequate standing next to the men being honored, each of whom has suffered terrible injuries. But, like the many wounded my MASH unit treats, they are genuine heroes.

"I must mention a couple of people who did more than me

and who should receive recognition. First is Private Charles Keyser, an orderly from the 100th MASH. The need for a swift evacuation meant we didn't have enough transportation for all patients. Twenty-three seriously wounded men had to be left for enemy capture. Private Keyser volunteered to stay and care for them, knowing he would be taken prisoner. His commitment to those patients is beyond description. Today, his fate is unknown."

"Next, Captain David Walsh, my partner in surgery. He saved countless lives with his medical skills. When we were separated from our unit, he created a distraction with the enemy that allowed another nurse and me to escape. Today, my surgical partner and good friend is missing in action."

"Last but not least, my fellow nurse, Lieutenant Grace Thomas. I wouldn't be here without Lieutenant Thomas carrying me back to Allied lines. They're the actual heroes in this story, sir. I pray each night for those three."

The audience erupted with applause. The general moved over to stand next to Mary as flashbulbs exploded.

Back at her bed, Mary tried to calm down. But a steady stream of patients and staff came by, saying how much they appreciated her words.

One soldier, hobbling on his crutches, would remain forever in her mind. "In my worst moment, ma'am, you nurses were all I had. Unfortunately, my buddy didn't make it."

Mary gripped him tightly. They both sobbed.

Later, Doctor Fischer appeared, pulling the privacy curtains. "Well done to tell that general you wanted the podium. Bravo! It might be the first time someone has gotten a microphone away from that man. That alone deserves a medal. How are you feeling?"

"Wrung out from nerves."

"Rest up. We'll get you out to see some of Japan in a few days. You'll get a list of hotels when they discharge you. Enjoy the sightseeing, but don't overdo it."

When he turned to go, Mary said, "I've been thinking about the two-week break and have an idea. Of course, it would require your approval. Do you have a minute to see if I'm crazy?"

The doctor returned to sit on the end of the bed. "Go ahead. I like out-of-the-box ideas, as long as they're not too wacky."

CHAPTER 24

The bus edged to a stop at Manchester Station. Mary awoke from one of the catnaps that had dominated her past two days. She couldn't believe she'd pulled this off and hoped that what happened over the next seventy-two hours would clarify the future. Three days would be all she had before starting back for Japan.

Doctor Fischer said no when she first laid out the proposal to head home instead of resting in Japan. "A furlough is for rest and recovery. Traveling halfway around the world to deal with stressful family issues isn't the best prescription for your health."

But Mary had doggedly described her situation and how much she wanted to make this trip. Eventually, the doctor came around, recognizing that resolving issues in New Hampshire would reduce her stress.

Fischer made an appointment with a neurology specialist at the San Leandro Naval Hospital in Oakland, California, prioritizing her transportation. The flights to California took almost three days, where a specialist squeezed her in. He concluded that her recovery from the concussion was progressing well.

She then rushed to the San Francisco Airport to travel on military standby. It took two more days to get to Boston, where she caught the bus to Manchester. Because of the uncertainty of getting on flights, she chose not to alert anyone at home. Surprising the family would be better than disappointing them.

As the bus pulled to a stop, Mary's heart beat faster. So many thoughts ran through her head. She hoped her mother would be home.

By chance, Tess, a high school classmate, had been on the bus. "I can't believe you're here telling no one you're coming. My dad is picking me up. I'm sure he'll give you a ride."

Tess's father insisted on carrying Mary's bag. "Let's get you home right away. Mary Belanger, our hometown hero. You were recently on page one of the newspaper, getting a medal. Wow."

Twenty minutes later, they pulled up in front of the family house. Tess's father said, "Do you mind if we watch you go in? I bet we'll hear some screaming."

"Dad, let Mary have her privacy. No gawking."

"You spoilsport, but you're right. Mary, as you requested, I promise not to go to the local paper and tell them you're in town."

"Thank you, sir, for the ride and confidentiality."

The car pulled away. Mary stood looking at the neat little house she'd dreamed of so many nights as she tried to sleep. In her old neighborhood, soft evening twilight cast long shadows. It looked cozy. A dusting of snow in the front yard framed the early holiday decorations. Although it was cold, Mary smiled. Tonight's weather didn't approach what she'd left in Korea.

Up and down the thoroughly American street, the peaceful beauty looked perfect. She wondered what her unit might be experiencing at this moment. In the sky, the North Star rose. *Like the Wise Men, this star guided me home.*

On the porch, she put down her bag, held her breath, and rang the bell. The sound of steps came from inside. The door swung open. There stood her mother.

Susan raised her hand to her mouth. Not a sound escaped. Mary stepped in to gather her mother in her arms. Tears flowed as they clung to each other.

From the hallway, Linda squealed, "Oh my God! It's Mary! Mary's home! It's a Thanksgiving present!"

CHAPTER 25

The helicopter lifted off, dipping toward the mountains of North Korea. Mary pulled her parka tight against the growing cold and rearranged her knees, now wedged between plasma and other medical supplies. The snow-capped peaks looked picturesque in the morning light, belying the intense fighting below where the Chinese and North Korean Armies continued their assault.

Anxious about rejoining her unit, she knew conditions would be as harsh as anything she'd experienced to date. Not just with the cold and medical challenges but because of her responsibilities now as First Lieutenant and Senior Nurse. Mary was replacing Sally, who had finally burned out. With Christmas coming soon, this would be a holiday unlike any other.

Events of the past weeks had resolved the issues she had wrestled with for months. Mary's most significant worry had been telling her mother about her decision to enlist for full-time active duty and commit to the Army for three more years. That decision brought the promotion and new assignment. Not surprisingly, Susan cried at the news but came to understand why her daughter chose this path. Her little girl was a woman with a future in Army nursing. Saying goodbye again so quickly had been painful, but the visit gave hope for more reunions.

Talking to Rob had been more complicated. By now, Mary knew what she wanted. Richard and Rob pressured her to stay married. When she refused, father and son proposed that the couple adopt, then allow Mary to go her way with a nice check from Richard. Mary didn't want a sham marriage or anything that required a long-term relationship. The bribe convinced her that Rob's custody would not be best for the baby.

At one point, Rob got mean, wondering how she could end their marriage since the Catholic Church did not allow divorce. Mary shared Father Phil's explanation that they could be eligible for annulment as they had no children of their own. She promised to work through that process.

Rob sputtered, "Who are you? You're not the girl I married. It's unacceptable for you to enlist for three years without talking to me. I'm your husband. What have you become?"

She found it easy to answer. "A woman who wants more than playing second fiddle to your selfish ways is what I've become. I've learned how rewarding it can be to work with dedicated professionals and save lives in the worst conditions. Those are the people I respect and who respect me. You, of all people, can't possibly understand who I've become."

After a tense day, Rob and his father reluctantly recognized the best option would be to have Linda and Stan apply to adopt Cindy. The couple was thrilled and made clear they wanted Rob and his father to stay involved in raising the baby. It was bittersweet holding Cindy one last time, but Mary felt content knowing that the child she loved would have parents who genuinely wanted her.

And then there was Ben. Once back in Japan, Mary wrote to share her decisions with him. The last paragraph was the most difficult to write since he had declared his love.

Ben, it's clear we have feelings for each other. However,

given all that I've been through and my decision to pursue a career in the Army, I believe it would be best to put our relationship on hold. It's too soon for me to think about another commitment with much to do to end my marriage. Despite my feelings for you, I need time to figure out my future. I hope we stay in touch. Who knows what tomorrow may bring? You're a wonderful man who's been nothing but kind and supportive when I needed that.

The helicopter began dropping toward the valley floor. Mary could see long tents with big red crosses. Already people were running toward the landing pad to unload. Mary knew Grace was now assigned to surgery, meaning she would not likely be one of those scrambling nurses.

When the aircraft settled on the landing pad, orderlies rushed to grab boxes, yelling quick hellos. Ginny stood there, directing the unloading, and quickly hugged Mary. Then she stood back, laughing and giving the new senior nurse a crisp salute. "We knew you were special when you joined us. Congratulations, ma'am."

Mary grabbed Ginny's arm, pulling it out of the salute. "Stop that. I'm the same old Mary. How are things here?"

"Typical horror and craziness. The enemy pushes us back, and the casualties keep flooding in. Besides the usual mess, you'll be earning your money. Your old friend Bones is head surgeon. He was none too happy when he heard you were named senior nurse—even tried to get you reassigned, from what we heard."

Mary heard scuttlebutt about Bones' efforts. It didn't surprise her he carried a grudge. "Where is the big guy? Might as well get this over with."

Ginny picked up Mary's duffel. "He's in surgery. You can confront the ogre soon enough. It's not just you; being in charge has changed that man. Whatever happens between you two, we nurses are glad you're back and totally behind you."

Mary pulled her collar tight against the familiar, bitter

wind. With a deep breath, she fought a flutter of nerves thinking about confronting her nemesis. No one said this job would
be easy. Despite Ginny's foreboding, Mary knew that for now,
this is where she belonged.

KEY FACTS ABOUT THE KOREAN WAR

Armed conflict ceased in the Korean War on July 27, 1953, with an armistice agreement that created the Korean Demilitarized Zone and returned the border between the two countries to the 38th Parallel. However, a formal peace agreement has never been signed. Officially, those two countries remain in a state of war.

Mobile Army Surgical Hospitals (MASH) were pioneered in the last six months of World War II in Europe and became the primary emergency treatment practice in the Korean Conflict. Technological developments and the evolution of fighting strategies led to the current configuration of the Combat Support Hospital (CSH). The concept and learnings pioneered by MASH units remain central to the current operations of the CSH. The US Army deactivated the last MASH unit on February 16, 2006.

Richard Hooker (the pen name of Richard Hornberger) wrote the novel *MASH*. In Korea, he served as a surgeon in the 8055 MASH. Hornberger started writing his war experiences in 1956, with publication in 1968. A series of sequels followed that have been credited to Hooker but were actually written by William Butterworth. Generally recognized as the real-life Hawkeye Pierce in the movie and television show, Hornberger had a tent in Korea that did carry a sign "The Swamp."

Besides the American MASH units, the Norwegian Parliament authorized a NORMASH on March 2, 1951.

Personnel were dispatched to Korea in May of that year, establishing a surgery of four operating tables. With the signing of the Armistice, the Norwegians transitioned from receiving wounded soldiers to general medical support. On October 17, 1954, NORMASH personnel received orders to return to Norway.

The 100th MASH is a fictional name I used for this book, similar to the MASH entertainment series with its fictional 4077 MASH. The numbering for actual MASH units was tied to the Army Unit identifications they supported.

The airlift of patients from Korea eventually carried over 300,000 patients. During various stages of the three-year war, air transport of patients within Korea became a significant activity.

Today, physician's assistants and nurse practitioners are an important element of US domestic medical service. In response to workloads in Korea and Vietnam for physicians, the increased responsibilities assumed by nurses and medical corpsmen served as a model to develop these fields of American civilian medical care.

Author David Halberstam quoted former Secretary of State Dean Acheson, who said, "If the best minds in the world had set out to find us the worst possible location to fight this damnable war politically and militarily, the unanimous choice would have been Korea." I am certain the nurses who served there would agree.

RECOMMENDED READING

Feller, Carolyn & Cox, Deborah. *Highlights in the History of the Army Nurse Corps*. Government Printing Office, 2016.

Halberstam, David. *The Coldest War: America and the Korean War*. Hyperion Books, 2007.

Hooper, Elise. *Angels of the Pacific*. William Morrow, 2022.

Kenneally, Thomas. *The Daughters of Mars: Nurses in Gallipoli*. Atria Books.

Pash, Melinda. *In the Shadow of the Greatest Generation: The Americans Who Fought the Korean War*. New York University Press, 2012.

Sarnecky, Mary. *A History Of The U.S. Army Nurse Corps*. University of Pennsylvania Press, 1999.

Weintraub, Stanley. *War in the Wards: Korea's Unknown Battle in a Prisoner-of-War Hospital Camp*. Presidio Press, 1976.

Westover, John. *Combat Support in Korea*. U.S. Army in Action Series, 2014.

ACKNOWLEDGMENTS

There are so many people to thank for their support and assistance in this long process to publication.

The many early experts, readers, and critics made the transition possible from my first efforts. They include Carole Ambroziak, Lis Ard, Mark Barbour, Robbi Calhoun, Michael Colvin, Dr. Marriane Dwyer, David Engberg, Terry Esvelt, Lori Ferreira, Dr. Henry Garrison, Paula Hagan, Shirley Henderson, Janice Matthews, Karen Meadows, Steve Morgan, John Linde, Melissa Owens, Catherine Rittenhouse, and Sandra Turnbull.

Special thanks to my editor Doctor Jill Kelly, Alexander Ko, Archivist, US Army Museum, and Melinda Pash, author of the important book *In the Shadow of the Greatest Generation: The Americans Who Fought the Korean War*.

As always, there is never enough appreciation for the critical feedback and love from my partner, Susan Weedall.

Most importantly, thanks to the nurses who served in Korea and those who continue to serve our country. There can never be enough recognition for what you do quietly and valiantly.

Printed in the USA
CPSIA information can be obtained
at www.ICGtesting.com
LVHW050037310124
770429LV00001B/59